"I'm sorry. I don't know what got into me. I never cry."

Haley wiped her eyes on her shirtsleeve, but tears still beaded in her long lashes.

"You deserve to cry. What they did to you..." Sully clenched his jaw against the reckless words crowding his throat.

"It happened a long time ago. I never think about them anymore. And the baby..." A sheen of tears sprang to her eyes again. "That was...hard. But I can't change the past. I've had to accept it and move on."

He reached out and smudged away a tear. She was amazing, the most courageous woman he knew. She'd fought for her sister, the teenagers in her shelter, even him.

But who had fought for her?

"Sully." Her whisper whipped through him.

His body went taut, the invitation in her eyes impossible to miss. She wrapped her arms around his neck and kissed him, her lips soft, almost tentative, a benediction to his aching soul.

Shuddering, he deepened the kiss....

Dear Reader,

I have the utmost admiration for the members of our armed forces. My husband was a career military officer. My father served in World War Two, and my youngest son is on active duty right now. I appreciate their sacrifices, including the time they spend away from their families, and the risks they take to keep us safe.

But my heart really aches for those men and women who come back damaged from their experiences, lost in horrific memories they can never escape. Sullivan Turner, the hero of *A Kiss to Die For,* is one such tortured man. Sully went to war with the idealism of youth, hoping to make a difference in the world, but returned a broken man, his failures made worse by addiction and guilt. I hope you enjoy his journey as he meets the woman who has the power to heal him and finds the redemption he desperately needs.

Happy reading!

Gail Barrett

A Kiss to Die For

Gail Barrett

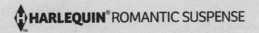
HARLEQUIN® ROMANTIC SUSPENSE

Recycling programs for this product may not exist in your area.

ISBN-13: 978-0-373-27836-7

A KISS TO DIE FOR

Copyright © 2013 by Gail Ellen Barrett

Printed in U.S.A.

www.Harlequin.com

Chapter 1

Trouble was brewing. Haley Barnes could feel it. She'd spent enough years living on the streets to know.

She stood on the steps of her shelter for pregnant teenagers, her gaze on the dusky street. No traffic rumbled by. No D.C. commuters hurried past, despite the evening hour. Even the homeless man who'd taken up residence in the empty row house several doors down had gone to ground, drowning who-knew-what demons in a bottle, no doubt. And her teenagers were safe inside the shelter, warming themselves before the fire.

Except for one. The one who worried her the most.

Ignoring the premonition of danger stirring inside her, Haley hurried down the steps to the sidewalk, then started up the empty street, heading toward the metro station where the runaways sometimes hung out. She should have watched Lindsey more closely. The teen had exhibited the classic signs of depression—refusing to eat, unable to sleep, rebuffing Haley's attempts to talk. Instead, she'd withdrawn into a sad kind of silence, slipping outside when no one was looking, and nine hours later, she hadn't come back.

Not that Haley blamed her for feeling depressed. Lindsey was fourteen and pregnant. Her boyfriend had dumped her, her family disowned her—and Haley knew *exactly* how that felt. She understood the despair that threatened to engulf her, the terror of her unknown future, the knowledge that her childhood had abruptly ended in the most fundamental of ways.

Haley had tried to offer her comfort, to give her a shoulder to lean on and pull her back from the brink. But the girl had rejected every overture of help. She'd retreated into moroseness, into the overwhelming dejection of someone who'd given up hope. Haley just prayed she hadn't done anything drastic—to herself or that unborn child.

Her sense of urgency mounting, Haley hurried down the cracked sidewalk, the low drumming of subwoofers a block away quickening her pulse. *Trouble was right.* The Ridgewood gang was on the prowl. No wonder everyone had fled the street. No one with any sense would risk confronting that violent group.

But she refused to give up. She'd made it her life's mission to help these troubled girls, to give them the acceptance and safe haven she'd lacked. She knew the desperation that drove them, the terrible dangers that awaited them on D.C.'s brutal streets.

And she didn't intend to lose one now.

The wind gusted hard, pushing loose strands of hair into her eyes, and she paused to shove them back. She scanned the row houses bordering the street, the late-model cars lined up along the curb, and searched for the missing girl. Her gaze landed on the dilapidated row house where the homeless man holed up. Another wounded soul. Another loner adrift in an uncaring world. Another stray she wanted to save.

One stray at a time. She had Lindsey to worry about first.

She just prayed she could find her in time.

Staff Sergeant Sullivan Turner slumped against the wall in his best friend's row house, the whisper of oncoming danger prickling his nerves. *Not his problem,* he reminded himself firmly. Fighting the bad guys hadn't been his problem in months—nine long months, to be exact. Not since he'd returned to civilian life.

He knocked back a swallow of vodka, then rubbed his aching leg. Dusk crept through the empty room, shrouding the corners in darkness, but it did nothing to subdue his nerves. He dreaded the night, dreaded battling the memories that inevitably flashed back, reminders of the ambush that had claimed his buddies' lives. And he especially dreaded confronting the failures he couldn't erase, no matter how much alcohol he drank.

He closed his eyes, inhaling around the desolation gripping his chest, and willed the images aside. He couldn't afford to go there. He couldn't afford to picture their grinning faces and remember the deaths he'd caused. And he definitely couldn't afford to envision his best friend Jason's cocky grin, that instant when he'd turned around, preparing to launch another laughing insult at Sully just as his world had come to an end.

By some miracle, Sully had survived. But his survival hadn't been a blessing; it was a curse. A curse that would plague him until the day he died.

Determined to hold off the flashbacks, he drained the bottle of vodka and hefted himself to his feet. It was going to be one hell of a night, his wounded leg already aching with a vengeance, unwanted memories bombarding him like those RPGs that destroyed his squad. He tossed the empty bottle onto the counter and twisted the cap on another, but a faint mewling sound made him pause. Frowning, he limped across the kitchen to the glass door leading to the patio, his steps thudding on the wooden floor.

A furry animal huddled on the step outside. *Great.* Just what he didn't need—a cat. If he could call him that. He was the most pathetic creature Sully had ever seen, with one missing eye, flea-bitten ears encrusted with filth and a scraggly, crooked tail. His fur was mangy and gray. A shock of white stuck up on his ruff, matching his face and legs. He had a lame front paw, a limp that matched Sully's own. His chest swelled with unbidden sympathy—a feeling he couldn't afford.

"Go away," he told the cat through the glass door. "I'm not taking care of you."

The cat meowed and gave him a beseeching look with his good eye. Then the wind bore down again, ruffling what remained of his matted fur. He hunched his back, his thin body so undernourished, Sully was surprised he didn't blow away. More kitten than cat, he decided. Lost and alone. Another misfit wandering the streets.

"All right," he grumbled. "But just this once."

Swearing, he shuffled back into the kitchen, his own stomach growling as he opened his last can of tuna—the sum total of his remaining food. But what the hell. The cat needed it more than he did. He cracked open the sliding glass door, nudging the cat back to keep him from slipping inside, and set the can on the ground.

"Don't think I'm doing this all the time," he warned him. "Don't start hanging around, expecting handouts. I don't need a damned pet."

He shut the door. He didn't need anyone to take care of—or another failure to add to the list. He'd already let everyone down enough.

Pushing aside thoughts of the needy cat, he crossed the empty room to the front window, his steps echoing in the gloom. The house had no electricity, no heat, no hot water. No furniture, except for the mattress Sully had hauled inside. Jason had cleared out before his last deployment, as if he'd known he wouldn't be back. And for some unfathomable reason, he'd willed the place to Sully, his best friend since childhood.

The best friend who'd caused his death.

Sully braced his forearm on the glass and worked his jaw, trying to control the flood of regrets. Shadows bled across the pockmarked yard. Bare tree branches scratched at the gloomy sky. His sense of foreboding grew stronger, and he frowned at the empty street. He'd once trusted his instincts for danger. But then, he'd once felt invincible. He'd once believed in good versus evil, the glory and necessity of war.

No more.

The rhythmic thud of subwoofers made the floor pulse, rumbling through the lug soles of Sully's boots. Tensing even more now, he skimmed the houses up the street, eyeing their peeling paint, their house numbers hanging askew, the weedy yards littered with trash. There was no sign of the approaching car, no sign of the gang that had been making inroads into the neighborhood. But he wasn't fooled. The bad guys were out there.

And evil always won.

He shoved away from the window, but a motion on the sidewalk caught his eye. A woman hurried into view, her long woolen coat flapping in the wind, her thick chestnut hair whipping around her face. *The woman who ran the teen shelter.* He'd seen her from a distance a couple of times. But this close he caught the elegance in her slender frame, the graceful way she moved. She had clear, creamy skin, an open, appealing face. She was in her early thirties, he guessed, and wholesome in a girl-next-door sort of way.

Wholesome. Right. Just what the world didn't need— another misguided do-gooder, idealistic and naive. A crusader out to save humanity.

He'd once been the same.

Well, he definitely knew better now.

A movement in the opposite direction grabbed his attention, and he turned his head. A teenager waddled into view across the street, heading the woman's way. One of the pregnant teenagers who stayed in the shelter. Her swollen belly gave her away.

The vibrations deepened and rattled the window. Rap music now boomed out, the spew of angry lyrics throbbing through Sully's skull. He shifted his weight from his aching leg, his nerves coiling tighter as he watched the street. A vehicle crawled into view, a black SUV with dark tinted windows, pimped out with flashy chrome. *Gangbangers.* He'd seen them cruising the neighborhood in the past few days, staking their claim to the territory, challenging anyone who stood in their way.

But this situation felt different. They were driving too slowly, inching down the street with lethal intent. Was a drug deal going down—or something worse?

What did it matter? This wasn't his problem. He had no reason to get involved.

And yet… He stood motionless at the window, his attention riveted on the unfolding scene. The young kid crossing the street. The SUV steadily approaching. The woman from the shelter scurrying along the sidewalk as she rushed toward the pregnant teen.

He didn't like this. His instincts were clamoring hard. He needed to get those women off the street *pronto* before someone ended up dead.

Kicking into gear now, he reached into his waistband and tugged out his Glock—a holdover from his army days. Then, keeping his gaze glued on the oncoming vehicle, he limped to the front door. He pulled it open and stepped outside onto the sagging porch.

The cold air brushed his skin. The heavy bass from the SUV thundered through his chest. The pregnant girl was halfway across the street now, her face registering fear as she caught sight of the gang.

The tinted windows on the SUV rolled down. The barrel of a rifle appeared, the shock of it halting his steps. *An E-13.* He couldn't mistake the experimental weapon with its distinctive bullpup configuration, even from this far away.

And they were going to use it to shoot that kid.

Without warning, the shelter woman darted into the street, straight into the line of fire, and his heart careened to a stop. She didn't have a chance. The gang would mow her down before she made it three more feet.

He leaped off the porch and charged.

* * *

She wasn't going to make it. She'd never get Lindsey to safety before the gang began to shoot. She'd just run out of time.

A shot barked out from the vehicle. The girl let out a panicked scream. Desperation erupting inside her, Haley lunged to Lindsey's side, staying between her and the SUV in an attempt to shield her and that precious babe.

But then a man barreled into the street out of nowhere. Startled, she whipped around. She caught sight of shaggy blond hair and furious eyes as he rushed toward her, a pistol in his left hand.

"Go!" he shouted. "Take cover behind the car!"

Haley didn't hesitate. Dragging Lindsey with her, she sprinted toward the curb while the man opened fire on the SUV, the sharp reports thundering through the air. She dove to the ground, pushing Lindsey behind the engine block, deliriously grateful for the mystery man's help. But who was he? Where had he come from? And where had he gotten that gun?

The gang returned fire, the staccato of semi-automatic gunfire making her flinch. Fearing bullets would penetrate the vehicle, she flattened herself over the teenager, determined to protect her at any cost. Their avenger ducked behind a nearby tree, but a new horror fisted in Haley's throat. He'd helped rescue the teenager—but now the gang was shooting at him. How could he possibly survive?

The shots went on forever, the rapid-fire stream of bullets shattering the windows on the house nearby. More shots slammed into the car, the force of the deadly blasts making it rock. Hardly able to think straight,

Haley covered the girl's head, total pandemonium breaking loose inside. *They'd never make it out alive.*

The shooting paused. Rap music drummed through the silence, the menacing sound stoking her nerves. Their rescuer sprang out from behind the tree, firing several rounds at the SUV as he raced over and dove behind the parked car. He landed close beside her, breathing hard.

She spared a glance his way, gathering a quick impression of dark, slashing brows, a steel jaw lined with heavy stubble, shoulders so broad they blocked the light. He ejected a spent magazine, then slammed another into his gun without looking at her. Whoever he was, whatever guardian angel had sent this commando to save them, they owed him their lives.

Assuming any of them survived.

"Stay right there," he shouted as more gunfire tatted out, and she covered her ringing ears. But the firefight raged, the noise horrific. Bullets sprayed the parked cars. Haley tried her best to shield the teenager, but the futility of their predicament hit her hard. How could they escape this? The three of them were doomed.

The din grew even louder, the cacophony so overwhelming she thought her head would splinter apart. Then the shooting abruptly stopped. Tires squealed and the SUV zoomed off. The thumping music grew fainter as the vehicle drove farther away.

For a minute, she didn't move. She gasped for breath, her pulse still chaotic at the close call. Her ears throbbed in the painful silence, the girl's frantic whimpers finally penetrating her daze.

"Are you all right?" the man asked.

His low, gravelly voice drew her attention, and she

turned her head. She met his grim, whiskey-hued eyes, and her belly made a little clutch, the reaction catching her unprepared. Startled, she took in his dark, furrowed brows, the stark angles of his craggy face. He had straight, collar-length hair dampened with sweat, a slightly off-center nose that hinted at less than a choirboy past. A few days' worth of razor stubble—several shades darker than his blond hair—covered his throat and jaw.

Her heart took another swerve. He wasn't exactly handsome. But man, oh man, was he attractive. Arresting. Thoroughly masculine in a decidedly carnal way. He looked like an old-fashioned gunslinger, like the loner who rode into town, risking his life to battle the bad guys and save the day. A solitary man in need of comfort who left behind a trail of broken hearts as he rode away.

This was the homeless man, she realized with a start. But he was nothing like she'd expected. He was younger—in his midthirties at most—and far more virile. He wore work boots and tattered jeans, a long-sleeved T-shirt he'd pushed up to his elbows, exposing the tendons roping his arms. His hands were big and lean. He cradled the gun with lethal ease.

He was the sexiest man she'd ever seen.

Her throat suddenly dry, she managed a nod. "I'm fine." *Thanks to you.*

"Well, you're damned lucky. What the hell were you thinking, running out into the street like that? You could have been killed."

His sudden anger took her aback. "I had to protect Lindsey. I couldn't let them…" Suddenly remembering the pregnant teenager, she rolled aside. "Oh, God. Lindsey. Are you hurt?"

The girl lifted her head, her eyes huge in her too-pale face. "I'm okay. But…what happened? Who was that? Why were they shooting at us?"

Haley's mouth went flat, her own anger stirring now. "The Ridgewood gang." Based primarily in Baltimore, the gang had recently begun making inroads into nearby Washington, D.C., in an effort to control the heroin trade. And she'd be damned if they'd chase her out.

Grabbing hold of the car's door handle, she pulled herself upright, more shaken than she cared to admit. She'd been in a lot of danger during her homeless years, but this incident ranked up there with the worst.

The man reached out his hand to the teenager and helped her to her feet. And Haley couldn't help but blink. He towered above them, his wide shoulders heavy with muscle, his lean body whittled of any fat. And he'd materialized by magic, like some sort of avenging angel.

A very earthly angel. Her heart made another lurch.

"Who are you?" Lindsey sounded just as awed.

"Sully. Sullivan Turner."

His deep voice rumbled through Haley like a caress. Braced for the sensual impact, she met his gaze dead-on. "Well, Sully Turner. I have to thank you. You saved our lives."

His eyes narrowed a fraction. "So why *were* they shooting at you?"

"Wrong place, wrong time, I guess. They're establishing their territory, and we got in their way."

"I don't think so."

She paused. "What do you mean? You think they were targeting us specifically?"

"That's how it looked from where I stood."

Her belly dipped. Dread whispered through her, a memory ghosting back from the past. *But that was nuts.* The killer couldn't have found her. There was no way he would know where she was—not after all these years. And even if he did, why would he want to harm her? The actual shooters were dead now. She couldn't implicate anyone else in that long-ago crime. She had nothing to worry about. She was safe.

"That's crazy. That shooting was random." It had to be. Because the alternative scared her down to her bones.

"If you say so." His eyes skeptical, Sully stuffed his pistol into the waistband of his jeans. "Come on. You need to get off the street before they come back."

Her heart skittered a beat. "Why would they come back?"

"I hit one. I'm not sure how bad he's bleeding, but they're going to retaliate."

He was right. The gang wouldn't let a challenge like that go unanswered, especially when they were determined to rule the street. They would insist on exacting revenge.

Which meant Lindsey wasn't safe. The other girls in her care weren't safe. Even this homeless man wasn't safe. He was a marked man now—because he'd rescued *her*.

She'd endangered the life of an innocent man.
Again.

Chapter 2

Sully limped up the sidewalk beside the woman, his hands trembling, his pulse jumping, a cold sweat beading his palms. That semi-automatic gunfire kept ricocheting through his mind in an endless loop, making it hard to distinguish his nightmares from fact.

But one thing was clear, even to his battle-fogged brain. Something was terribly wrong here. The gang gunning down two unarmed women to establish their territory didn't make sense. It would bring the police force out in droves, giving them unwanted scrutiny, something they'd never risk. And he'd seen the doubt flitting through the woman's eyes, that flicker of remembered fear. She was hiding something. Something important. Something to do with that ruthless gang.

Stuffing his shaking hands into his pockets, he slid her a sideways glance. She didn't look like the type to consort with gang members. She looked too innocent, too *decent* with those wide, hazel eyes, that lush and tempting mouth. Her thick hair gleamed in the twilight, streaks of sorrel and mahogany mixed with the chestnut brown. But after her reckless dash into the street—defying bullets to save that kid—he could imagine her doing something foolhardy and ticking them off.

But who she was, what the gang wanted from her—none of that mattered to him. *It couldn't.* He'd already interfered in her life enough. He'd just accompany her to her shelter, make sure she and the kid got inside safely and leave. He refused to get more involved.

They reached her row house a minute later, and the pregnant teenager rushed up the steps. Sully hung back, taking in the freshly painted black shutters, the pale yellow bricks of the facade. Pumpkins lined the porch. An autumn wreath hung on the door. The place was an anomaly on the rundown street, an oasis of cheerfulness and warmth. But he guessed that was the point of a shelter. The small plaque beneath the wreath read Always Home.

She paused on the step above him and turned around. "I'm sorry. I never introduced myself. I'm more rattled than I thought. I'm Haley. Haley Barnes."

For a moment, he couldn't answer. Her greenish-brown eyes held him spellbound, the lilt of her voice derailing his thoughts. His heart sped up, the sudden punch of adrenaline catching him off guard.

But then the door swung open behind her. She turned and hurried up the remaining steps. Stunned at his reaction, he followed more slowly, trying to wrap his head around what had occurred. What the hell was he thinking? Sure, she was pretty. And even though he deserved to be, he wasn't exactly dead.

But this woman was beyond off-limits. She came from a different world. And the last thing she needed in her life was a man like him—a washed-up, wounded ex-soldier, an alcoholic plagued with flashbacks, a man so haunted by his failures that he could barely make it through the night, let alone take care of her.

Shaking himself back to his senses, he stepped over the threshold into the room. The shelter had the same layout as Jason's row house, but the similarities ended there. This place had gleaming hardwood floors, a banked fire smoldering in the fireplace, the embers glowing red and orange. Oversize armchairs surrounded the fireplace. A basket of pinecones sat on the hearth. Beneath the window was an inviting sofa, piled high with faded quilts. The place even smelled appealing, like cinnamon and pumpkin pie.

Always Home. She'd created a home, all right, a cozy refuge for the teenage girls. The kind of place he had no right to after that debacle in the desert sand.

He shifted his gaze, taking in the half-dozen girls clustered by a wooden staircase—all pregnant, all young, their eyes too knowing for their tender age. Like the kids he'd seen in Afghanistan. They'd had those same half-dead, traumatized eyes.

"We need to leave," Haley told the girls. "Right away, before that gang comes back. Gather your things and meet me back here. *Fast.*" Her voice was soft and calm, but authoritative—the voice of a woman used to taking charge. And the girls obeyed without question, racing up the staircase while she pulled out her phone.

"You have somewhere to go?" he asked, catching her gaze.

She nodded, but a small crease marred her brow.

"There's another shelter near here. I'm calling them now to see if they have room."

Sully crossed his arms and waited while she murmured into the phone. In less time than he'd expected, the girls traipsed back down the stairs. They all traveled light, each carrying a single knapsack slung over their backs.

A siren broke out in the distance. A second later, another one joined in. Haley pocketed her cell phone and turned to the girls. "All right. Is everyone here?"

The teenagers murmured assent.

"Good. I want to get out of here before the police show up."

Sully didn't blame her. The cops would descend in droves. They'd cordon off the street and canvass the neighbors, questioning everyone multiple times. He'd resigned himself to the scrutiny; he could hardly avoid it since his pistol shell casings littered the road. But Haley couldn't afford the delay. She needed to get those kids to safety before the gang regrouped.

"We need to stick together," she continued. "It's not far, just a few blocks. Walk as quietly and quickly as you can."

Sully's head came up. "Wait a minute. You don't have a car?"

Her gaze swung to his. "It's in the shop. They're going to meet us by the bridge and take us there."

Frowning, he rubbed his bristly jaw. He didn't like this. They'd be too exposed on foot. They'd been lucky enough to survive the first attack with just one kid in tow. An entire group of pregnant teenagers made them sitting ducks.

"I'll go with you."

"That's not necessary."

"The hell it isn't. What if that gang shows up?"

Her face paled, but she raised her chin. "We'll deal with it. You've done enough. I appreciate your help, a lot. But—"

"I'm armed, and you're not. You need somebody to guard your back. Now, let's get going. We're wasting time."

Doubt flickered in her eyes. She glanced at the girls and back, clearly reluctant to agree. But then she gave him a nod. "Fine. Thanks."

He knew she didn't want to involve him. And who could blame her? Who'd want a derelict like him around? But he had to give her points. She did what she needed to protect the girls.

Or she knew more about that gang than she'd let on.

She turned back to the pregnant teens. "Let's go, then. We'll leave through the back."

Careful to keep his distance, Sully followed the girls through the kitchen to the fenced-in patio, then waited while she locked the door. She paused to embrace Lindsey, then murmured something to another teen, evoking a shaky smile.

The girls liked her, he realized. And why not? There was something comforting about her. She was gentle and warm, but in a take-charge sort of way. She radiated confidence, reassurance. She was the kind of woman they knew they could depend on, a woman who'd confronted a gang to save their lives. No wonder she drew them in.

Without warning, a wistfulness rose inside him, a yearning to bask in that soothing warmth. To forget the past, forget the evil lurking in the world, to feel whole and happy again.

Shocked, he pulled himself upright. What was wrong with him tonight? That gunfire hadn't only triggered a flashback, it had knocked something loose in his head. Maybe once upon a time, he could have pursued her. Maybe before he'd lost his illusions. Maybe before he'd gone to war.

But not now. *Not ever.* He hardened his jaw, determined to keep his focus on what mattered—getting her and those kids to safety fast. Then he'd head back into exile where he belonged.

Before he succumbed to his sudden insanity and lost what little remained of his common sense.

Haley led the way out the back gate and through the alley, her senses sharp, the persistent feeling of danger mounting with every step. She scoured the deep shadows blanketing the tomb-like lane, the bushes frothing in the cold, night breeze. The sirens began to draw closer, the eerie sound ratcheting her tension up another notch, adding to the urge to flee.

But she had to give the girls credit. No one complained. No one panicked or lagged behind. They padded along in silence, the faint crunch of dried leaves under their feet the only sound. Now if she could just get them to that van in time....

She stole a quick glance back at their protector looming behind the girls. He walked with a decided limp, his steps amazingly stealthy despite his size. An ex-soldier, without a doubt. Possibly suffering from post-traumatic stress, given his reaction to the attack—sweating, shaking, his entire body bristling with the need to bolt.

She turned around with a sigh. She hated involving him in her problems. He'd already risked his life enough—and he'd clearly wanted to leave. But frankly, she needed his help. She had the lives of six pregnant teenagers on her hands, not to mention their unborn babes.

And she had to admit that he intrigued her. That naked longing she'd glimpsed in his eyes—that hint of vulnerability he'd quickly masked—had aroused every nurturing instinct she possessed. He was an enigma, a strong, taciturn man wrapped in a body that vibrated with sexual hunger—nearly impossible to resist.

But she definitely had to resist him. She had no business thinking about Sully Turner that way. She had nothing to offer a man like him long-term. Short-term, either, if her nightmares had come true and her past had caught up to her at last.

She stopped at the end of the alley and waited for the girls to catch up. Her apprehension growing, she glanced around, wondering if she'd made a mistake. She thought they'd have time to escape before the gang returned. But what if they didn't? What if the gang came back sooner than she'd anticipated and caught them out here alone? Even with Sully providing cover, they wouldn't stand a chance.

The girls formed a circle around her, waiting for instructions. The wind blew hard, and she shivered inside her wool coat. "Okay, listen up." She didn't want to scare them, but she had to make sure they understood. "There'll be a white panel van waiting on the corner of Massachusetts Avenue. I don't think anything will happen, but if it does, if you hear gunshots or we get separated for any reason, just run to the van. Don't look back. Don't wait for me. As soon as you're all there, just go. I'll catch up later. All right?"

The girls murmured their agreement, but she could sense their dismay. "Don't worry." Giving them each a hug, she did her best to keep them calm. "We're all going to be fine." *She hoped.* She'd never forgive herself if they came to harm.

Letting the girls precede her, she fell in beside Sully at the rear. They crossed the road at the corner market and continued up a quiet side street, past an empty lot. A car drove by, quickening her pulse, but it didn't stop. A city bus lumbered past, heading the opposite way. But still no sign of the gang.

They made it to another cross street and started up the following block. The street was residential, the faint light from the row houses casting a gleam across their path. She slid Sully a glance, taking in the jut of his rugged jaw, the leashed power in his muscled frame, the intensity in his eyes as he scanned the street. Thank goodness he'd come along. Even with the odds against them, he made her feel less exposed.

The road curved. She spotted the white panel van, just one more block ahead. *Almost there.* She opened her mouth to say so, but gunfire suddenly broke out, the sharp reports shattering the calm. Sully whipped out his gun and spun around. "Run!"

The teenagers scattered at once. Frantic to protect them, Haley raced after them up the street. More shots rang out and she put on a burst of speed, praying they'd make it to the van in time. Up ahead, the fastest girls leaped inside.

Just three more kids to go.

But then, Lindsey stumbled and fell, landing on the

pavement with an anguished cry. Haley darted over and pulled her up.

"I'm fine," the girl gasped, staggering upright. Another shot erupted, and she let out a panicked shriek.

"Go!" Haley urged, and the teenager sprinted away. But where was Sully? *Had he been hit?* She whirled on her heels to see.

Then he charged toward her out of the darkness and seized her arm. "Over here! Come on!"

Still gripping her biceps, he dragged her toward an alley behind a house. Haley caught a glimpse of Lindsey at the corner, climbing into the van. The passenger door slid shut, and the van roared off into the night. *The girls were safe, thank God.* But she and Sully were exposed now, the gang in full pursuit.

She raced with him down the alley, their footsteps hammering the ground. Her lungs heaved. Her thigh muscles burned, but she forced herself to go on. Then Sully jerked her to a halt, dragging her behind a Dumpster along the fence. "Stay here."

"What? No way. You're not fighting them alone." Not after she'd caused this mess.

"You're not armed. Just stay put, and I'll be right back." Not waiting for an answer, he crept away.

Clinging to the Dumpster, she gasped for breath. She wasn't about to let him face that gang without her, no matter what he thought.

But he was right about the weapon. She wouldn't do any good unarmed. Standing on her tiptoes, she lifted the lid on the Dumpster and peered inside, but all she could make out in the darkness were mounds of plastic bags.

The rapid thud of approaching footsteps reached her

ears. *Not Sully.* The steps were too even. They lacked his distinctive limp.

Her desperation surging, she searched the shadows around the Dumpster for a way to defend herself. She spotted a two-by-four and picked it up, then flattened herself against the metal container to wait.

Her palms began to sweat. Her heartbeat ran completely amok. She listened intently, every sense focused on the person coming her way.

The footsteps slowed. She held her breath, keeping her body completely still. Then a man stepped into view, holding a gun. Knowing she'd only have one chance, one split second to surprise him and knock him out, she raised the board, then slammed it against his skull. A sickening crack rent the night. Pain radiated up her arms, and she bit down hard on a moan. The man sank to the pavement, his body limp. His pistol skidded away.

But more footsteps pounded nearby, the sudden flurry of activity jump-starting her pulse. She lifted the board again, preparing to strike.

"It's me," Sully called out. A second later, he emerged from the darkness and limped to her side.

Her breath rushed out. She staggered to the Dumpster and slumped against it, dizzy with relief. "What happened?"

"They're gone. There were only a couple of them this time, and I chased them off."

"Not all of them." She gestured to the man on the ground.

"Hell." His eyes shot to hers. "Are you all right?"

Pressing a hand to her chest, she gave him a nod. "Just winded." And her arm ached. "He dropped his gun. I'm not sure where it went."

He held her gaze for a heartbeat, his expression impossible to read in the dusky night. Then he turned away and searched the ground. "Here it is." He retrieved the gun, then dropped to one knee beside her attacker and rolled him onto his back.

"He's not dead, is he?" Even though he'd intended to harm her, she hated to think that she'd killed the man.

"No, just unconscious. You recognize him?"

She tossed aside the board and stepped closer, trying to make out his features in the dark. He looked young, not much older than the girls in her shelter, with light-colored hair and skin. Blood trickled down his jaw toward a dark form writhing across his neck. "Is that a snake tattoo?"

"Looks like it."

"Then he's a member of the Ridgewood gang. That's one of their signs."

Sully grunted. He checked the gang member's pockets, unearthing a wicked-looking knife, several magazines for the handgun and a cell phone. He tucked the weapons into his pockets and rose, then turned on the phone and checked the calls.

Suddenly, he went stock-still.

"What is it?" Her apprehension rising, she searched his face.

His gaze cut to hers, the sudden suspicion in his eyes jolting her heart. "What did you say your name was?"

"Haley Barnes."

"Not Burroughs?"

Her lungs stopped dead. *Burroughs.* No one had called her that in years. Fifteen years, to be exact. Fifteen terrifying years spent running for her life. *But how would the gang know her name?*

"I...I go by Barnes now. But Burroughs..." She tried to swallow, but failed. "That used to be my name. Why do you ask?"

Sully's gaze stayed on hers. Several charged seconds crawled past. Dread pounded inside her, so fierce she could hardly breathe.

Then Sully held up the cell phone for her to see. "This guy got a text message. There's a reward for the capture of Haley Burroughs—and it's double if you're brought in dead."

Chapter 3

She had a price on her head.

Haley jogged down the alley beside Sully, the revelation making her reel. That shooting hadn't been random. They'd targeted her specifically. *Her*. Haley Burroughs.

They knew who she really was.

And they'd put a bounty on her head. Now every criminal on the east coast would be gunning for her to claim the prize. And if that weren't bad enough, she was more valuable dead than alive.

Sully slowed to a walk and she followed suit, trying to come to grips with that awful thought. "So what's going on?" he asked.

She glanced at his steely face, knowing she had to explain. He'd rescued the girls. He'd risked his life for her. *Twice*. She'd swept him into this lethal mess, painting a gang target on his back—and all because he'd tried to help.

"This can't be a typical turf war if they're after you," he added.

She pressed her hand to her belly to quiet her nerves. "You're right. It's not." It was far, far worse. Her past had come back to haunt her. Her worst fear had just come true.

"It's complicated," she hedged.

"Try me."

Hesitating, she looked away. She never revealed her past. She'd concealed her identity and stayed on the run for years. And even though she'd thought the danger had finally passed, that it was safe to return to the mid-Atlantic area, she still used a pseudonym and stayed out of the limelight in case someone recognized her.

But she could trust this man. He'd leaped into the path of danger, putting his life on the line on her behalf. And she owed him the truth after all he'd done.

But first they needed to find a place to hide. They couldn't stay on the street, exposed. Her shelter would do no good; the gang would have it staked out. And neither could they join the teenagers and risk leading the danger to them.

She caught Sully's gaze. "All right," she said. "I'll tell you. But we need to find a taxi first. A friend of mine lives in Baltimore with her fiancé, and I need to let them know what's going on."

"Baltimore? That's forty miles away."

"I know. The fare's going to be through the roof. But they're involved in this, too. And my friend's fiancé is a cop. We can talk while we're on the way."

He frowned at that. She didn't blame him if he wanted to bolt. He probably regretted setting eyes on her considering the disaster she'd mired him in.

"A cop, huh?"

"Yes. His name's Parker McCall. He's a detective with the Baltimore Police Department." A sudden thought gave her pause. "Is that a problem?"

His gaze snapped to hers. "You think I'm a criminal?"

"No, of course not." She trusted her instincts about people. She'd had to as a runaway if she'd hoped to survive. And whatever tormented Sully was inside him. Deep inside. If he was fleeing, it was from himself.

He plowed his hand through his shaggy hair. "All right. I'll go with you."

"Good." She started across the street. "We can catch a taxi at the Colonial Hotel. It's just a few blocks from here."

Inhaling, she tried to regroup. She eyed the traffic whizzing past, the people standing across the street, waiting for the metro bus. The normality of the scene felt bizarre. They'd barely lived through a gun battle, and yet the world went on unaffected with people continuing their usual lives.

But she couldn't let the peacefulness fool her. She had the Ridgewood gang hunting her down. Someone was determined to see her dead. But was it really that long-ago killer? *How could he have discovered her name?*

"If I'm right," she finally began, "this goes back to when I was a teenager. When I ran away from home."

Sully turned his head. "You were a runaway?"

"Yes." She picked up her pace, as if walking faster could help her escape the past. But she could never out-run that painful time—pregnant, her parents insisting on an abortion, her boyfriend unwilling to help raise the child. So she'd run away, determined to keep the baby, convinced she could make it on her own.

She'd been wrong. Her baby had paid the price.

So had she.

But Sully didn't need to know all that. And it didn't matter now. She'd come a long way since then. She was no longer that naive girl. "I was fifteen. It was tough."

"I'll bet."

She slanted him a glance. He'd obviously seen enough of the streets to know. "I got lucky, though. I met two other girls. We stayed together for protection and became best friends. We still are."

They stopped to wait for a red light. "Go on," he said in his rusty voice.

The light changed to green, and she stepped into the street. "One of those girls was Brynn, the friend we're going to see. She had a camera she always carried around. She wanted to be a photographer, even then. She'd decided to take some pictures of an abandoned warehouse. We tried to talk her out of it. Baltimore didn't have many gangs back then, but there was one, the City of the Dead, and they ruled the neighborhood where the warehouse was. But we couldn't convince her to stay away.

"Nadine and I went with her, but I was scared so we waited on the street outside." A mistake she'd regretted ever since.

She swallowed hard, her belly tightening at the memory, but she forced herself to go on. "We were right to worry. She stumbled across a crime scene, a gang execution. She caught it on film."

"They saw her?" Sully guessed.

She nodded. "They chased her. They chased us all."

"So you saw them, too?"

"No. Brynn came flying out of the warehouse, shouting at us to run, so we did. I didn't look back. And then I heard shots...."

Lost in the gruesome memory, she tripped. Sully lunged over and steadied her arm. She glanced up at his face, intending to thank him, but for an instant, his dark gold eyes held her riveted, the sheer maleness of him arresting her thoughts. And once again, his incredible appeal rolled through her, making her breath back up in her lungs.

He dropped her arm and stepped away.

Her face burned. Embarrassed at her reaction, she looked away. *Lovely.* This was all the poor man needed. They had their lives on the line, a vicious gang hunting them down—and her hormones chose this moment to go berserk.

Steering her thoughts back to her story, she cleared her throat. "Anyway, another runaway we knew was nearby. Tommy McCall. He was Parker's younger brother. He got in their way, giving us a chance to escape. He saved our lives."

"Was?"

That was the worst of it. "The gang killed him." Tommy's gallantry had cost him his life.

She lapsed into silence again, the guilt plaguing her even now. Tommy had died because of them.

Several cars sped past. The cold wind picked up, and she hunched deeper into her coat to escape the chill.

"So you never saw the shooters?" Sully asked, drawing her attention back to him.

"No, but they didn't know that. And they saw me."

"But your friend took pictures. So you know who they are."

"Yes, but both of the shooters are dead now. The last one died a couple of weeks ago."

He angled his head to meet her eyes. "Then who's trying to kill you? And what does this have to do with the Ridgewood gang?"

She sighed. "I told you it was complicated. About ten years ago, the City of the Dead disbanded. Most of their members were dead by then. The ones who'd survived ended up merging with the Ridgewood gang. And it seems the leader of the original gang—the head honcho who ordered that execution in the warehouse—was one of the ones who survived.

"We don't know much about him, just that he now has power. Lots of power. We think he even has ties to the police. In fact, he had Markus Jenkins released from jail—he's the head of the Ridgewood gang."

"And that's who's after you."

"It's the only explanation that makes sense right now. No one else would want me dead. What's ironic is that none of us can identify him. We don't have a clue who he is. But I guess he doesn't want to take the chance.

"I don't understand how he found me, though. We went on the run after that shooting. We changed our names and moved around the country for years. I only came back here a couple years ago to be closer to Brynn. And I've kept a really low profile since then."

"But somehow he found you. He sent his gang after you."

It was worse than that. She came to a stop. The dread inside her grew. "I haven't used the last name Burroughs since I left home. I told you, I go by Haley Barnes now.

So this killer knows who I really am. He's figured out where I live.

"And he knows that you helped me." Fear for him chilled her heart. "He'll come after you, too, now. You'll never be able to escape."

And unless she managed to stop him, history would repeat itself. And another innocent man who tried to help her would lose his life.

Sully didn't know what disturbed him more, to think of Haley as a teenage runaway or that she had a gang contract on her head.

He sat across from her in her friends' Baltimore apartment, still reeling from what she'd revealed. She looked so damned fragile huddled on the sofa, her face drained of any color, her full lips flattened with worry, dark circles smudging her soft eyes. Every instinct inside him urged him to drag her off to a distant cave, to hole up with her somewhere safe and keep the danger from coming her way.

Not that she was defenseless. Far from it. She'd taken down that gang member. She'd run straight into a firefight to save that pregnant teen. But a powerful killer wanted her dead, a man who'd hunted her for fifteen years. How was she going to fight that?

It wasn't his business. He'd done his job. He'd gotten her to Baltimore and informed her friends about the attacks. They'd added some details to Haley's story—that the victim executed in the warehouse had been a junkie named Allen Chambers, and that one of the shooters had been a cop.

But he'd done his part. And now it was time to go. Her friends could take it from here.

They emerged from the kitchen just then. Brynn Elliot, a diminutive redhead with a heavily bandaged shoulder, settled next to Haley on the couch. Her fiancé took a seat on the armchair opposite his. Parker McCall was tall, nearly Sully's height, with a steady, unflinching gaze—a man who inspired trust. He had one arm in a sling, courtesy of the same gun battle that wounded Brynn.

"We made some calls," Brynn told Haley. "Parker can get you into a safe house. Both of you," she added, glancing Sully's way.

"Thanks, but I'll be all right on my own."

"I'm not going into hiding, either," Haley said.

"It's not forever," her friend told her. "Just until we track this guy down."

"But—"

"Haley, you've got a reward on your head." Exasperation tinged Brynn's voice. "The Ridgewood gang's going to be searching for you everywhere. You've got to go somewhere safe."

The cop shifted forward, drawing their gaze. "Brynn's right. It's too dangerous. You need to go to a safe house."

"You're not hiding," Haley pointed out. "And you're in as much danger as I am."

The redhead shook her head. "No, I'm not. There isn't a contract out on me."

"That you know of."

"Right. But I've also got Parker to watch my back."

Whereas Haley was on her own. Sully clasped his hands, trying not to care. *Not his business,* he reminded himself fiercely. He needed to forget her plight, forget the fear shadowing her lovely eyes, forget how soft she'd felt when he'd held her arm.

"It's only for a while," her friend argued. "Only until we find out who's behind all this."

"And how long will that take? Months? Years? You said you aren't making progress."

Sully frowned at that. "You don't have any leads?"

"No." Parker grimaced. "It's someone high up. We know that much. Everyone's running scared. All our snitches refuse to talk."

"All the more reason to hide," Brynn pointed out.

But Haley only shook her head. "Look. I know you mean well. It makes sense to lay low for a while. And the runaways don't need me now. They're safer if I stay away.

"But I don't want to hide. I've spent too many years on the run—and the danger *still* hasn't gone away. And I'm sick of it. I'm tired of looking over my shoulder, wondering when he's going to catch up. I have to at least try to fight back."

"How?" Sully cut in, not liking how this was going. "You can't fight a gang like that. Christ, you saw them. They even had an E-13."

The cop shot him a startled glance. "What?"

Sully exhaled. "I forgot to tell you. They had one in the car."

"An E-13? Are you sure?"

"Yeah. I fired one in Afghanistan. I recognized the design—the bullpup configuration, the top-mounted magazine. And those high-velocity cartridges made Swiss cheese out of those cars. We're lucky they couldn't control their shots."

"Then the rumors on the street are true...."

"What rumors? What's an E-13?" Haley asked. Both women looked confused.

"It's an experimental weapon," Parker told her. "A shoulder-fired submachine gun with a really short barrel. It's similar to the P-90 but smaller. It has the same ambidextrous controls, but a better feeding system, and it fires more rounds."

"Our military's field-testing them," Sully added. "Production's limited. They aren't on the market yet. Not even the black market."

Or so they'd thought.

"What that means," he continued, returning to the point, "is that you're out armed. There's no way you can fight them alone."

Her frown deepening, Haley rose and walked to the window, her slender spine straight, her hips gently swinging in her low-slung jeans. He took in the glossy hair tumbling over her shoulders, the seductive curve of her back, trying to ignore the sensual tug. He understood her reluctance to hide, and he sympathized with her need to fight back. But she'd never fend off that gang, even without the E-13s. She *had* to go somewhere safe.

She turned around and sighed. "I know you're worried, but I'm not completely defenseless. I've got some high-powered connections, too."

Brynn swiveled around to face her, grimacing as she moved her arm. "You're not serious."

"Why not? They know everyone in Baltimore and D.C."

Sully frowned. It was his turn to be confused. "Who does?"

"My parents. My father's a criminal defense attorney. He represents a lot of gang members. He knows everyone—the police, people in the criminal justice system, politicians. And my mother knows even more people than he does. Her ancestors helped found this town. If the person behind this is that high-level, they'll know him for sure."

"Assuming they agree to help you," Brynn said.

Haley crossed her arms, worry darkening her eyes. "I know. It's a long shot. We didn't exactly part on friendly terms. But it's worth a try."

Her friend didn't look convinced. "I guess a phone call wouldn't hurt."

"No. I need to see them in person. Otherwise they'll just hang up. There's a fund-raiser tomorrow night for area shelters. I wasn't going to go, but now…" She shrugged. "It's at Hunter Hall in Virginia. All the bigwigs will be out in force."

"I heard about that," Parker said. "The police commissioner's going to attend."

Sully's frown deepened. The uneasy feeling inside him grew. "Wait a minute. You said the guy who's after you has power. What if he's there?"

"Then I can draw him out."

The hell she would. Outraged, he rose and limped to her side. "Are you crazy? You can't take a risk like that. You saw that text message. You can't just walk around in the open with a bounty on your head."

"So I'll take a bodyguard along."

He still didn't like it. He glowered back, his protective instincts raging, needing to force her to listen to sense. But he didn't have that right. And neither did he want it. This woman meant nothing to him.

Then Parker spoke up from across the room. "I can

get a cop to go with you. I know a few who moonlight as bodyguards."

Sully shot him a look of disbelief. "You can't be serious. She needs to hide, not appear in public, risking her life."

But Haley broke in. "It doesn't matter. I can't use the police. The killer could recognize a cop. I need someone less obvious. Someone I can pass off as my date." Her gaze returned to his.

Realization sank in. He took a quick step back. "Forget it."

"Why not? You obviously know how to shoot. And you're in this as much as I am. That gang's after you now, too."

He didn't care about himself. He should have died months ago. But Haley needed protection—protection he couldn't provide.

"I can't." He had a bum leg. He suffered from chronic flashbacks. Hell, he was so messed up he could barely function without a drink, let alone safeguard her. And his intuition was off. The last time he'd relied on his instincts, he'd screwed up—and his men had paid the price.

"He's right," the cop told her. "No offense to Sully, but you need a pro, someone who can keep his eye out for trouble in a place like that."

Someone who could stay sober, he meant.

Sully worked his jaw, suspecting his bloodshot eyes had given him away—or the way he'd guzzled the beer Parker had offered him when they'd first arrived. But even if it humiliated him to admit it, Parker was right. Haley didn't need a ruined man like him for her bodyguard.

But she only raised her chin. "I don't want anyone else."

"Too bad. I'm not going to do it."

Her eyes held his. The air between them pulsed. But then she glanced at her friends again. "Would you mind giving us a moment alone?"

"Sure. We'll be in the kitchen." Brynn struggled to her feet. Her fiancé helped her up, and they exited the room.

Sully folded his arms, steeling himself for the argument he knew would come. He didn't have long to wait.

"Listen, Sully. I don't blame you for not wanting to get involved in this."

"I can't."

She gave him a nod. "I understand."

"No, you don't. You don't know anything about me."

She tilted her head, her dark-lashed eyes on his. "I know some things. You saved my life today. You rescued the girls. If you hadn't been there we'd all be dead."

"I got lucky, that's all."

"It was a lot more than luck, and you know it."

"No, it wasn't. Don't twist this around. And don't make me into something I'm not. Your friends are right. They know I can't protect you. You need to listen to them."

Her eyes went soft. She moved even closer, her nearness muddling his thoughts. "They're wrong. You're wrong. But if you don't want to do it, I understand."

"Then you'll do what they say? You'll go to a safe house?"

"No. Not yet. I can't," she added when he hissed. "I have to try to get answers. If my parents won't talk, if I don't learn anything at the fund-raiser, then I'll reconsider my plan. But I have to give it a shot."

Frustrated, he gripped the back of his neck. He was starting to realize how she'd survived the streets—she was too damned stubborn to quit. "Then at least take a cop as your bodyguard."

"No. It's either you or no one. I won't change my mind about that. I can't. I'll never figure out who's involved if I tip him off."

His jaw clenched. Dread mingled with desperation at the thought of her taking on the killer alone. "That's not fair."

A sad smile curved her lips. "Don't worry, Sully. I don't blame you for not wanting to do this. I've already involved you enough."

Suddenly feeling cornered, Sully turned to the window and scowled out at the city lights. She'd just given him an out. He should leave right now while he still could. But he couldn't let her go to that fund-raiser alone. He'd never forgive himself if she got killed.

But how could he protect her? He was the worst possible man for the job. He swung around to face her again. "For God's sakes, Haley. Why can't you understand this? I'm not the man you need."

"But you're the one I want."

His hopes plummeted hard. He gazed into her hazel eyes, her gentle beauty swamping his heart. He was all wrong for this mission. He knew it. She knew it. Even her friends knew it.

But it was the resignation in her eyes that demolished his resolve. She spent her life helping others, yet expected nothing in return.

Feeling doomed, he released a sigh. "All right."

"You'll do it?"

"Yeah. I'll do it." He just hoped he didn't screw up.

Or he'd have this woman's innocent blood on his already-guilty hands.

Chapter 4

Despite what she'd told Sully, by the time they arrived at Hunter Hall, the eighteenth-century estate in the northern-Virginia countryside where the charity gala was being held, Haley's bravado was fading fast. She stared out the passenger-side window of their borrowed car at the thousands of acres of dusky woodland rolling toward the Shenandoah River and struggled to contain her nerves.

She dreaded confronting her parents. She feared exposing her presence to the killer who wanted her dead. Every instinct she possessed warned her to run, take cover, hide. Instead, she was going public, revealing her identity, setting herself up as a target—and putting Sully's life even more at risk.

But she had no choice. She couldn't go on looking over her shoulder. She couldn't keep fleeing the killer when he'd only find her again. And she couldn't continue to jeopardize those teenage girls. Unless she brought him down now, she could never return to her shelter. She would lose everything she'd worked for— her dreams, her sense of security, her *home*.

Still, she never should have involved Sully. She should have kept him far from the gang trying to murder her instead of coercing him to help. So what if he'd saved her life? She had no business endangering him further—no matter how badly she needed his support.

Battling back a flurry of anxiety, she cast him a glance, taking in the wide, muscled shoulders straining his tuxedo, the appealing contrast of his swarthy skin against his stark-white shirt. He'd combed his shaggy hair into submission and shaved the beard stubble from his face, revealing the hard planes of his cheeks and jaw. But somehow, his attempt to tame his appearance only emphasized the power of his features, making him look even more uncivilized.

He turned his head and his gaze connected with hers. And for one unguarded instant, that raw heat tangled between them, those whiskey-colored eyes wreaking havoc on her insides. Then he lowered his gaze, traveling over every inch of her, unleashing a frenzy of nerves in her chest.

She jerked her gaze to the windshield, her pulse on a wild stampede. *She didn't need this.* It didn't matter if he compelled her. It didn't matter if he radiated an inner pain she found hard to resist. She couldn't afford to let him distract her, no matter how much he stirred her blood. She had to track down the man trying to kill her—or they both would end up dead.

The long drive began to curve, the centuries-old oak trees and tulip poplars closing in on her like a gauntlet on either side. Then the mansion came into view, its huge white pillars spurring her pulse into another sprint. Sully stopped in front of the imposing entrance, and a teenage valet rushed over to open Haley's door. She stepped out of the car, trying to attribute the chills skidding down her spine to the cold, autumn breeze instead of fear.

Sully joined her at the portico steps. "Some place."

"It's on the historic register." The exquisitely restored mansion was the epitome of antebellum gentility with a huge central hall built of local limestone flanked by two-bay wings. Not exactly where she'd expect to confront a killer. But that's why they were here.

A burst of laughter drew her attention to the side of the house. Stopping, she studied the people crowded around a sports car parked beneath a tent. "They always have a raffle at these events," she explained. "People donate cruises, vacations, cars."

Sully raised a brow. "Must be nice to have that much money to give away."

"They don't do it to be kind. Well, maybe a few of them do." She had to be honest about that. "But for most of these people, money's a means to an end—status, power. That's how they measure your worth—by what you can do for them. And if you can't help them get ahead, they discard you without a thought."

Oh, God. Where had that tirade come from? Her face warmed as she realized how bitter she sounded, at how much of her past she'd disclosed. "I'm sorry, I—"

"Haley." Closing the distance between them, he reached out and cupped her jaw. His touch was gentle, barely there, but his warm, calloused skin sent a blaze of heat rushing through her, both thrilling and steadying her somehow. "We don't have to do this. We can leave right now."

His husky words rumbled through her. His eyes and voice held her captive, anchoring her in place. And for a minute, she was so darned tempted to take the easy way out, to jump back in the car and leave before anyone noticed them here.

But she'd never forgive herself if she gave up. This killer was threatening her friends, her pregnant girls, the dreams she'd spent years working to make real. She had to stand and fight.

"No. I need to talk to my parents. But let's make it fast, all right?"

He lowered his hand, a crooked smile warming his eyes. "A 'shoot and scoot' it is, then. A quick attack and then retreat," he added when she gave him a quizzical look. "We'll get the information we need and go."

"That sounds good." Especially the part about *retreat*. But she refused to run. She could handle her parents. She was older now. She had a satisfying life helping troubled teens. She didn't need their approval, didn't need them to validate her self-worth. And she wouldn't let them shake her composure, no matter how nervous she felt.

Sully offered her his arm. "Ready?"

"As much as I'll ever be." Gripping his arm for courage, she turned to the entrance and accompanied him through the massive door.

But one glance at the crowd milling beneath the chandeliers—their diamond jewelry flashing, their forced laughter rising above the strains of the string quartet—made her want to bolt. She despised this world—power brokers making deals over old-fashioneds. Women plotting remarriages over caviar. Do-gooders who wouldn't dream of getting their hands dirty, writing checks to absolve themselves of any real responsibility for fighting the evil plaguing the world.

But this wasn't the time to indulge in a rant. And no matter where the money came from—or why—it went to a worthy cause, supporting shelters like hers.

Assuming she survived long enough to collect the check.

While Sully took care of her shawl, she headed to the reception table tucked discreetly to the side of the foyer. Exquisite millwork covered the walls, along with museum-quality portraits in huge gilt frames.

"Haley Barnes and Sullivan Turner," she told one of the women manning the desk. "From Always Home Teen Shelter in D.C." The woman consulted her list, then murmured to the worker beside her. "I was late sending in my RSVP," she added, waiting while they shuffled through the names.

"Haley!"

Her heart lurching, she whipped around. A middle-aged man strode toward her with his hand outstretched. *Senator Alfred Riggs.* In his early sixties now, he looked stockier and grayer than when she'd seen him last. But he still had that aura of power that commanded respect, even in this moneyed crowd.

"It's great to see you." He sounded surprisingly genuine as he shook her hand. But then, he was a consummate politician, one of his party's rising stars. Rumor had it he was contemplating a run for the White House should the current vice president decide to retire.

Years of debutante training kicked in. She glued a smile on her face. "It's wonderful to be here, especially for such a worthy cause." Thanks to his own troubled childhood, the senator worked tirelessly on behalf of at-risk youth—which also endeared him to the voters, paying off at the ballot box.

"Thank you for hosting this gala," she added. "I appreciate the donation to my shelter."

"I didn't realize you worked in this field."

"Yes, I—" Sully came up beside her. Grateful for the interruption, she turned his way. "Senator Riggs, I'd like you to meet my escort, Sullivan Turner."

The senator's eyes turned speculative as he shook Sully's hand. "Have we met before? Your name sounds familiar."

"I doubt it."

Haley jumped into the breach. "Senator Riggs went to law school with my father."

The senator smiled. "That's right. And I had the pleasure of watching this lovely young woman grow up." He waved at someone in the crowd. "Here comes someone else you know. We'll catch up later," he promised, then strode away.

Haley peered over Sully's shoulder, experiencing an unexpected burst of pleasure as a woman in her early forties approached. "Gwendolyn Shaffer," she murmured to Sully. "The senator's chief of staff." One of the few genuinely nice people she knew.

"Haley." The woman gave her a kiss. "I didn't know you'd be here," she added after Haley had introduced Sully.

"I run a shelter in D.C. now. But I'm afraid I accepted the invitation at the last moment. They can't find us on the list." She motioned toward the women still rifling through pages of names.

"Latecomers are on the addendum," the chief of staff told them, and Haley smiled. Gwen had always been a "fixer," one of those competent, take-charge people everyone relied on to get things done. Apparently, that hadn't changed.

But her appearance had. Never slender, her hips had grown broader, her waist thicker over the years. Gray hairs now streaked her classic bob. But she still had that brisk, efficient attitude that had been her hallmark, propelling her formidable career.

And if anyone deserved success, it was Gwendolyn Shaffer. She'd helped make Haley's teen years tolerable, offering sympathy and support, especially after her sister's death.

"Oh, here we are." Apology in her eyes, the woman at the table handed Haley their raffle tickets and brochure. "You're automatically entered in the drawing. The winners are posted on the board near the orchestra as they're announced."

"Ms. Shaffer," another woman called out.

"Another crisis." Gwen rolled her eyes, but her smile softened the complaint. "We'll talk again later." She turned and hurried off.

"So your father went to school with the senator," Sully said, taking Haley's arm.

"He knows everyone. That's why I need to talk to him."

And there was no reason to delay. Inhaling deeply, she walked with Sully to the edge of the ballroom and scanned the crowd. Her belly churned. A clammy sweat moistened her upper lip at the thought of confronting her parents after all these years. But she'd come here to smoke out a killer.

And it was time to start.

* * *

An hour later, Sully limped beside Haley through the stifling room, no longer bothering to fake a smile. His head throbbed. His hands shook from the need to drink. His bum leg ached so badly he grimaced with every step.

And he was sick of the endless introductions, the air kisses and backslapping from vain, vacuous people who'd elevated chitchat to an art form, millionaires displaying surgically enhanced women to pump up their egos, men who wouldn't last two minutes on the battlefield posturing to exude an air of virility and power. He'd met celebrities, politicians, diplomats. The Virginia attorney general was here, along with the commissioner of the Baltimore Police Department. Across the room, the ambassador of Jaziirastan stood talking to Dean Walker, a high-powered CEO.

The place was a logistical nightmare. There were too many people, too much commotion beyond his control. The patio doors were wide open, allowing people to enter and exit at will. And with every passing moment, the uneasy feeling drumming inside him grew. Danger was here. He could feel it. But which direction it came from, he didn't know.

Damn, he needed a drink.

He eyed a passing waiter, tempted to indulge in a shot of whiskey to take the edge off his mounting nerves. But he couldn't take the chance. He couldn't afford to dull his reactions with Haley's life at risk. She was too vulnerable, too exposed, despite the crowded room.

He grabbed some water from the tray instead and gulped it down. Then he turned her way, skimming the graceful lines of her profile, the curve of her slender neck. She wore her hair up, but silky tendrils fluttered loose, softening the effect. And he had the strongest urge to move closer and inhale her seductive scent. To feel her softness wrapped around him and taste her sultry lips.

The dress she was wearing didn't help. Long, black and tight, it showed off her curves to perfection, hugging her full, round breasts and hips. The dress dipped low in the back, exposing a heart-stopping expanse of naked skin.

Skin he had no business ogling right now. He jerked his attention back to the jam-packed room. It was bad enough that he couldn't control their surroundings. Worse that he needed to drink so badly his heart was starting to race. But the last thing they both needed was to have lust fogging his brain, making it impossible to keep her safe.

The string quartet ended their piece. The emcee, a local radio personality, announced another batch of prizewinners to a smattering of polite applause. They were down to the final five.

Haley pulled out their ticket stubs from her little purse, then wrinkled her brow. "That's your ticket. You're one of the finalists."

He shot her a frown. "Forget it. We're not staying to the end."

"I know. I just need to find my parents, and then we can go."

Sully scanned the room, the crush of people making him sweat despite the open doors. He tried to loosen his collar, but failed. The rented tuxedo was too damned tight. "You're sure they're here?"

"Yes. They make a big show of supporting causes like this. They put on quite a show when I ran away, pretending to care. And events like this give them a chance to cash in on that sympathy again. Besides, I checked with my mother's secretary. I said I was on the attendance committee."

He tried to absorb all that. "Your mother has a secretary?"

Haley's bare shoulders rose. "She has a busy social calendar."

"Right." He shook his head, wondering exactly how wealthy her family was. "How long since you've seen your parents?"

"Fifteen years. I talked to them on the phone once after I ran away, but..." She lifted her shoulders again, that wounded look flitting back through her hazel eyes, the same hint of vulnerability he'd glimpsed on the porch.

And all of a sudden, the need to comfort her stirred inside him, the desire to erase the tiny frown marring her brow and let her know that she wasn't alone.

"I don't see my family, either," he confessed, then blinked, stunned that he'd let that slip. He never talked about his family. He tried not to even think about them after the mess he'd made of his life.

"Don't they want to see you?"

They wanted to see him, all right. But he couldn't stand the shame. He'd failed them all too badly, destroying their confidence and respect.

Not wanting to go down that disturbing track, he tugged on his collar again. "Something like that. It doesn't matter now."

But Haley's perceptive gaze lingered on his. And for one unguarded moment, he wanted to tell her the truth, to confess how horribly he'd screwed up. To reveal the guilt, the regret, the pain.

No wonder the kids in her shelter liked her. There was something soothing about this woman, something solid and warm and kind. Her soft eyes promised compassion, absolution. *As if she could make the world all right.*

But then her gaze shifted to someone behind him. Her spine stiffened, snapping his attention back to the ballroom and the danger shadowing their heels. His pulse accelerating, he wheeled around. "What is it?"

"My parents."

The dense crowd parted, revealing a couple heading their way. Sully's gaze zeroed in on her father, Oliver Burroughs. About six feet tall, the prominent Baltimore defense attorney had Haley's dark hair and hazel eyes, but the similarities ended there. His stride was an arrogant swagger, his eyes sharp and impatient as they skimmed the crowd. An egotist, Sully decided. A man consumed with his own inflated sense of power.

Sully's gaze shifted to the woman beside him. Haley's mother, Catherine, was tall, blonde and still strikingly beautiful, despite her advancing age. She had a slender build and a blade-thin nose in an impossibly flawless face. Like Haley, she wore her blond hair up, but not a strand was out of place. Diamonds glittered around her swanlike throat.

He swung his gaze to Haley, marveling at the difference. Haley certainly couldn't match her mother in looks. Her mother was more beautiful, at least in a superficial way. But Haley radiated an inner warmth he found far more appealing. She was softer, more authentic.

More tense. She clutched his arm with a death grip despite the smile pasted on her face. And his admiration for her rose. No matter how much she dreaded this confrontation, she didn't intend to let them know.

"Hello, Mother." Her voice was calm.

"Haley." The woman shifted her eyes to Sully. She sized him up and dismissed him in one cool glance. Not worth her time, he guessed.

Her gaze skipped back to Haley. She didn't bother to do the air-kiss thing. "How lovely to see you after all this time."

He'd never heard anything less sincere.

"It's been a while," Haley agreed. "Since I was a teenager, I think." She paused, but when her mother didn't answer, she soldiered on. "Hi, Dad."

Oliver Burroughs spared a glance at his daughter, his eyes lacking any warmth. Sully could see this attorney ripping his opponents in court to shreds.

"I was hoping to talk to you," she added.

"We don't have anything to say."

Haley's chin went up. Her smile didn't slip, but her fingers dug into Sully's arm so hard he expected bruises to form. "Please. It's important. I need information. It has to do with the Ridgewood gang."

Her father's eyes turned even colder. He glanced at Sully, then back to his daughter again. "You know I don't discuss my clients." He grabbed a drink from a passing waiter, then turned away.

But Haley released Sully's arm and blocked his path. "Please, Dad. I only need information. It won't take long, but…my life could be at risk. Can't we go somewhere to talk?"

Her mother's pinched nostrils flared. "Really, Haley. Your imagination always did get the best of you. And you heard his answer. Now please don't act crass and create a scene. You've damaged the family enough." She took her husband's arm and pulled him away. A moment later she stopped to greet the senator. Her forced laughter floated back.

Sully glanced down at Haley. She stood stock-still, her eyes stricken in her flushed face. His anger rose, his own face heating at the need to avenge the slight. What the hell was wrong with her parents? How could they ignore Haley's plea for help? Their daughter's life was at stake.

He balled his hands and stepped forward, determined to make them talk.

"Don't." She tugged his sleeve, the flayed look in her eyes twisting his heart. "It's not worth it. I was wrong to come here. I thought… It doesn't matter. Let's…let's just go."

"Good idea." This was a waste of time. Finding the killer in this crowd was futile, like searching for a diamond in a gravel pit. It could be anyone—or no one. There wasn't any way to tell. And people were already whispering, spreading word of Haley's humiliation at her parents' hands.

Even more anxious to leave now, he placed his palm at the small of her back and steered her toward the door. But the crowd had tripled since they'd arrived, making it difficult to move.

Behind them, the music stopped. "Ladies and gentlemen," the emcee announced. "This is the moment you've been waiting for. We'll now announce the three finalists in our auction. Please come up when I call your names."

Good. The distraction would draw the crowd's attention to the stage, enabling them to sneak away without another scene.

"Kenneth Jones, Camille Henson and Sullivan Turner," the man boomed out. "Please come to the stage."

Haley stopped and turned back. "You have to go up there."

"I don't care about the raffle. Let's get out of here."

"Please." Her eyes pleaded with his. "If we leave now, they'll think they drove us out."

He knew she meant her parents. And he couldn't blame her for wanting to preserve her pride. "It's not just that. I can't leave you alone in the crowd."

"I'll go up with you."

"You'd be too exposed." And even though he had his sidearm, he couldn't risk opening fire in a crowd this size. The collateral damage would be too high.

But she didn't budge. "Nobody's going to shoot us in the ballroom. And it will only take a minute. We'll accept whatever the prize is and leave right after that."

He glanced around. People were pointing and looking his way. His heart sank. She was right. They'd look like cowards if they slipped out now.

"Fine." Not seeing an alternative, he trailed her to the small corner stage where two other people waited with the emcee. Taking his position beside Haley, Sully scowled at the audience, watching for signs of animosity.

Haley leaned toward him. "Try to look happy. You're about to win something."

"Right." He bared his teeth.

The emcee introduced Senator Riggs, who thanked an endless stream of sponsors for their help. He finally wound down, and the emcee took the microphone again. While a drum rolled, he reached into a clear, plastic ball and pulled out a ticket stub. "In third place, a two-week cruise to the Black Sea, Camille Henson."

Sully clapped. But he caught sight of Haley's parents in the crowd and it was all he could do not to glare.

The drum roll sounded again. "In second place, for ten thousand dollars, Kenneth Jones. That means Sullivan Turner is our grand-prize winner, the proud owner of a new Chevrolet Corvette."

Cameras flashed. Haley turned toward him and gave him a squeeze. But his heart began to race, the light from the cameras flickering through his memory, yanking him into the past. And suddenly, he was back in that desert valley, the world exploding in a roar of flames, surrounded by bodies and blood and screams.

His limbs began to shake. A clammy sweat broke out on his brow. And that god-awful panic consumed him, the frantic need to fight back. He grabbed Haley's arm, struggling to anchor himself to the present, knowing if he lingered another minute he was going to lose it and come undone. He had to get away from the flashing lights *now*.

But the senator stepped into his path. "If I could have your attention for another moment," he boomed into the microphone. "I've just discovered that our winner is none other than Sergeant Sullivan Turner from the United States Army, who not only earned a Purple Heart, but a Silver Star, one of the highest commendations there is. He's a real-live hero! I'm sure you'll all join me in thanking him for his service to our country."

Applause broke out. Sully's gut tightened to steel. *Hell.* This was all he needed, for the senator to broadcast that. Desperate to hold it together, he gripped Haley's arm even harder and turned to go.

But a man carting a camera blocked his way. "Sir, we need you to come outside and stand by the car for a couple of photos."

"We'll be right there," Haley promised before Sully could refuse. Then she towed him through the crowd. "A Silver Star?"

Ignoring the people surging toward him, he mopped his brow with his sleeve. "It's no big deal."

"No big deal?" She shot him a look of disbelief. "How can you say that? That's a huge award."

An award he didn't deserve. "It's nothing."

"But—"

"Forget the damned medal. Let's just get out of here." He knew he sounded surly. But there were too many people, too much noise. And they all seemed to be pressing toward him, offering congratulations, making it impossible to breathe.

Haley pulled him out the doors to the patio. His pulse still chaotic, he inhaled deeply, filling his lungs with the fresh night air. Light spilled from the mansion, illuminating the garden beyond the wall. But past the perfectly trimmed hedges lay acres of unlit fields and woodland— where a shooter could easily hide out.

"Come on." Hurrying, he limped toward the side of the mansion where the Corvette was parked. The photographer was waiting by the car, along with the senator and another man Sully didn't recognize. Several teenage valets hovered nearby.

"Man, this thing's loaded," a tall, dark-haired boy was saying to his friends. "Seven-speed manual transmission…" He ducked his head under the hood and rattled off a list of stats.

The photographer motioned Sully over, then turned

to the valets. "Sorry, boys. I need you to step aside for a minute."

Haley waved him on. "I'll wait over here." She joined the valets near a stand of trees.

Anxious to get this over with, Sully strode to the Corvette. The photographer got to work, taking photos of him shaking hands with the senator and accepting the keys from the dealer who'd donated the car.

Sully's jaw started to ache. The pounding in his temples increased. And with every passing second, the uneasy feeling inside him grew. He didn't like this. The guests were beginning to leave. Several lights near the tent had gone out. And Haley was too far away.

He pushed away from the car. "That's enough."

"We just need one more shot," the photographer said. "In front of the mansion this time. If you could drive the Corvette around to the portico, we'll take it from there." Without waiting for an answer, he jogged off.

Haley caught his eye. "Go ahead. I forgot my shawl inside. I'll go get it while you drive the car around."

He hesitated. He still didn't like this. The feeling of danger kept getting stronger, despite the thinning crowd. And no matter how damaged his instincts, he wasn't going to let Haley out of his sight.

He glanced back at the car. The valets still lingered nearby, salivating over the Corvette.

"Hey," he called to the tall kid who'd recited the stats. "You want to drive the car to the front for me?"

The kid's eyes widened. "Sure."

Sully tossed him the keys. Then he pulled Haley toward the entrance, away from the unlit grounds.

Male laughter erupted behind him. Sully glanced back as the kid swaggered to the Corvette, putting on a show for his friends. Another valet pulled out his cell phone and took a picture of him leaning against the car.

Sully shook his head. He'd once been that young, that cocky. *That idealistic and naive.* Back when he'd still felt immortal, when his life had been blessedly simple, when all that mattered were girls and cars.

The kid opened the door. More raucous laughter broke out. He got in and cranked the engine. Still smiling, he punched down on the gas pedal and took off.

The car exploded in a ball of fire.

Chapter 5

Haley sprawled facedown in the grass beside the mansion, Sully lying atop her, his heavy body plastering her into the ground. Heat scorched her skin. Smoke billowed past, the thick, acrid stench choking her lungs. A huge roar filled the air, punctuated by panicked screams.

Stunned, she struggled to think, to make sense of the shocking scene. That car had blown up. *With the valet inside.* Sully had knocked her down to keep her safe. But why didn't he move? Was he all right? Terrified, she bucked against him, desperate to make sure he'd survived.

But then he rolled to his feet and hauled her upright, and she risked a dazed look back at the car. Flames shot up in a towering inferno. Heat and smoke roiled up in oily waves. People scurried and raced around, total pandemonium breaking out in the dark.

"Come on!" he shouted, grabbing her arm. Coughing, she staggered forward, the nightmarish scene too surreal to take in. How had it happened? *Surely it wasn't intentional?* She stumbled after him toward the patio, then skirted a garden hedge. A second later Sully came to a stop.

He whipped around to face her, then ran his hands over her shoulders and arms. The flickering light from the explosion painted macabre stripes on his sooty face. "Are you all right?"

She wheezed, then coughed, struggling to suck air through her fiery throat. "Yes. Are you—"

"I'm fine. Let's go." Taking hold of her hand again, he pulled her along the gravel path.

"But our car's back—"

"No key. It's with the valets. And we can't risk going back that way."

His meaning penetrating, she skidded to a halt. "You're not saying...you don't think that was a bomb?"

"It can't be a coincidence that we won that car."

Horrified, she spun around. She gaped at the roaring fire—the smoke pouring out, the flames boiling into the sky, the brave souls darting through the shifting shadows in a futile attempt to save that boy. Then a boom thundered out, hurling the blaze even higher and driving the rescuers away.

Nausea swelled inside her, and she clamped her hand over her mouth. Oh, God. Sully was right. She hadn't wanted to believe it, but someone had just tried to kill them.

That boy had died instead.

Sully pulled his gun from a hidden holster. "Come on. We need to get out of here before they figure out we survived." He cut through the shrubs and exited the gardens, then took off across the field.

Still reeling, she raced after him through the dark, stumbling over the uneven ground in her flimsy heels. Her eyes watered and stung. Her throat seared as she gasped for air. And the ghastliness of it all spiraled through her, the horror too awful to bear.

But she couldn't think about it now. She couldn't dwell on that poor boy's death. They weren't out of danger yet.

Moments later, they reached a barn. Sully stopped beside an open door, then waited for her to catch up. She slumped against the side, coughing so hard she nearly retched. "What now?" she managed to gasp.

"We need to find a ride. Wait here while I check it out."

He disappeared into the building. Still struggling to subdue her cough, she glanced back at the mansion a hundred yards away. A deep rumble filled the air. An eerie orange glow lit the sky. Beyond the house, cars had begun snaking through the inky blackness, their taillights forming undulating ribbons of red.

That should have been us inside that car. Shuddering, she willed the thought aside. Then she inhaled, pressing her fist to her chest to quell the spasms racking her lungs, and followed Sully into the barn.

The bright, overhead lights were on, making her blink. Squinting, she scanned the vehicles crowding the space—tractors, trucks, several farm machines she couldn't identify. In the back of the barn was an office, its door hanging ajar. Tinny music from a radio wafted out.

She crept to the office and peeked inside. *Deserted.*

The explosion must have sent whoever was in there running to help. But he'd be back. Knowing they couldn't dawdle, she rushed down the central aisle, then spotted Sully headed back her way.

"Over here," he called. "I found the key to one of the trucks."

"Good." She jogged after him to a small pickup truck that was parked by an open bay door. "Go ahead and back out," she told him. "I'll close the door."

Sully leaped into the driver's seat and cranked the engine. Her heart missed a beat, the memory of that bomb prompting a spasm of nerves. But he backed out without a problem, and Haley joined him in the cab. With the headlights off, they drove into the nearest field, jostling over the uneven ground.

"Where are we going?"

"To the main road, I hope. This tractor trail should meet up with it somewhere. I don't want to go back to the house."

Tensing at the reminder, she twisted around. A heavy layer of smoke blanketed the mansion, making it hard to see the fire—and them, if anyone looked their way.

But if their attacker knew they'd escaped that blast... he might have followed them to the barn. He might be watching them cross the field, even with their headlights off. And he might anticipate their route and lie in wait on the road ahead.

Thoroughly rattled, she hugged her arms, struggling to make sense of the awful night. But her thoughts were too disjointed, flitting through her mind like a hummingbird too wired to land.

Sully turned his head. "Are you sure you're all right?"

All right? Hysteria bubbled inside her. A gang had

gunned them down. She had a bounty on her head. Now they'd barely survived a bomb blast—and the would-be killer could be waiting ahead.

"I'm alive." Which was more than they could say for that poor valet.

Still unable to believe it, she shook her head. Someone at that gala had tried to kill them. Who it was, she didn't know.

But she did know one thing. To have any hope of survival, she had to find the answer fast.

By the time they checked into a small, rundown motel outside of Winchester an hour later, Haley felt completely numb. She perched on the edge of the queen-size bed, her eyes stinging, her teeth chattering, so cold she doubted she'd ever warm up.

She still couldn't believe what had happened. How could her life have changed so drastically in just two days? It seemed unreal, as if she'd crash-landed into a nightmare. And that valet...

"Here." Sully draped his tuxedo jacket over her shoulders, then settled beside her on the bed, his weight making the mattress dip.

Grateful for the warmth, she pulled the jacket closer around her and met his bloodshot eyes. Dark beard stubble coated his jaw. Soot streaked his craggy face. His hair was wild, the collar of his shirt smudged with black. She knew she looked even worse—her hair hanging askew, her feet filthy, her long dress shredded and torn. Even her eyelashes felt singed.

"Do you think we're safe here?" she asked.

"For now." His deep voice had turned even raspier thanks to the smoke. "I doubt anyone saw us leave with everything else that was going on. And they probably won't notice the missing truck right away. But even if they do, they don't know which way we went. So we'll definitely be all right for tonight."

Shivering, she gave him a nod. But her pulse continued to race. Images collided behind her eyes—the billowing smoke, the valet's beaming face, the Corvette engulfed in flames. And without warning, tears sprang to her eyes, the horror she'd held at bay crashing through her like a breaking wave.

Appalled, she struggled to blink them away. She never cried. Not anymore. She was strong, steady, a rock, the person everyone else always turned to for help. She never wallowed in self-pity or indulged in tears.

Wrapping his arm over her shoulder, Sully tugged her close. "Don't worry. We're safe now."

"I know." But her mouth wobbled badly. Her throat thickened with a rush of dread. "It's just…that poor boy…"

"Shh." He pulled her even closer, the solid weight of his arm anchoring her in place. Giving in to the need for comfort, she burrowed against him, relishing the hard, iron feel of his muscles, the slow, steady thud of his heart. He smelled of smoke and sweat and warm, male skin—proof that they were alive.

But it had been close. Way too close. If she hadn't forgotten her shawl…

"Breathe," Sully ordered, rubbing slow circles on her back with his hand. "Take a deep breath in, hold it for several counts, then exhale. It'll help manage the adrenaline dump."

Obeying, she drew in a breath. But thoughts kept circling in her jumbled mind. This was her fault. She'd caused that valet to die. Even Sully had nearly lost his life because of her. How were they going to survive?

Tremors shuddered through her. She released her breath, then inhaled again, struggling to block out another onslaught of gruesome memories—the screams, the flames, the teenager mugging for the camera as he climbed inside the car....

"I don't know how you do this," she said.

"Do what?"

She lifted a hand. "This. Deal with bombs and death when you're at war."

"Who says I do?"

She raised her head and searched his eyes. And for one unguarded moment, emotions flickered through those amber depths—pain, dread, horrors only he could see. And she realized in that instant that the war had wounded him badly, that despite his heroic actions, this man hadn't come through unscathed. He carried a terrible burden, feelings no medal could ever heal. And now he'd risked his life to save hers—reliving the nightmares he was trying to escape.

"I'm so sorry," she whispered. "I didn't mean to put you in danger."

"It's not your fault."

"I never thought...I really didn't think he'd try anything at the gala."

"I said it's not your fault."

"But you could have died protecting me." *Just like Tommy McCall.*

"Well, I didn't, so forget it."

But if he had, it would have been her fault. Her throat clenched tight, the thought of this brave soldier dying on her behalf too much to bear.

And as much as it frightened her to admit it, she had no right to involve him in her problems, not with the risk to his safety so high.

"Listen." She swallowed again, pushing aside the panic licking her nerves. "I appreciate your help. I don't know what I would have done without you tonight. But this bomb…it changes things. You don't have to stay—"

"Stop."

"But—"

"But nothing. We're in this together now." He paused. "Unless you'll take your friend's advice and enter a safe house?"

"No. I have to fight back." It was the only thing she was sure of right now. "I've got too much at stake— my shelter, my friends, the safety of the girls…I'm not going to let him win."

"He just tried to kill me, too. And I'm not leaving you alone."

She slowly eased out her breath, more grateful than she could express that he'd agreed to help. Because the thought of fighting that killer alone… "Thank you."

He gave her a nod. His gaze stayed on hers, the emotions swirling in his eyes holding her prisoner, making it impossible to look away. But suddenly, she realized she was sprawled against him, her breasts brushing his chest, her face mere inches from his. That she could trace the whiskers emerging on his jaw, smell the warm, soapy scent of his skin beneath the smoke. And that his hand had stilled on her back, his body vibrating with a different sort of tension now.

Without warning, she had the overwhelming desire to stroke her hand up his bristly jaw, to plunge her hands through his tousled hair. To feel his mouth covering hers and forget the night, forget the danger and pain and lose herself in the pleasure of this man's kiss.

His hot, whiskey-hued eyes tangled with hers. Awareness sizzled between them, jolting her heart into a reckless sprint. His gaze fell to her mouth, causing every part of her to go insane.

But then he abruptly rose. While she struggled to push herself upright, he limped to the window, pulled aside the curtain and stared out. And even from across the room, she could see the rigid set of his shoulders, the unyielding line of his ramrod back.

"I'm going to get more cash." His voice was gruff. "Lock the door. I'll knock three times when I come back." He opened the door and strode out.

Haley jumped as the door slammed shut, his brusque departure leaving her stunned. What had just happened? That desire hadn't been one-sided. She'd seen the hunger in his potent eyes. But then he'd fled.

Which was good. She was relieved. She didn't want Sully Turner to kiss her. So what if he intrigued her? So what if he was a hero who'd saved her life multiple times? And so what if he brought out needs she'd repressed for years, making her hormones blaze to life with those sexy, magnetic eyes?

She couldn't romanticize this man. She knew next to nothing about him. And the little she did know pointed to a man with issues, a war-damaged man barely hanging on to his sanity, a man living way too close to the edge.

And with their lives on the line, this situation was complicated enough.

No matter how compelling he was.

Shaking herself out of her stupor, she rose and bolted

the door, then sank onto the bed again. But the memory of his hot, carnal eyes flooded her senses, and she flopped onto her back and groaned.

Because she had a feeling she was heading down the road into trouble—and it had nothing to do with that deadly bomb.

Sully sat in the truck outside the motel room two hours later, wondering if he'd lost his mind. He had no business being around Haley. There was no damned way he could protect her; tonight's near miss proved that. She'd only survived by luck.

And to make matters worse, he'd nearly kissed her. He closed his eyes and groaned, his mind flashing back to her soft, beckoning mouth, those gorgeous, moss-green eyes, and how right she'd felt in his arms.

Right? Was he nuts? He took another long swallow from the bottle of whiskey he'd bought, then held out his hand to see if the trembling had stopped. Because the stark truth was that he was a drunk. An ex-soldier tormented by flashbacks. A man who'd led his friends to their deaths. He was the last man she needed at her side.

But what could he do? He couldn't leave her unprotected. Their enemy was brazen, determined. Planting that car bomb had taken audacity and skill. And Sully sure as hell didn't intend to roll over like a coward and turn tail—no matter how much power their assailant had.

So inadequate or not, he was in this thing for the duration. It was up to him to protect her.

Even from himself.

Knowing he couldn't hide out in the parking lot forever, he recapped the bottle of whiskey and stuck it under the seat, then took a swig of water to mask the smell. At least the alcohol had subdued the shakes. Now to see if it quieted the flashbacks. He didn't want to burden Haley with that.

Grabbing the bags of supplies he'd bought, he climbed out and locked the truck. Then he paused for a moment, letting the frosty air clear his head. He scanned the late-model cars crowding the lot, the motorcycle parked by the neighbor's room, the No Vacancy sign shining above the office door. Steeling himself for a long night cooped up in the tiny motel room, he limped to their door and knocked.

"Who is it?" Haley called out.

"It's me." The security chain rattled as she slid it off. Then she swung the door open and he stepped inside, his gaze arrowing straight to hers. She'd showered while he'd been gone. Her hair was damp and loose, falling in thick, dark waves over her shoulders and back. She'd scrubbed her face, giving her a younger, more approachable look. She'd ditched the dress, wrapping a spare blanket around her instead. The scent of her shampoo filled the air.

Trying hard not to notice her tempting softness, he made a beeline to the table beside the window and set down the plastic bags. "I got some things. A laptop, some clothes." He handed her one of the bags. "I didn't know your size, so it might not fit. We can get something better tomorrow."

She peered at the bag. "Where did you find a store?"

"About a mile away." A block from the liquor store. But she didn't need to know about that.

"Great. I'll change right now. I couldn't bear to put my filthy dress back on."

He nodded, not wanting to envision her naked beneath the blanket. "I got some other stuff, too." He handed her another bag, this one filled with toiletries.

She headed across the room. "I started a list," she called back. "I was writing down everyone I could remember at the gala. It's on the notepad." She went into the bathroom and closed the door.

Deciding to delay his own shower until later, he pulled off his reeking dress shirt and donned one of the T-shirts he'd bought. Then he grabbed the list and sat at the table, determined to keep his mind off Haley stripping in the bathroom and focus on keeping them alive. But after a minute, he gave up. The names meant nothing to him. He needed her help to sort them out.

The bathroom door opened a moment later. And before he could stop himself, he skimmed her lushly curving hips, her long legs encased in the too-snug jeans, the baggy T-shirt that did nothing to disguise her breasts. Her feet were bare, her eyes hesitant. A soft blush suffused her cheeks.

His jaw tightening, he dragged his gaze back to the list and stared blankly at the names. *Focus,* he ordered his wayward mind. He had to concentrate on finding a killer. She took the seat across from him a minute later, her clean scent taunting his nerves.

"I don't know how we're going to narrow it down." She nodded toward the notepad. "I left off the staff and celebrities, but the list is still too long."

"Maybe we should let the police handle this."

She wrinkled her brow. "You heard what Parker said. This guy has contacts inside the police. We can't depend on them to figure it out."

She was right. If they hoped to survive this thing,

they had to investigate it themselves. Besides, they had the most at stake.

He leaned back in his chair, resigned. "All right, then. Let's go over this again. You said a gang executed that man in the warehouse fifteen years ago."

She nodded. "The City of the Dead. The victim was a junkie named Allen Chambers. It happened in Baltimore near the Inner Harbor."

"So whoever is behind this was in the area back then."

"Right."

"And since that Ridgewood gang just put a price on your head, he has contacts with that gang, too."

"That doesn't give us much to go on. I mean, most people don't exactly advertise their involvement with criminals. Well, Senator Riggs does. He talks about his troubled childhood all the time."

"It's also someone who knows you."

"But that doesn't mean *I* know *him*."

Unable to argue that point, Sully frowned. "Let's not overthink it for now. Let's start with the people you know and go from there."

She reached out and took the list. Nibbling her bottom lip, she crossed out several names. Then she blew out her breath, making wisps of hair flutter around her face. "That still leaves a lot of people."

He glanced at the list again. "I bought a laptop. We can check their online bios, see where they were fifteen years ago. We can probably eliminate a few more that way."

"Can we connect to the internet here?"

"Yeah. The hotel's got Wi-Fi. I asked when I checked in." He paused. "I say we start with your father."

"My father? Why him?"

"He meets the criteria, for one thing. He was in the area back then, and he defends gang members now. And he was at the gala tonight."

"Maybe so, but I can't see him trying to murder me."

"You're probably right." Her father didn't seem to care enough about her to want her dead. "But let's use him as a starting point."

"All right."

"So what can you tell me about him?"

She tilted her head. "What do you want to know?"

"Tell me his background to begin with."

Her eyes turned thoughtful. "Well, he married my mother for her social connections. At least that's what my sister told me. I think they met at a regatta on the eastern shore. My mother comes from money, really old money. Not that my dad was poor by any stretch, but her ancestors were shipping magnates back in the day. Sugar, lumber, the whole nine yards. They made a mint during both world wars. She inherited the house in Guilford. It's on the historic register.

"And she's all about status—the country club, the summer house in St. Michaels, attending the right events. They're listed in the Baltimore Blue Book— the Society Visiting List."

"What's that?"

"A list published every year about who's acceptable to invite to parties."

He laughed. "You're joking, right?"

"I wish I were. My sister was a debutante. She came out at the Bachelor's Cotillion. I was supposed to be next. My mother sent me to comportment classes when I was young."

He could see that. Despite her disheveled appearance, Haley radiated class. He could see it in the graceful way she held her head, her elegance when she moved. And he'd seen her in action at the gala, mingling with the wealthy patrons like a pro.

"My father's family was in finance," she continued. "He's more into power. He attended Georgetown Law with Senator Riggs. And he's ruthless in court. He takes on the high-profile cases and always wins."

Sully nodded at that. The man had struck him as a bully. "So how did you fit in?"

"I didn't."

The hurt in her voice stopped him cold. The last thing he wanted to do was cause her more pain. "Sorry. You don't have to tell me—"

"No, it's fine. It's ancient history now."

"You're sure? You really don't have to talk about that."

"I'm sure. And if it helps us figure this out…"

She rose and walked to the bed, then sank onto the mattress, her gaze turning inward now. "To make a long story short, I disappointed my parents. My sister Lauren…she was four years older than I was, and everything they wanted—beautiful, smart, popular. I couldn't come close to matching her."

"I don't believe that." Haley wasn't just pretty. She had a gentle compassion about her that was far more appealing, at least to him.

"My mother certainly thought so. She was always comparing me to Lauren. I was too plain, too fat."

"Fat?" His gaze dropped to her breasts. "I wouldn't say that." She looked damned near perfect to him.

"I had a weight problem growing up. And I didn't

have any real talents, nothing they could brag about, at least. So they pinned all their hopes on her. But being perfect took its toll. The pressure finally got to her and she became bulimic. She got thinner and thinner…."

Her eyes turned raw. "I begged my parents to get her help, but they wouldn't listen to me. They thought I was making it up, that I was jealous because I wanted to be thin like her. And Lauren hid her illness well."

Acting on instinct, Sully rose and went to the bed. He sat down beside her, his shoulder touching hers. "What happened?"

"She died when I was fourteen. Sudden cardiac arrest from an electrolyte imbalance."

And suddenly, he understood. "You blame yourself."

"I loved her so much. You wouldn't think so, considering the age difference and how my parents compared me to her. But we were really close. I tried to help her, but—"

"It wasn't your fault. It was your parents' responsibility to get her help."

"I know." Guilt strained her voice. He understood how she felt. He'd lost his best friends in Afghanistan— good, brave men who died because of him. And he'd do anything to go back and do it over, to take their place in the desert sand.

Her gaze clung to his, the suffering in her eyes impossible to ignore. Sensing she needed comfort, he wrapped his arm around her and pulled her close. Then he ran his finger over her jaw, tracing the delicate slope of her cheek, drowning in her gorgeous eyes.

"Sully," she whispered, the soft plea twining around his heart. His gaze fell to her mouth. His pulse kicked into a sprint. He knew he had to resist her. She needed his compassion, not lust right now. He tucked a strand of hair over her ear, relishing the silky feel, her amazing scent, trying to conquer the overpowering need to move closer yet.

But her eyes fluttered closed. His heart thudding, he lowered his head. And then his lips claimed hers, the sultry feel of her searing his blood. He meant for the kiss to be tender, comforting, but it ignited a yearning inside him, a pull so powerful it caught him unprepared.

He tugged her even closer, drowning in her feel and scent. He ran his hand down her curving back, inhaled the fragrance of her hair and skin. She was soft and welcoming and warm, inciting a longing he couldn't name.

Like an angel beckoning him home.

A very erotic angel. Her lips opened under his. His thoughts shut down, his body shuddering as she drew him into her velvety mouth. Stark hunger ripped through him, his entire body hardening with need.

A car door slammed in the parking lot. Jolted back to reality, Sully ended the kiss and let her go. His breath sawed. His heart sledgehammered his chest. The sight of her dark, limpid eyes, her sultry, swollen lips nearly demolished his control. It took every ounce of willpower he possessed not to pull her back into his arms and kiss her senseless, sating the fierce hunger scorching his blood.

But this was wrong. He had no business touching Haley. He wasn't what she needed right now.

Disgusted at himself, he rose. "Sorry. That was a mistake." Arousal still pounding inside him, he staggered to the table and grabbed his bag of clothes.

"Sully…"

"Forget that happened, all right? I was way out of

line. It's late," he added, not daring to look her way in case he caved. "You take the bed. I'll sleep in the chair."

"But—"

"I'm going to shower. We'll work on the list in the morning."

Determined not to buckle, he limped into the bathroom and shut the door. But the sight of her underwear hanging on the towel bar caused an onslaught of sensual images—her wet hair slicked back, her naked skin glistening beneath the spray, her full breasts pouting for his touch....

Swearing, he braced his hands on the sink and grappled for self-control. Then he lifted his head and took a long, hard look at himself in the mirror. A haggard-looking man with bloodshot eyes and badly hollowed cheeks stared back. It was a face he hardly recognized. The face of a worn-out man who'd lost his illusions. The face of a man who had nothing left to live for.

The face of a man who'd failed.

And the last thing Haley needed was a man like him ruining her life.

Vowing not to forget it, he peeled off his clothes, turned the shower on cold and stepped inside.

But he had the sinking feeling it was going to be one hell of a miserable night.

Chapter 6

"Where are you? What happened? Are you all right?"

Haley squinted in the brittle lamplight and adjusted her grip on the motel's phone. "I'm fine," she told Brynn. Or as well as she could be after barely surviving a bomb blast, then suffering through a sleepless night. Every time she'd closed her eyes, those horrific images came flashing back—the explosion, the flames, the valet's face before he'd climbed inside that car. And in the rare moments when she *had* managed to forget those gruesome scenes, Sully's kiss came winging back, disturbing her even more.

"I've been so worried," Brynn persisted. "Why didn't you call me last night?"

"I dropped my purse and lost my cell phone. And by the time we got to the motel…I'm sorry. I should have called. It's just…I was pretty shaken up."

Especially after Sully's kiss.

The tap came on, drawing her gaze to the bathroom, where Sully was showering again. That kiss had blown her away, devastating her senses, making it impossible to keep her mind off him. His touch, his eyes, the mesmerizing sound of his husky voice…

She couldn't deny that he appealed to her—and not only because she had an affinity for strays. He was strong, brave and sexy as all get out, the most attractive man she'd ever seen. But it was the shadows in his eyes that kept her riveted, touching her in ways she couldn't quite name.

But while she longed to know more about him, she knew better than to ask. She first had to build his trust. Years spent working with skittish runaways had taught her that.

"Anyway, you don't need to worry," she told her friend. "We're both all right." *For now.*

"When I heard about the bomb… And then when Parker said they couldn't find you and the car was still at Hunter Hall…" Brynn's voice broke, betraying her fear.

"I know." She closed her eyes, sudden pressure tightening her throat. The past few days had stripped away her sense of security, proving that the safety she'd worked so hard for had been an illusion, resurrecting the terror of a life on the run.

The shower turned off. She opened her eyes, the thought of facing Sully scattering her pulse. "Listen, Brynn. I need to go."

"Wait. Parker wants to talk to you first."

A second later Brynn's fiancé came on the line. "Haley? Where are you?"

She realized she didn't know. She glanced at the stationery beside the phone. "The Oak Leaf Motel. It's just outside of Winchester."

"How did you get there? They said my car is still at Hunter Hall."

She winced. Even though their lives had been at stake, they'd still stolen a truck—and Parker was a cop. "We borrowed a truck from the barn. We were going to return it today."

"That can wait. I need to meet with you right away. Sergeant Delgado from the gang unit wants to interview you, and the ATF needs information about those guns. Can you get to Chevy Chase by nine? We can meet you there."

Haley studied the gray light peeking around the edge of the curtains. It was barely dawn, and D.C. was only an hour and a half away. "I think so."

"Good." Parker gave her the address for a chain restaurant outside of D.C. and she jotted it on the pad. After warning her to be careful, he disconnected the call.

The bathroom door opened just then. Straightening, Haley clutched the list they'd made and tried to look unfazed. Even though it had rocked her world, Sully had called that kiss a mistake. Now she had to put it out of her mind and pretend she'd forgotten all about it, before she did something foolish and mortified them both.

He emerged from the bathroom in a cloud of steam. Despite her attempts to control it, her gaze instantly flew to him. She took in his still-wet hair, the dark circles underscoring his red-rimmed eyes, the worn-out pull to his rough-hewn face. A drop of water ran down his clean-shaven jaw, then over his corded neck. His white T-shirt clung to his wide shoulders. His jeans hugged his hard, lean thighs. And, she had the strongest urge to run her hands up those sculpted arms, over his broad shoulders and muscled back, and inhale his compelling scent.

His gaze collided with hers, and he paused. A sudden flurry of excitement erupted inside her, little bursts of remembered pleasure skipping through her nerves.

Her face warming, she cleared her throat, wrestling to get her wayward thoughts under control. But his molten eyes sizzled through her, the memory of that kiss hovering between them like smoke from that deadly bomb.

But he'd apologized, called it a mistake. And he was right.

"Did you sleep all right?" Her voice came out breathless.

"Yeah. You?"

"Great." She knew he wasn't fooled. Neither had slept a wink. While she'd tossed and turned, he'd spent the night working on the computer and pacing around the room. But the last thing she wanted to discuss right now was how often she'd relived that kiss. Not only had he insisted they forget it, but they had more important problems to deal with right now—such as trying to stay alive.

He joined her at the table, his limp heavy as he crossed the room. Determined not to let him distract her, she forced her gaze to the list. But someday, before this thing was over, she would discover what plagued this man.

He took the seat opposite hers. "I did some research online last night, tried to find out where everyone was when Allen Chambers got killed. I eliminated a few people from the list."

She skimmed the names he'd crossed off, along with those that remained. "Senator Riggs? You really think he could be involved?"

"He belonged to a gang growing up. I read it online."

"That's true." The senator didn't make a secret of his background. In fact, because of his violent childhood, he advocated for at-risk youth. "I can't see him trying to kill us, though. He's one of his party's rising stars. There's even talk he'll be on the next presidential ticket as VP." Putting him in line for the presidency someday.

Sully leaned back in his chair and crossed his arms, his flexing muscles drawing her gaze. "That gives him a motive. If he masterminded that killing, he won't want it to come out, especially now. He'll need to clean up any loose ends."

"Maybe." But could a U.S. senator—a man she'd known since childhood—really be that coldhearted? "He definitely has the connections. He knows a lot of cops. He was even mentoring Colonel Hoffman before he died. And he went to Georgetown Law, so he has contacts in the judicial system, too."

His expression thoughtful, Sully rubbed his jaw. "What about his chief of staff?"

"Gwendolyn Shaffer? What about her?"

"Any chance she could be involved?"

Haley snorted at that. "I'd be shocked if she was."

"Why's that?"

"She's too young, for one thing. She was still in law school back then."

"Gang members aren't usually very old."

"Still… She worked at my father's firm part-time. That's how we met. And she's nice. She always made a point to talk to me." Which had meant the world to an awkward teen.

"Just because she's nice doesn't mean she's not a

criminal. And she's the chief of staff to a powerful senator. She has almost as much to lose as he does."

"I suppose." Haley didn't doubt she enjoyed the power. And she certainly could have changed in fifteen years. "But I still can't see her trying to kill me now."

Sully tipped back in his seat, studied her for a moment, then gave her a nod. "Cross her off the list, then. We can always put her back on later if no one else pans out."

Haley eyed the remaining names—a banker, a local philanthropist, several attorneys and high-level CEOs. Her father, Oliver Burroughs. "I don't think my father is trying to kill us, either. I can't see him dirtying his hands that way. He's too much of a snob."

"But he does defend gang members." Sully paused. "Any chance you can get into his office? I'd like to check his records and find out who he represents, see if we can make a connection that way."

"Not his office, no. The security would be too tight. But he stores his inactive files at home...or at least he used to. I can probably get us into the house."

"Today?"

Dread made her belly tense. The last thing she wanted to do was to revisit the house where she'd grown up. But she had to do her part.

"I think so. It's Sunday, so the staff is off. And my parents always go to the country club for brunch, assuming their routine hasn't changed. I can call the club and find out."

"They might not go after that bomb blast."

Haley snorted. "On the contrary. They'll be anxious to talk about it and spread the news."

"What time do they leave the house?"

"Around eleven. They're usually gone for a couple of hours."

He checked his watch. "We've got time. We can stop for breakfast on the way."

She paused. "Speaking of breakfast, I called Brynn while you were taking a shower. Parker wants to meet at a restaurant in Chevy Chase at nine. He's bringing someone from the gang unit and the ATF."

"You think that's a good idea?"

"Why wouldn't it be?"

"Your friends knew we were going to that gala." He raised a pointed brow. "They were the *only* ones who knew."

She sat up straight. "No way. They're not involved. They can't be. Brynn's a target, too."

"And her boyfriend?"

Haley opened her mouth to defend him, then stopped and forced herself to think it through. She didn't know Parker well. But she trusted Brynn's judgment. They'd relied on each other for years. And Parker's brother had died in the warehouse, protecting them. He wanted to catch the man responsible for his murder as much as they did. "I'd trust him with my life."

"That's exactly what we're doing. We can't afford to make a mistake."

"You don't need to worry. He's on our side."

Sully drummed his fingers on the table, doubts flickering through his golden eyes. At last, he gave her a nod. "All right. We'll trust him for now. But we'd better go. I don't want to hang around here long."

Her heart changed its beat. "You think the bomber might catch up?"

"I don't know."

But he could. She rose and went to the window, then inched aside the drape and peeked out. An SUV was warming up in the parking lot. A young couple walked past, pulling their suitcases behind them as they headed to their car. Somewhere in the building, a door slammed shut, the absolute normalcy of the scene at odds with the mounting threat.

The killer was out there, hunting them down. But she couldn't let him win. She couldn't let him destroy the shelter she'd worked to build, the safe haven she'd created for those runaway girls. She couldn't let him harm her friends. And she especially couldn't let him hurt Sully—not when his only crime was protecting her.

Sully clamped his hand on her shoulder. Startled, she lifted her gaze to his. And for an eternity, she couldn't breathe, his cognac-colored eyes holding her in place.

"Don't worry. We'll find him," he finally said, his gravelly voice echoing her thoughts.

"I know. I just hope he doesn't find us first."

By the time they arrived at a chain restaurant on the outskirts of D.C. two hours later, second thoughts threatened Haley's resolve. Was Sully right? Could they really trust Parker? Or were they walking into an ambush? And what about the two men Parker was bringing along—could they rely on them?

She scanned the area around the restaurant, her tension ratcheting higher as Sully backed into a parking space, angling the truck for a quick escape.

"Listen, Haley..." The urgency in his voice echoed hers. "I'm going to leave the truck unlocked. If there's any sign this is a trap..."

"We run."

"Right." His flinty gaze stayed on hers. "I mean it. I don't care how much you trust this guy. We're not going to take a chance."

"I understand." They had to attend this meeting. They needed help if they hoped to identify their assailant before he caught up with them. But given his connections, they had to stay on guard—even from the police.

Praying they wouldn't regret this, she opened the passenger door and climbed out. The cold wind caught her hair, whipping it around her face, and she shivered inside her new coat. She took another close look at the parking lot, but nothing seemed out of place.

Still, she had a hard time relaxing as she followed Sully into the restaurant and spotted Parker at a corner booth. "Over there," she said.

The detective rose as they approached and introduced them to the other men. Special Agent Roger Foley was from the Bureau of Alcohol, Tobacco and Firearms. He looked about her father's age with a broad nose, thick, black-framed glasses and a comb-over that made her cringe. But his eyes were sharp in his ruddy face, his gaze assessing as he shook her hand.

The other man was Sergeant Enrique Delgado from the gang unit in the Baltimore Police Department. Delgado had dark hair, dark eyes and a handsome Latino face—a fact he seemed to be aware of, judging by the way he lingered over her hand. Exasperated, she pulled away.

Sully slid into the booth beside her when she took her seat. Her nerves still edgy, she scooted as close to him as she dared, reassured by his solid strength.

A waitress deposited a stack of menus on the table

and filled their coffee cups. After promising to return for their orders, she hurried away.

Parker cleared his throat. "To begin with, we need your statements about last night. Our phone's ringing off the hook—every law-enforcement agency and media outlet on the Eastern Seaboard wants details, especially since that kid got killed. You'll have to give a formal statement later, maybe a couple of them, depending on what agencies end up involved, but this should give us a start."

"Right." Sully went first, telling Foley and Delgado about the shooting near her shelter, as well as the previous night's events. Haley added several details, including the warehouse execution that had started it all. She finished after they'd ordered and their food arrived. Ravenous, she dug into her scrambled eggs.

"What makes you think that car bomb was meant for you?" Sergeant Delgado asked.

"Who else would it have been meant for?" Sully answered. "You heard what we said. There's a price on Haley's head."

"Yeah, but a car bomb?" Delgado didn't look convinced. "That's not typical for the Ridgewood gang. The street shooting is more their style."

"Who knew you were going to be there?" Parker asked.

Haley swallowed a mouthful of eggs. "You did. I don't know who took my call when I RSVP'd for the gala. Someone on the senator's staff, I guess."

"I'll check on that." Parker took out a small notebook and wrote it down.

"How about you?" the ATF agent asked Sully. "You have any enemies?"

"Not that I know of."

"You were the one who won that car."

"Yeah, but I was Haley's guest. And I didn't know anyone there. What would they have against me?"

The ATF agent tugged on his bottom lip. "They must have arranged for you to win the raffle. That couldn't have been easy to do."

Parker jotted down something else. "I'll find out who set up the raffle and had access to the ticket stubs."

Her mind on the raffle, Haley polished off her eggs, then started in on a slice of toast. But she'd spent a sleepless night mulling over the logistics and still didn't have a clue.

The ATF agent looked at Sully again. "By the way. We got confirmation from ballistics that the weapons you saw were E-13s. They were manufactured by Walker Avionics at their West Virginia plant, part of a shipment that went missing a few weeks ago."

Haley blinked. "Walker Avionics? As in Dean Walker?"

The ATF agent turned to her. "You know him?"

"Not really. I mean, I can recognize him. He attends a lot of charity events. I saw him at the gala last night." Her mind raced. Could there be a connection between the weapons and the attack on her? But how could there be? It didn't make any sense. Fifteen years ago, those experimental weapons didn't exist.

"We're still trying to track down Markus Jenkins," Delgado added. "He's the leader of the Ridgewood gang, the one who got released from jail around the same time those weapons went missing. Once we bring him in, we'll try to strike a deal, see if he'll tell us who's involved in this."

"Any idea where he is?" Parker asked.

"No. He vanished. And none of our informants will talk."

"Can you blame them? Everyone associated with this case so far has died."

A chill scuttled through Haley at the thought. But Parker was right. This wasn't a game. Their assailant wanted them dead.

The ATF agent slid her his business card. "If you think of anything else, let me know. We need to get those weapons off the streets."

"I will." Although she didn't see how she could help.

Sully glanced at his watch, then caught her eye. "We need to go."

They had to get to her parents' house. Wishing she could avoid it, she took her leave of the agents and followed Sully outside. But while she dreaded visiting the site of so much of her childhood suffering, they desperately needed clues. And if Sully could face his ghosts, defying a gang to safeguard her, she could do the same.

"Wait!" She turned at Parker's call. Catching up, he tugged out a set of keys. "Take my SUV. It's the black one over there. I've got a meeting at Hunter Hall, so I'll return the truck and bring back my other car."

Haley released her breath. "Thanks." At least one good thing had come from the meeting. They didn't have to keep driving a stolen vehicle.

"There's a sports bag in the backseat," Parker added while Sully retrieved their shopping bags from the truck. "Brynn packed some clothes and stuff you might need." He took the truck key from Sully and turned to go.

But then he stopped. "I can still arrange a safe house, you know."

Haley hesitated, tempted. A safe house sounded good right now. She'd been shot at twice and barely escaped a car bomb. What if her luck didn't hold? Or worse, what if Sully got killed, instead?

But she couldn't run. She'd never be safe, not really, not with the police involved. No matter where she hid, no matter how many times she changed her identity, her pursuer would eventually catch up. She had to stay put and face him, and put an end to this for good—not only for herself and Sully, but for her friends, Brynn and Nadine. Until she defeated their enemy, they were all at risk.

"Thanks, but we'll be all right." She hoped.

Parker's eyes turned grim. "Be careful. This person's determined, whoever the hell he is. And if you change your mind…"

"We won't." They were committed now. No matter the cost.

Sully glanced in the rearview mirror as he drove through the historic neighborhood of Guilford, the uneasy feeling that had hounded him since they left the restaurant growing stronger with every mile.

"What's wrong?" Haley asked.

He studied the mirror for several seconds, then returned his gaze to the road ahead. "Nothing."

Haley twisted around in her seat. "Is someone following us?"

"I thought I saw a dark van behind us, but it's gone now." At least he hoped so.

Haley shot him a worried glance. "Those guys at the restaurant, Delgado and the ATF guy, Foley…you don't think they're involved in this?"

"No." They'd seemed trustworthy enough, despite his initial concerns. But something about this still felt off.

Maybe it was the neighborhood. He gazed out the windshield at the huge lawns dotted with oak trees, the mansions lurking behind gated drives—a far cry from the crowded, middle-class suburb where he'd grown up.

More likely it was that kiss. He slipped Haley a glance, taking in the compelling lines of her profile, the curve of her bowed lips. He'd spent the entire night battling his hunger, reliving her taste, her scent, fighting the insistent yearning to pull her close.

At least he hadn't suffered any nightmares. Of course, he hadn't exactly slept....

She shifted forward, her thick hair tumbling over her shoulders in glossy waves. And once again, the stark need hit him, the longing to plunge his hands through that silky mass and feel it sliding over his bare skin.

"That's Sherwood Gardens." She pointed toward a tree-lined park. "It's not far now."

Battling to regain his focus, he glanced at a Tudor-style mansion across the road. "Nice area to grow up in."

"Looks can be deceiving."

His gaze met hers, the strain in her expression too obvious to miss. And suddenly, he understood what this visit might cost her, confronting her painful past.

And damned if he could bear to see her hurt.

"Listen, Haley. You don't have to go inside the house if you don't want to. Just tell me where to look for the files. You can stay and stand watch at the car."

"Don't worry. I'll be fine."

He doubted that, given the dread he saw in her eyes. He knew he shouldn't care. He needed to keep his distance from her, not worry about how she felt.

But he *couldn't* stay detached. She already appealed to him too much. He admired her courage, her drive, her concern for those runaway girls.

And the way she'd responded to that kiss…

He stifled a groan. *Oh, hell.* This wasn't good. He had no business thinking of Haley that way. She did not need him in her life.

"There it is." She pointed to a house on the left. "Drive past it."

Sully peered out the window, his jaw sagging at the three-story brick mansion she'd pointed out. Huge columns fronted the house. Six double chimneys jutted up from a black slate roof. A high stone wall bordered the perimeter of the estate, keeping undesirable elements at bay, no doubt.

If he'd needed proof they'd come from different worlds, that house was it.

"Keep going past the alley," she said. "We'll park on the next street and walk back."

"Got it." Still marveling at her family's wealth, he glanced in the rearview mirror, but the dark van was nowhere in sight. Reassured, he turned onto a quiet residential street, then pulled to the curb and parked. "So what's the plan?"

"We'll go through the back gate. As long as they haven't changed the code I can get us in."

"And if they have?"

"We can climb over the wall, but I'd rather try the easy way first."

He hopped out of the SUV, then dumped the contents of the sports bag on the backseat. Taking the empty bag with him, he joined her at the curb. "You said your parents have servants?"

She led the way up the street. "They have a cook, a couple of caretakers and maids…and my mother's secretary. But they shouldn't be around today."

Trying to imagine her affluent childhood, he walked with her into the alley, his feet crunching over fallen leaves. The wind whispered through the pines. A flock of sparrows soared by. The neighborhood felt hushed and safe, worlds away from Baltimore's more violent streets.

They reached the gate at the rear of the mansion and Haley punched in a code. The iron door slid open without a hitch. "They always use my sister's birthday. It's a number they can both remember."

"Not yours?"

Her lips made a bitter quirk. "No. I told you. They'd prefer to think I don't exist."

Wondering at her callous parents, he followed her through the manicured gardens, past a gazebo and a stone fountain to the house. A gray squirrel bounded past. Majestic trees dominated the grounds, their centuries-old branches stretching into the morning sky. Sully studied the mansion's mullioned windows, watching for signs that someone was home.

But nothing moved. No one sounded the alarm. They reached a small door just off the patio and Haley punched in the code again. "I doubt anyone is here, but be quiet, just in case."

They crept into a small room lined with cabinets, then entered a narrow hall. A moment later they reached the two-story foyer, and Sully stopped to stare. An ornate ceiling soared overhead. A crystal chandelier anchored by a carved medallion towered above them like a waterfall suspended in time. Massive oil paintings hung on the walls. The sun gleamed off the marble floor so brightly he had to shield his eyes. Even the wooden banister was a work of art.

The house was a showcase, dripping with studied elegance—but oddly sterile and cold. There was no mess, no hint of the people living within its walls. It was too perfect. Too structured. Even the flowers in the Oriental vases matched, their colors exactly symmetrical, not a single petal out of place.

He couldn't imagine Haley living here. She was too soft, too natural. How had she escaped unscathed?

She hadn't. She'd fled this place, carrying wounds that would last a lifetime. But unlike his, her scars were all inside.

He frowned at that. He'd hit the jackpot with his family. They didn't have much money, but they'd always made him feel loved—which is why he couldn't face them now. He couldn't bear to see their disappointment after the way he'd let them down.

Pushing his mind away from those thoughts, he padded after her through the foyer, then into her father's library in an adjacent wing. The room faced the front of the mansion, its huge windows overlooking the rolling lawn. Floor-to-ceiling bookcases—complete with a library ladder—lined the other walls. An executive desk occupied a spot near the fireplace, along with leather chairs. The smell of fine cigars lingered in the air.

Haley crossed the room to a small door in the paneling beside the shelves. "The files should be in here." She opened the door and flipped the light switch, then came to a halt. Sully peered over her shoulder at the empty room.

"There used to be boxes and file cabinets in here." She sounded confused.

"Maybe he scanned everything onto disks."

"Maybe, but that would have taken years. He had thousands of files."

"So maybe he threw them away."

She shook her head. "No, he saves everything related to work. He must have moved them somewhere else."

But where? The mansion was huge. They didn't have time to search it all.

Sully turned and scanned the room. Noticing a sideboard, he limped over and looked inside. It was a treasure trove of liquor—and not the rotgut he usually drank. He hesitated, torn, tempted to take a swig while he had the chance, but closed the door, instead. He'd deal with his trembling hands later, when Haley couldn't see.

He spotted her kneeling behind the desk. "What are you doing?"

"He has a secret drawer. My sister found it when we were kids." She popped it open and took out a scrap of paper. After studying it for a moment, she put it back.

"It's the combination to his safe," she explained, turning to a painting beside the desk. She tugged it aside to reveal a wall safe, then punched in the code she'd found.

"What do you think you'll find in there?"

"I don't know. His appointment book, maybe. It wasn't in the desk."

"He probably keeps his schedule on his cell phone these days."

"Probably. But it doesn't hurt to check."

While she inventoried the safe, Sully double-checked the desk. A framed photo caught his attention, and he picked it up. It was a picture of Haley's parents with a beautiful, fair-haired child. Her sister, Lauren, without a doubt. She was a younger version of their mother with the same striking face and blue eyes.

He set it down. Curious now, he circuited the room, spotting dozens of family pictures—Lauren riding a horse, Lauren dancing at a ball, Lauren holding a trophy and competing in a tennis match. He didn't see a single photo of Haley, nothing to chronicle her childhood, nothing to prove she'd even lived in the same house.

"I'm done."

Stunned by her parents' indifference, he took the folders Haley had collected and stuffed them in the bag. "We'd better go. Your parents might be back soon."

"I want to check the solarium first. It will only take a second. My mother does her correspondence there. And she keeps records of everything. She's really obsessive about it. She'll have files from the time that I left home, maybe even before."

Still marveling over her hard-hearted parents, he followed her down the hall into a sunny side room with a pale pink sofa and claw-foot desk. More flowers decorated the room, their perfectly matched arrangements bugging him like hell. The place was as lively as a funeral home.

Haley crossed the room to a cabinet and opened a drawer. Hundreds of old-fashioned floppy disks were inside, arranged by date. "She's a perfectionist," Haley explained, thumbing through. "She keeps records of all her parties—what food she served, what she wore, who she invited, things like that."

"How is that going to help us?"

"It might not. But we'll find out who they socialized with back then."

While she sorted through the disks, he walked to the

nearest window and looked out. A shadow raced over the lawn. A bird swooped past the patio and landed on a nearby branch. Then a movement caught his eye—a man darting behind the shed.

His heart stopped dead. "Someone's here."

She whipped around. "My parents?"

"No. Someone else."

Haley hurried over, her arms laden with floppy disks. He unzipped the sports bag and she dumped them inside, then joined him at the window and peered at the empty yard.

Seconds passed by. The wind blew again, making the shrubs beside the windows bow. But just when he'd decided he'd imagined it, the man crept back into view, a snake tattoo on his jaw.

The Ridgewood gang.

Chapter 7

Sully had screwed up. He'd ignored his instincts about that van and led Haley into a trap. Why had he taken the chance?

A thump came from the foyer. Tugging out his sidearm, he whipped around. *Hell.* Either they escaped right now or they'd be dead. "They'll block the doors. Is there another way out?"

Haley paled but didn't panic, adding to his respect. "The wine cellar. They might not know it's there. This way." She turned and fled the room.

Sully hugged her heels, his guilt growing with every step. He'd seen that suspicious van. He should have trusted his gut, even after the van disappeared. Instead, he'd discounted his premonition of danger, leading them straight into an ambush—just as he'd done in Afghanistan.

And probably with the same result.

No. He wasn't going to fail this time. No matter what it took, no matter how many gang members came in pursuit, he wasn't going to let Haley die.

She threw open a door near the end of the hallway and lunged inside. Sully trailed her down a stone staircase toward the below-grade floor. The air grew musty, the temperature colder as he tramped down the narrow steps.

At the bottom, she flipped a switch. A row of overhead lights came on, revealing a long stone corridor that ran the length of the house.

"The wine cellar's at the end." Not waiting for an answer, she took off running again.

His gun in one hand, the sports bag slung over his shoulder, Sully hurried to keep up. At the end of the corridor, they entered an even colder room. Haley hit another switch and low lights penetrated the gloom, illuminating hundreds of dusty wine bottles arranged on wooden shelves.

"Over here." She wove through the stacks to the exterior wall. A modern, hermetically sealed door separated the wine collection from the original cellar entrance—a dozen steep steps topped with overhead doors. She rushed up the steps and tried the latch. "It's locked."

"Let me try." He tucked his gun into his waistband and climbed the steps. Putting all his force behind it, he shoved on the double doors. *Damn.* "There must be a padlock on the outside."

Now what were they going to do?

Footsteps pounded close by. Haley's panicked gaze flew to his.

Signaling for her to stay with him, he drew his sidearm and went back down the stairs. He peeked into the wine cellar, then inched inside, searching for the man they'd heard. A thud came from the next aisle over. Sully stopped and spun around, flattening Haley behind him against the wall.

For a moment, he didn't move. His blood hammered in his skull. Every muscle in his body tensed, shifting into battle mode. But he forced himself to wait, his senses focused on the predator prowling through the neighboring aisle.

How many men had entered the cellar? One for sure, but he might not have come alone.

The footsteps stopped. Sully stayed immobile, his adrenaline pumping, sweat streaking down his jaw. Then the man started walking again, heading the opposite way.

Sully eased out a silent breath. Gesturing to Haley, he crept toward the hallway door. They had to go back through the corridor. There wasn't another way out. But damn, he hated going in blind.

Just as he had in Afghanistan. He'd led his men into that valley where they hadn't stood a chance. *And all because he'd wanted to help those kids.*

He cracked open the door to the corridor and peered out. *Empty.* His heart still thundering, he crept into the hall and started toward the basement stairs.

But more footsteps headed their way. He whipped around and swore, searching for a place to hide. But Haley beat him to it. Motioning for him to follow, she threw open the door to the nearest room and dove inside. He lunged after her a second later and closed the door.

Breathing hard, he glanced around. They were in the furnace maintenance room, judging by the maze of pipes and heating ducts. "Is there a way out?" he asked. "A window?"

"I don't know. I hardly ever came in here." Her voice revealed her despair.

There had to be some sort of access to the outside. A house this age hadn't always had modern heat. Hoping he was right, he limped past grumbling machinery to the outside wall, looking for a way to escape.

A sheet of plywood caught his eye. It was tacked at ground-level height, about seven feet off the floor. "What's that?"

"I have no idea."

"Step aside." He handed her the sports bag. Then he reached up and pulled on the plywood, wincing at the noise it made. Putting even more muscle behind it, he finally worked it free, exposing a rectangular metal door. "An old coal chute." Or what was left of it. He just hoped to hell it opened—or they were doomed.

Knowing they only had seconds, he laced his fingers and crouched. "Come on. I'll boost you up."

Haley gripped his shoulder and stepped into his cradled hands. He rose, heaving her up to the metal door.

She tugged open the chute, exposing the shrubs beside the house and bringing in a rush of air. He thrust her up even higher and she scrambled through.

The sound of the door crashing open behind him jolted him into gear. Sully leaped up, seized the iron pipe running along the ceiling, and swung across it monkey-bar style to the chute. Then he twisted through the opening, squeezed into the bushes beside Haley and shut the door.

They'd made it—but barely. And they wouldn't avoid detection for long. Still breathing heavily, he pushed aside the branches and surveyed the yard. One man watched the gate. More gang members stood guard nearby. They'd need a miracle to get out alive.

Haley leaned close, her soft hair brushing his ear. "There's a way out behind the gardens. I used to sneak out that way. Follow me."

Taking hold of the sports bag, he crawled after her through the bushes, trying not to make any noise. But twigs crunched under his feet. Bare branches snagged his T-shirt, snapping off as he pulled free. They made it to the patio a few minutes later and stopped again. Beyond the patio lay the gardens, a sprawling landscape filled with flower beds, carefully manicured hedges—and wide-open stretches of lawn.

They'd never make it. They'd be too exposed. But at least they could count on surprise. And what other choice did they have?

Haley's eyes met his. "Ready?"

"Yeah." Sully rose as she took off. Then he sprinted after her across the patio and veered down a flagstone path. They raced past a marble statue and cut across the lawn, skirting a gazebo and a small stone hut. At a tree bordering the perimeter of the property, they stopped, and Haley grabbed a branch. By the time Sully had made it to the bottom limb, she'd disappeared over the wall.

He joined her in the alley a split second later. His breathing labored, he followed her through the neighbor's yard, relieved no one had raised the alarm. *So far.*

Which seemed damned odd. How had they managed to avoid detection during that run through the open yard? Unless the gang had let them escape for a reason…

He shook away that rogue thought as they reached the SUV. "Stay back."

"What?"

"Stand away from the curb until I've started the car."

"Sully, you can't! If there's a bomb…"

Ignoring her protests, he leaped inside. Holding his breath, he cranked the engine, exhaling when it purred to life. He waited for Haley to join him, then peeled away from the curb, speeding through the hills of Guilford, zigzagging across town on various side streets, finally merging with heavier traffic to blend in.

But his heart refused to slow. His hands continued to shake, the close call spooking him more than he cared to admit. He tightened his grip on the wheel, longing for that bottle of whiskey he'd left behind in the truck. But he didn't have time to coddle himself, not with that gang anticipating their steps.

He flicked his gaze to the rearview mirror, a bad feeling seeping through his gut. Something was wrong here. Really wrong. That gang was too damned smart.

Haley's gaze connected with his, her eyes dark in her pallid face. "How did they find us?"

"Good question." One they needed to answer— because their time was fast running out.

Haley sat in the parked SUV a short time later, still not able to catch her breath. They hadn't told anyone about their plans. No one knew where they'd gone. And yet that gang had magically found them. But how?

Stifling a swell of panic, she turned her gaze to the park where they'd pulled off. She eyed the children playing on swings, the mothers sitting on nearby benches, chatting in the chilly air. Two young women jogged by, their blond ponytails swinging in tandem, wearing windbreakers and spandex tights.

She had to stay calm. Their assailant wasn't omnipotent, no matter how powerful he might seem. Somehow, she'd find a way to defeat him. She couldn't let Sully or her best friends die.

Feeling marginally more under control now, she pushed open the door and hopped out. Sully crouched on the driver's side of the SUV, inspecting the area around the tires. "What's wrong?"

"I'm not sure yet." Running his hands along the side-wall, he squatted beside the tire. Then he lowered himself onto his back and scooted under the SUV.

Her nerves still edgy, she skimmed her gaze up his dirt-stained jeans to the apex of his muscled thighs. Annoyed by the direction of her thoughts, she rolled her eyes.

But then he scooted back out and stood. "Found it." He opened his hand to reveal a small black box.

"What is it?"

"A tracking device."

Her jaw dropped. "They're tracking us?" No wonder the gang had caught up. But who'd planted it—and when?

"Get in the car. We'll talk about it as we go." He hurried to a nearby trash can, stuck the magnetic tracking device underneath it, and then came back to the SUV and leaped inside.

Still reeling at the discovery, Haley climbed inside the cab. She latched her seat belt as he started the engine and they sped away from the park. "It couldn't have been Parker," she said. "I can't believe he'd track us." It didn't make sense. He wanted to find that killer as much they did, and he'd never do anything to harm Brynn.

Sully made a U-turn, then turned down another road.

"I agree, and the gang wouldn't have known that he'd lend us his SUV. So maybe they hoped he'd lead them to us. Or the cops could have planted the device. We know whoever is behind this has infiltrated the police force."

"Then why didn't they attack us at the restaurant? They probably knew we were meeting him there."

"Too public. They wouldn't want to risk being seen."

"They risked invading my father's house. How did they know he wouldn't be home?"

Sully hesitated, then met her eyes. "Maybe your father told them. Maybe he's involved in this."

Not wanting to believe it, she massaged the dull ache forming behind her eyes. "I don't know. It doesn't seem right. But we still need to warn Parker, either way. I can try Brynn's cell. She's using a disposable one right now. They won't be able to track that."

"All right. We can pick up a couple of burner phones for ourselves. We need to find a different vehicle, too, now that they know we're driving the SUV."

Her mind still whirling, Haley gazed out the windshield as they drove west through Druid Heights. She eyed the weed-filled yards, the boarded up homes and stores. Men congregated on the corners, rubbing their hands to warm them in the frigid air.

"What about Delgado?" she finally asked. "You think we can trust him?"

"He's a cop. We'd better not take a chance."

"How about Foley? He's with the ATF, not the police."

"That's still law enforcement. And if we trust the wrong person…"

She hugged her arms, the realization of just how vulnerable they were hitting home. They were completely on their own.

And the killers were fast closing in.

Even worse, they had no clues, no idea where to search, no way to protect themselves, aside from Sully's gun.

He turned off the street at a fast-food restaurant and swung into the drive-through lane. "Are you hungry?"

"Not really." But she deserved some comfort food after the terror of the last few days. "I'll have a large vanilla shake, though."

Sully placed their order and they snaked through the pick-up line. Haley tried to stay objective, but she still couldn't see her father attacking them. But how else had the gang members known he wouldn't be home? And where had he moved those files?

Sully handed her the bag of food, then drove to an automotive store in the strip mall and parked. Not wanting to waste time, she took several long swallows of her milkshake and set it aside, then dragged the sports bag onto her lap. "We need a way to read these old floppy disks."

"You really think they'll tell us anything?"

"They'll tell us who attended their parties back then. My mother keeps records of everything. No detail is too small. Heaven forbid that she wear the same dress or serve the same wine twice."

"They wouldn't invite gang members to their parties."

"No. My mother would never risk inviting anyone the least bit questionable. She cares about her standing in the community too much." She even labored over her seating charts like a general devising a battle plan, determined to benefit from every guest. "But the killer might have been their guest. And since we didn't find those files…"

Sully polished off his burger and shrugged. "Yeah, it's worth a try. We can pick up an external disk drive just about any place they sell electronics. We'll get our phones there, too."

"I'll pay you back. I don't have my debit card with me right now."

"No need. I'm not broke."

Wondering at that, she picked up her milkshake and took another sip. She'd assumed he was penniless, since he was staying in that empty house. But he probably received an army pension, maybe disability pay. In fact, he probably had more money than she did, considering the expenses her shelter incurred.

"How do you fund your shelter?" he asked, his thoughts apparently echoing hers.

She sucked on the straw again. "We get some state and federal grants, and donations from private groups, like that charity gala last night. But Brynn pays the bulk of the bills."

"Brynn?"

"She's a photographer. B. K. Elliot. She specializes in runaways, photos of street life." *People like him.*

"The Pulitzer Prize winner? You're joking."

Haley smiled, unable to mask her pride. "She does beautiful work, really amazing stuff. She uses some of the proceeds to fund my shelter. She also helps Nadine, our other friend. Nadine's a plastic surgeon in New York now. But she does charity work, too, mostly pro-bono work on battered women. Right now she's in South America, helping villagers who can't afford medical care. Brynn helps pay for those trips, too."

"Isn't that risky? Funding your shelter, I mean. That killer could follow the paper trail."

"We don't use our real names anymore. We all have fake documents—everything from driver's licenses to school records. If anyone checks, we look legit. You'd be surprised what you can buy these days if you have the money. There's a whole underground industry in creating fake identities."

He seemed to consider that. "So you reinvented yourselves, and now you all spend your lives helping others."

She took another long draw on her straw, wondering how to explain. "None of us had an easy childhood. We thought running away would solve our problems, but it only made them worse. Life on the streets is dangerous, especially for girls. If we hadn't had each other's help, we probably wouldn't have survived. But not everyone's as lucky as we were. So now…we try to help the people we can."

Sully looked away with a frown. She wondered if she'd touched a sore spot, prompting his shift in mood. She didn't ask. She didn't know him well enough to pry. But someday she would discover what made this brooding man tick.

Forcing her mind back to the gang members, she dug through the athletic bag and pulled out the folders from her father's safe.

"Anything of interest?" Sully asked a moment later.

"Not really. Just insurance policies and stock certificates…" She set that folder aside and picked up the next. More documents. "His birth certificate, marriage certificate…" Her voice faltered.

"What is it?"

A terrible tightness constricted her throat. "A death certificate."

"Your sister's?"

She managed a nod. "You'd think it wouldn't matter after all these years. But the grief…it never goes away." Not completely. The crying jags had stopped. She didn't think about her sister constantly anymore. And the terrible loneliness that plagued her after losing the one person on earth who'd actually loved her had faded to a fleeting ache.

"It's always the little things that set it off." A song, a whiff of the jasmine-scented perfume Lauren used to wear, seeing her death certificate…

Sully's eyes met hers. "I saw her picture in your father's study."

"My parents…they never recovered from her death."

"I get that. But why don't they want to see you? Why don't they have your picture there? You're still their daughter, the only one they have left."

"It's not the same. They idolized Lauren. We all did. And I couldn't come close to measuring up. They made that clear."

His eyes flashed. He reached out and cupped her chin, forcing her gaze to his. "You don't believe that crap."

"No, not anymore."

"They're idiots, Haley. If they don't appreciate you, it's because there's something wrong with them."

"I know that."

"Good." His angry eyes stayed on hers. Her heart increased its beat. And warmth infused her veins, something beyond the lust, beyond the attraction for a sexy man, beyond the excitement shimmering through her at the feel of his calloused hand. Sully was on her side. He was indignant on her behalf. He cared.

The folders slid from her lap to the floor. Sully released his grip and leaned back. Shaking herself back to the present, Haley bent to scoop up the papers, struggling to get her off-kilter pulse under control. But she had the feeling that something had changed between them. Something important.

Something she couldn't deal with right now.

Gathering the jumbled papers, she stuffed them into the files. But a pink sheet went in sideways, and she pulled it out. *"You Save Self-Storage."* She frowned. "That's weird. Why would my father rent a storage unit?" And hide the receipt in his safe, no less.

"The same reason people always do, for the space."

She shot him a skeptical look. "You saw the house. They've got three floors, plus the attics and basement. He could move the contents of an entire warehouse in there and still have room."

"So it's for something he didn't want in the house."

"Like what?"

Sully shrugged. "Who knows? Where's the unit located?"

Still frowning, she studied the header on the receipt. "On West Lafayette. That's not far from here. But how can we get in? I'm sure they have security. And it's Sunday, so the office is probably closed."

He started the engine. "People stop by to check their stuff on the weekends. Maybe we'll get lucky and we can follow someone inside."

She hoped so. A dark van passed by on the road, raising goose bumps along her spine. They needed all the luck they could get.

* * *

You Save Self-Storage was located in an aging commercial complex just off West Franklin Street. They parked beside a vacant gas station where they had an unobstructed view of the gate—and the security camera monitoring the grounds.

While Sully worked on their list of suspects, gaining access to the internet via a neighbor's unprotected router, Haley paged through the rest of the folders to no avail. Finally giving up, she put them back into the sports bag and sighed. If this was all they had to go on, they were doomed.

Suddenly weary, she slumped back against her seat and closed her eyes. The restless night, the horror of the past few days, had left her in desperate need of sleep. But memories kept flicking back—the bomb, the gang members creeping through her father's house, the heat in Sully's kiss....

With a shudder, she opened her eyes. She couldn't afford to go there. She couldn't obsess about how amazing he'd felt with the danger they were in. She glanced at his tanned hands tapping the keyboard, the taut set to his whiskered jaw, and released another sigh. No matter how much he appealed to her, she had to keep her mind on track.

A red Honda drove up to the storage unit's gate, catching her eye. "Someone's there."

Sully closed his laptop and set it behind the seat. "Good. That's our ticket in." He started up the SUV, then pulled in behind the car, staying on its bumper as the motorized gate slid aside.

The Honda entered the compound. Sully gunned the

accelerator, barely clearing the gate before it shut again. "Now where?"

"Unit number 19." Leaning forward, she studied the sign. "Turn right."

Sully steered through the rows of one-story buildings, past Dumpsters covered with gang tags and overflowing with trash. Then he parked beside a chain-link fence. "There it is." Incredulous, Haley climbed out of the SUV. She glanced at the weed-filled lot beyond the fence, discarded papers cartwheeling down the empty lane, the garage-sized storage unit with its battered metal door. "I don't believe this."

"What?"

"This. Any of it." She waved her hand around. She couldn't imagine her father coming here in his fancy Italian shoes and bespoke suits, driving his customized Lexus sedan. "It's just not like him."

"And yet he had the receipt in his safe."

"I know, but still…"

Sully walked over to the keyless entry pad mounted beside the door. "You want to try this?"

"Sure." She punched in her sister's birthday, shocked when the door started to rise. So her father really had rented this unit. *But why?*

The door creaked to a stop overhead. "It's empty." Even more confused now, she walked into the unit, her steps hollow on the cement floor. "What on earth? Why pay for a storage unit he doesn't use?"

"Maybe he did use it, but he doesn't need it now."

"Then why keep it?"

"Because the contract hasn't run out?"

That made sense. But why did he have it to begin with? And where had he put his missing files?

Unable to come up with an answer, she waited while Sully prowled around the empty space. A second later, he stopped and retrieved a scrap of paper from the dirty floor.

"What's that?"

"Maybe nothing." He handed it to her.

She carefully flattened the tattered fragment, trying not to damage it even more. On it were several numbers and a symbol—or what was left of one. "This looks like a logo. You think it's part of a label?"

"It could be. We can check online and see if we can find a match. But let's get out of here first. I don't want to risk having the cops show up."

"Good idea." Hurrying now, they closed the door, then piled back into the SUV. Leaving the complex was easy, thanks to a sensor that triggered the gate.

Sully parked several blocks away on a quiet side street. He booted up his laptop and met her eyes. "What do you want me to look for?"

She studied the paper again. "This could be the edge of a W. Try Walker Avionics."

"You think your father helped steal those weapons?"

"I don't know what to think. None of this seems like him. The gang, the storage unit…" Not to mention stealing weapons and planting a bomb. "It's just so bizarre."

Sully tapped on the laptop. A moment later, he angled it her way.

The Walker Avionics logo filled the screen. She held the fragment up, and her heart skipped several beats.

It matched.

Chapter 8

"I don't believe it. My father *can't* be the one behind all this. It doesn't make any sense."

"Sure it does," Sully argued. "We know he rented that storage unit. If we're right about the label, he had those stolen weapons inside. And we know he represents gang members. That makes him the obvious link between the guns and gang."

"But stealing weapons? My father?" Her voice rose. "He'd never dirty his hands like that. He'd never even talk to a gang member outside of work."

"And yet they just showed up at his house."

She collapsed against her seat and massaged her eyes. "I know it looks bad. And he *is* the obvious link. But putting a contract on my head? Sending a gang to kill me? *His own daughter?* I can't believe he'd stoop that low."

And it hurt, more than she'd expected. She thought

she'd inured herself to his indifference long ago. But the idea that her father would go so far as to want to kill her…

Sully reached over and squeezed her hand. Her gaze tangled with his, the sympathy in his eyes unraveling the tightness in her chest a notch, reminding her that she wasn't alone—which meant more than she cared to admit.

"Maybe he didn't have a choice." His voice was gentler now. "Maybe he got in over his head. Or he was doing it as a favor for a client."

"He doesn't do favors. I told you, he's all about power. If he's involved in this, it's because it benefited him."

But how? There had to be more to this story. No matter what her father thought of her, no matter what kind of bully he was in court, the idea of him leading a secret gang life didn't make sense.

A car passed by on the road. Sully released her hand and sat back, looking thoughtful now. Haley pressed her fingers to her gritty eyes, completely drained. It was all too much to process—the bomb, the gang, discovering that her father might want her dead.

"We need to tell Parker what we found," she decided. "I'm sure we can trust him."

"But we can't trust the people around him. The killer has connections within the police. And someone put that tracking device on his SUV."

That ruled out Delgado. "How about Foley?"

"He's still law enforcement."

"But the ATF is federal, not local. He wouldn't have any influence with the Baltimore police. And he's investigating the stolen weapons. He'll need to know what we found.

"What else can we do?" she continued when he didn't answer. "We can't confront my father directly. We already tried that, and he refused to talk to me. I could call Brynn—"

"No. She's too close to Parker. Let's keep her out of this for now."

"Then we don't really have a choice. We've got to get help."

A crease cleaved Sully's brow. He tapped his fingers on the steering wheel, then finally met her eyes. "All right. Foley it is. But we're going to take precautions. I'll be damned if they'll catch us off guard again."

Three hours later, Haley lay facedown next to Sully on a wooded hilltop, her binoculars trained on the phone booth beside a convenience store. Sully hadn't been kidding about taking precautions. First they'd driven to an ATM where he'd withdrawn cash. Then they'd stopped at a chop shop masquerading as a used-car dealership and picked up a junker car. They'd made a quick detour to buy supplies—binoculars, a couple of disposable cell phones and a floppy-disk reader to view her mother's files—then telephoned Foley and arranged to meet him at the convenience store. In case his line was tapped, they hadn't told him why.

Lowering her binoculars, Haley kneaded a crick in her neck, then glanced around her at the weedy brush. "Shouldn't we call Parker and tell him where we left his car?"

"He'll find it. As soon as they trace that ATM withdrawal, they'll send someone here to look for us."

"But then…"

"Don't worry. We'll be gone by then. Here comes Foley now."

Haley peered through her binoculars again. "Is he alone?"

"It looks like it so far."

A rusted green hatchback—more suited to a suburban soccer mom than an ATF agent—shuddered to a stop beside the telephone booth. Foley got out and glanced around, his hands braced on his hips. After a moment, he lumbered to the booth and stepped inside.

Her heart beat fast. "He's picking up the note."

A split second later, Foley crumpled it in his hand. Not looking happy, he exited the booth, climbed back inside his car and drove off.

"Let's go." Sully helped her to her feet and they returned to the small, silver Kia they'd bought. So far, so good. Everything was going according to plan. So why didn't she feel reassured?

When they reached the church where they'd sent Foley, Sully didn't stop. "Where are you going?" She peered back at the parking lot—empty except for Foley's car.

"Around the block. I want to make sure he came alone."

Glad for his sense of caution, she continued scanning the area as they drove past. "I don't see anything suspicious."

"Yeah. I think we're okay." Using the back entrance, Sully swung into the church's parking lot and pulled up beside his car.

"What's with the cloak and dagger routine?" Foley asked when they both got out.

"The gang followed us this morning." Sully leaned

back against the Kia and crossed his arms. "They put a tracking device on our car. You know anything about that?"

"Me?" Foley's face turned red. He sputtered, appearing outraged at the thought. "I've been in my condo watching TV all day."

Which didn't exactly answer their question. And he still could have directed that gang.

"So what happened?" Foley asked, his face still flushed.

Haley glanced at Sully again. He shrugged, letting her decide how much to say.

Hoping they wouldn't regret it, she filled Foley in on the tracking device and handed him the items they'd found. "This was in a storage unit my father rented. We think it's part of a label, possibly from those E-13s. The pink page is the rental-unit receipt."

Foley adjusted his thick glasses and studied the receipt. "You got this from your father's safe?"

"That's right. We were hoping to find notes about his clients, who the gang members are and what their hierarchy is. We found that receipt instead."

Foley examined the label again. "What makes you think this is from the stolen shipment?"

"It looks like the Walker Avionics logo, for one thing. And why else would he have a storage unit? He must have had something to hide."

Foley scratched his jaw. A gust of wind came up, shifting the long strands of hair he'd combed over the bald patch on his scalp. "Have you shown this to anyone else?"

"No. After that tracking device, we didn't know who to trust."

"I'll take care of it. I can't use it as evidence, but it's a good lead. It gives me a starting point."

Haley hugged her arms. "Whatever you do, be careful. If he catches on…"

"Don't worry. He won't find out." Foley slid the papers into his jacket pocket, then took out a notepad and pen. "Where are you staying—in case I need to contact you again?"

"We don't know where we're staying yet," she admitted.

But they needed to find a place soon. Night was approaching fast, and she could barely stand on her aching feet. And Sully looked just as exhausted, his wide shoulders slumped, his eyes even more bloodshot. If they didn't rest soon, they might make a deadly mistake.

The ATF agent tucked his notepad away. "I know a place you can stay if you want. My old house in Arlington. It's been on the market since my divorce. There's still some furniture inside. The Realtor said it would sell better that way." He grimaced. "Not that I care if it sells or not. Any profit goes to my ex."

The offer tempted her. They desperately needed to sleep. That tracking device and car bomb pointed to a level of sophistication they'd need all their wits to combat. And the longer they stayed in the open, the more likely that they'd be seen—or that another innocent bystander would get caught in the crossfire and lose his life.

But could they trust Foley? As Sully had pointed out, the ATF was still a law-enforcement agency. And yet, he'd come to this meeting alone. He'd worried about the legality of the evidence, indicating that he followed the rules. And while he obviously harbored resentment against his ex-wife, he had no reason to wish them harm.

And a hotel had risks of its own. Unless they stayed at someplace seedy, they'd need a credit card or ID to check in—which could tip off the police.

"Where are you staying?" she asked him.

"Falls Church. I rent a condo there. That's all I can afford after my ex-wife cleaned me out."

Haley glanced at Sully, but he shook his head. "Thanks anyway, but we'll find a place on our own."

Special Agent Foley shrugged. "Fine, but if you change your mind…"

"We won't."

"Right. Call me tomorrow around nine in case I have questions." He opened his car door, then paused. "And good luck."

Fearing they would need it, Haley shivered as he drove away.

To her surprise, Sully headed south to Annapolis, then continued for thirty more miles to a small clapboard cottage on the western shore of Chesapeake Bay. Set in an aging, blue-collar neighborhood, the house had trees and shrubs on one side and a tidal swamp on the other, providing both privacy and a place to rest.

Haley closed the long, plaid drapes in the family room, then joined Sully in the kitchen, the aroma from the pizza they'd picked up making her stomach growl. "You said your grandparents used to live here?"

Sully looked up, his gaze colliding with hers, the impact raising goose bumps along her arms. "Yeah. My family uses it as a vacation place now."

She could see that. While clean, it had a faded, worn-out carpet, fishing rods piled in the tiny mudroom, and battered, mismatched furniture that had definitely seen better days. But it also had a beautiful stone fireplace and a huge deck overlooking the wetlands—providing the perfect place to unwind.

"So tell me about your family."

"There's nothing to say. I poured you a glass of wine."

"Thanks." She lowered herself onto a stool at the counter and took a sip. "Do you have brothers and sisters?"

"Yeah. What kind of pizza do you want?"

She glanced at the boxes. "Both. I'm starving." She took another swallow of wine. "So, where do they live?"

He shot her a frown. "Look, I don't want to talk about them, all right?"

"Sure." But his abrupt refusal to discuss them struck her as odd. This house reeked of a happy family. She could envision kids doing puzzles at the kitchen table, adults reading by the fireplace, teens paddling canoes through the wetlands or fishing from their private dock. Surely Sully had good memories here. He wouldn't have brought her to a place he despised.

Even more curious, she studied him as he loaded pizza on their paper plates, taking in his red-rimmed eyes, the fine tremors in his big hands, the sheen of sweat moistening his brow.

He handed her a plate. Then he picked up the wine bottle, hesitated for several beats and set it back down without pouring himself a drink.

He was an alcoholic. The realization made her blink. She'd seen the signs, of course—the trembling hands, the dark circles signaling chronic insomnia, the faint taste of whiskey when they'd shared that kiss—but hadn't realized the extent of his problem until now.

Is that why he didn't talk to his family? Did he think he'd let them down? And what about that Silver Star he refused to discuss? Had that contributed to his need to drink?

She didn't ask; he'd already warned her off. And she didn't want to rob him of the dignity he was trying to preserve. She'd have to wait until *he* brought the subject up, assuming he ever did. But it was hard. The more she got to know him, the more she wanted to learn everything about this wounded man.

Not sure what to say, she dug into a slice of pizza, the warm, creamy cheese making her moan.

"Is the pizza all right?" he asked.

"Perfect." She was totally blowing her diet, but after nearly getting killed, she found it hard to care.

Three slices later, she finally summoned enough willpower to push her plate away. Sated, she refilled her glass of wine, her gaze drifting back to the taciturn man brooding at her side. She studied the bristles emerging on his solid jaw, the intriguing fullness of his bottom lip, the squint lines radiating from his sexy eyes.

His sensual appeal washed through her, propelling her pulse into another sprint. She ached to run her hands up his iron arms, feel his muscles flexing beneath her palms, plunge her hands through his shaggy hair. And she yearned to know his past, his pain, the secrets that made him tick.

He swung his gaze to hers. Thrills skidded inside her, frissons of excitement rippling over her skin as the memory of that kiss flashed back. *But he'd called the kiss a mistake.* And no matter how much she longed to touch him, no matter how much she wanted to console him and ease his pain, she had to remember that.

Her face warming, she cleared her throat. "So about this guy who's following us…I know you think it's my father, but I still can't see it. I think we need to keep researching the people on that list."

"Like who?"

Still trying to corral her scattered pulse, she spread her hands. "I don't know. Maybe I'm too close to this. It's hard to imagine anyone I know wanting me dead." And yet someone obviously did. And unless they identified him quickly, he might succeed.

Sully set his plate aside. "How about the senator?"

Trying hard to be impartial, she considered that. "He knows everyone, that's for sure. He doesn't strike me as a criminal, though."

"You know him well?"

"Not really *well*. But he's my father's friend. I told you they went to law school together. He came to our house a lot when I was growing up."

Sully rose and retrieved his laptop. While he connected to the internet, she dumped their trash in a paper bag, then sat beside him again. A moment later, he linked to an article about Senator Riggs.

She scooted forward, her shoulder bumping Sully's as she skimmed the bio on the screen. The article contained the usual information about the senator's childhood in D.C., his teen years in a gang, the military service that set him straight.

"I didn't realize he was in the army," Sully said.

"He enlisted after high school. It was either that or go to jail. That's how he got to college, on the GI bill. He talks about it all the time, how the army turned his life around. He tries to do the same for other people now, give them a helping hand, especially kids from his community. That's how he connected with Gwendolyn Shaffer."

"His chief of staff?"

"Right. She grew up in the same neighborhood he did. She was a lot younger, of course, only five or six years older than my sister, Lauren, but he got her a scholarship."

"Tell me about her."

"Gwen?" She took another swallow of wine and sat back. "She's nice. She worked for my father part-time while she was at the Georgetown Law Center. The senator recommended her for the job."

"A scholarship *and* a job? That seems like a lot for him to do. Unless he had some other interest in her."

His meaning sunk in. "No, he was married back then. His wife died on 9-11. And I've never seen Gwen date. She's too busy, I guess. Regardless, she deserved his support. She's brilliant. My father was really impressed with her work."

"So how did you meet her?"

"She started coming to the parties he held at our house. I was in high school then. She always went out of her way to talk to me." The corner of her mouth edged up. "I was the classic wallflower, awkward and overweight. I huddled in the corners and escaped the minute I could.

"But she helped my sister, too. Not socially. Lauren definitely didn't need help with that. She was so beautiful that everyone gravitated to her. She was a hit as a debutante."

Sully's eyes flickered. "Yeah, I saw her photo."

"Then you saw how beautiful she was."

His broad shoulders rose. "You're prettier than she was."

She laughed at that. "You need to get your eyes checked."

"My eyes are fine."

Her face warmed at the compliment, even though it wasn't true—particularly back then. "Gwen did favors for her sometimes, like inviting her to law school parties to meet men."

"She made herself useful."

"She still does. She's the go-to person when you need to get anything done. She's amazing, really. Efficient, smart…"

"You think she could be behind all this?"

Haley wrinkled her nose. "I doubt it. For one thing, she wasn't around when Allen Chambers got killed. She left for the Caribbean just before I ran away. She spent a semester abroad there. In Trinidad and Tobago, I think."

"She could have run the gang from a distance. Or maybe she came home on a holiday. It's not that far away."

"I guess." But it seemed a stretch, at least to her.

"So what's the other reason you don't think it's her?"

Her heart skipped a beat, the sudden burst of anxiety catching her off guard. "It's a long story."

"We've got time."

She held his gaze for a moment, her belly doing somersaults at the thought of revealing her past. But it had happened years ago. Her parents didn't have power over her anymore. There was no reason she couldn't discuss Lauren's death.

And even though Sully hadn't told her much about his life, she had the sense that he'd understand.

Trying to figure out where to begin, she took her wineglass into the living room, then sank onto the sofa, the worn cushions embracing her like a long-lost friend. Sully settled beside her a minute later and stretched out his injured leg.

She took another sip of wine and sighed. "Around the time Lauren graduated from high school, I realized she had bulimia. They'd talked about it in health class, and I recognized the signs.

"I told you I tried to tell my parents, but they wouldn't listen to me. In fact, they warned me to stay quiet. They didn't want me spreading rumors that might reflect badly on them. That's all they cared about, their image. My mother, especially. She didn't want me to damage Lauren's chances to make the perfect match."

She shook her head, their behavior appalling her even now. "By the time Lauren started college, I was desperate. I could see her wasting away. But I didn't know who to talk to. She lived in a dorm, so she was away at Georgetown most of the time. That's where she'd enrolled. She just came home on weekends sometimes."

"So you went to Gwendolyn Shaffer?"

Nodding, she took another sip of wine. "At least she took me seriously. She agreed that we needed to be concerned. She promised to talk to Lauren and convince her to get some help."

Her belly clenched, the pain still hard to bear, even after all these years. "But I'd waited too long. Lauren died before she could talk to her."

"I'm sorry."

Her throat tightened around a swell of grief. "I was

devastated. So was Gwen. She felt so guilty. But it was more my fault than hers."

"Baloney. If it's anyone's fault it was your parents'. They should have believed you. Or at least they should have taken her to a doctor and checked her out."

Haley drained her glass and set it on the end table, then folded her hands in her lap. "I know that now, but at the time… You have to understand. Our family revolved around Lauren. She was the center of our lives. She was everything my parents had hoped for—beautiful, talented, popular. My mother was convinced she'd land a good husband—maybe even a European with a royal title. And when she died… They lost everything."

"They still had you."

The constriction in her throat grew worse. "I was the last person they wanted around. They hated me. I'm not sure why. Maybe it was because of their grief. Or guilt. Or because seeing me reminded them that they'd failed to get her help. Or they just couldn't stand that their perfect daughter had died, and they were left with me—a social dud—instead."

Sully threw his arm over her shoulder and pulled her close. "They were self-absorbed idiots. They still are."

Her heart warming, she dredged up a smile. "I won't argue with that."

"And Gwendolyn Shaffer?"

Another pang knotted her chest. "They wouldn't have survived without her. They clung to her as if she were all they had left of Lauren. She became more a daughter to them than I was."

"That's even more ridiculous."

She met his gaze again. The compassion in his eyes, his fierce anger on her behalf assuaged the ache, making her feel less alone. And suddenly she had the urge to tell him the rest. Maybe it was the wine. Maybe it was the death threats and the fact that she might not survive. And maybe it was Sully, the first man who'd said she was beautiful and taken her side. But she wanted to tell him everything, details she'd never revealed, not even to her closest friends.

"I didn't make it easy for them," she admitted. "I couldn't control my grief. And I was angry—not just at them, but at Lauren, too. Why hadn't she listened to me? Why hadn't she gone for help? *Why had she left me alone?*"

She pressed her hand to her mouth, realizing for the first time that she'd felt abandoned, rejected, *betrayed.* Her best friend, the one person she'd thought had loved her, had chosen death over her.

Sully pulled her even closer, the feel of his strong arm steadying her somehow. "Your sister was sick. Bulimia's an addiction, isn't it? She probably couldn't control what she did."

He would know. She searched his eyes, but when he didn't elaborate, she expelled a breath. "You're right. I was too hurt to understand that then, so I lashed out. I'd always followed the rules, always tried so hard to please everyone, and where had it gotten me? My sister was dead. My parents rejected me. So I went wild.

"I met a guy. Jeremy. He went to the public school. I started sneaking out at night to see him. It was dumb, but I was so lonely. I'd convinced myself that he loved me." She shot him a rueful smile. "Pathetic, huh? Of course, I got pregnant."

Sully's eyes darkened. "It wasn't pathetic. You were a kid."

"I'd just turned fifteen." Grief mushroomed inside her, the memory of the child growing inside her setting off a wave of desolation so painful, she blinked back a sting of tears. Her precious, precious babe…

"What happened?" Sully asked.

"I told him I was pregnant. He freaked out and dumped me on the spot." She closed her eyes, still able to envision that night in excruciating detail. "My mother was having a party that night. I snuck back in through the garden, trying to avoid everyone, but she was in the hall."

"You told her?"

"I'd been crying. It was obvious something was wrong. She handled it worse than Jeremy did. She was furious. Livid. So was my dad. They insisted on an abortion. My mother even scheduled one at a private clinic in Philadelphia where no one would recognize me. So I ran away. I wanted that baby more than anything in the world."

She returned her gaze to his. "I wanted someone to love. Someone to fill the void Lauren had left. Someone who would love *me*."

And that was the crux of it, right there. When Lauren had died, she'd lost the only person who'd ever loved her. Lauren had left her utterly alone.

Sully reached out and clasped her hand, threading her fingers with his. "I'm sorry," he murmured, giving her the courage to go on.

"I was so naive. I thought I could raise a child on my own. I had no idea. You saw my house, how I grew up. And I had some money put aside. But I wasn't prepared for life on the streets.

"I got robbed straight off. That left me broke. Then I

miscarried a couple weeks after that. That's how I met Brynn and Nadine. I was bleeding, and they took care of me."

Losing that child had destroyed her. But what had happened next was even worse.

"What I didn't realize was that Jeremy hadn't only gotten me pregnant, he'd given me an STD."

She lifted her gaze to his, sorrow twisting inside her, the pain she could never escape. "It left me infertile. I can never have children now."

"Haley…" His hand tightened on hers. Sympathy shimmered in his dark gold eyes, as if he understood the agony she'd gone through. And then he pressed her head to his neck and held her against him, his strong arms sheltering her, the steady beat of his heart like a lifeline, the warmth emanating from his sturdy body a balm to her wounded soul.

"You didn't go back home?" he finally asked.

"No. I called my parents. I thought they'd want to know about their grandchild." She closed her eyes, fighting off another stab of pain. "I told them I was infertile. I thought they'd beg me to come home, that they'd want to take care of me."

Tears crowded her eyes. She blinked, appalled, furiously fighting them back. She didn't cry. She never cried, especially over them.

"I was a fool. It was the last straw for them, just another proof of my deficiency in their eyes. Not that they had intended to be doting grandparents, but this made me damaged goods."

She sat up and faced him, needing to unburden the rest. "They started laying down rules, conditions I'd have to follow if they did me the favor of allowing me back home. Ways they could hide how ruined I was. My self-esteem was already low. I knew it would kill me to face that censure every day. So I didn't go back. I never talked to them again…until yesterday."

Sully muttered a vicious curse. He tugged her close, pressing her head to his chest again, cradling her in the safety of his arms. "They didn't deserve you, Haley."

No, but she'd needed them. Her vision blurred. A deep, slashing ache swarmed her chest, like a rogue wave breaching a breaker wall, releasing a flood of pent-up pain. And for the first time in fifteen years, she wept.

Chapter 9

Sully held Haley in his arms, stunned by what she'd revealed. Not that she'd gotten pregnant. He could picture that part all too easily—rejected by her worthless parents, mourning the loss of her beloved sister, searching for comfort any way she could. And he sure as hell didn't blame her. God knew he'd made worse choices than hers at an even older age.

What shocked him was her strength, that she'd suffered a trauma that severe and hadn't turned out broken like him.

She pushed against the cushions and sat upright, then shot him an awkward smile. "I'm sorry. I don't know what got into me. I never cry." She wiped her eyes on her shirtsleeve, but tears still pearled in her lashes, glimmering in the lamp's low light.

"You deserve to cry. What they did to you…" He clenched his jaw against the reckless words crowding his throat. She didn't need to hear his opinion of her parents. It would only add to her distress. But he couldn't imagine parents acting that barbaric toward their child. His would welcome him home in a heartbeat, no matter how badly he'd screwed up.

She tilted her head, and her silky hair shifted against his arm. "It happened a long time ago. I never think about them anymore. And the baby..." Her mouth quivered, a sheen of tears springing to her eyes again. "That was...hard. But I can't change the past. I've had to accept it and move on."

He reached out and smudged away a tear clinging to her soft cheek. She was amazing, the most impressive woman he knew. She'd faced down the gang to protect that teenager. She'd taken down the man pursuing them. She'd fought for her sister, the girls in her shelter, even him.

But who had fought for her?

Her two runaway friends had. They'd found her bleeding and rescued her. And for the first time he understood why she was so determined to keep them safe. They'd saved her life. Now she refused to let their enemy cause them harm.

He respected loyalty like that. He would have gladly sacrificed his life to save his buddies in Afghanistan.

Instead, they'd died because of him.

Haley rested her head on his shoulder again. He shifted his aching leg, relishing the feminine feel of her—her soft, enticing breasts, her round hip nestled against his, her thick, shiny hair sweeping his arm, the mesmerizing scent of her skin.

But the anguish he'd heard in her voice kept echoing in his mind, impossible to ignore. Of all the women to end up infertile… Haley was a nurturer. He'd seen how fiercely she battled to protect those girls. She'd make the perfect mother—loving, compassionate, strong.

His throat thick, he rested his cheek against her head. She was strong, all right. Instead of trying to avoid the pain, she spent her life helping expectant mothers, reminded constantly of what she couldn't have. She had to face her loss every day with every one of those pregnant teens. The courage that took humbled him. *Shamed him.* Hell, he'd run away from his problems, drowning his pain in a bottle, rather than confront his mistakes.

She tightened her grip on his waist. His pulse slowing, he closed his eyes, feeling oddly at peace despite the danger hounding their heels. Maybe it was because she'd suffered as much as he had. Maybe because she understood how deep a loss like that could sear. But he realized that he liked being around Haley. He respected her. Admired her.

He was falling for her. *Hard.*

His stomach sank. He had no right to pursue her. He was the last person she needed, unsuitable in every way. She needed someone who could protect her, defend her, not an unstable wreck like him.

But he couldn't seem to resist her. Everything about her impressed him—her loyalty, her determination to safeguard others, her refusal to run from the enemy dogging their steps.

And God help him, but he wanted to feel that again, that idealism, that drive to make a difference in the world, that need to battle the bad guys and keep the defenseless safe.

To be the man that he once was.

She lifted her head, and he gazed into her mossy

eyes. Unable to restrain himself, he stroked his finger down her jaw, traced the delicate arch of her eyebrow, then lingered on her bottom lip. She was so soft, so graceful—and yet so resilient. He bracketed her fine-boned jaw with his hand, skimmed the hollow at the base of her throat with his thumb and felt her pulse trip under his palm.

His gaze dropped to her sultry mouth, the sheer beauty of her washing through him, and his heart began to thud. And before he could stop it, memories flooded back—of her kiss, her scent, her incredibly erotic taste. The provocative way she'd melted against him, the glaze of desire in her eyes.

That kiss had rocked his world. And he longed to experience that again. He wanted to feel her naked skin slick against his, caress the heaven of her breasts, to hear that arousing catch in her throat and make her breath come shallow and fast. And he wanted to bury himself deep inside her, slaking his hunger, his need, obliterating the unending pain.

"Sully." Her whisper whipped through him. His body went taut, the invitation in her eyes impossible to miss.

But he had to resist her. He closed his eyes, his hands trembling against her jaw. He should stand up and move. He had to put some distance between them before he did something they'd both regret.

But then she shifted against him. She wrapped her arms around his neck and kissed him, her lips soft, almost tentative, a benediction to his aching soul. He drank her in, consuming her like a starving man, his need for her more powerful than any drug.

Her lips parted under his. He invaded her sultry mouth, her soft moan rocketing through him, stoking his need. He plunged his hands through her satin hair, lost to the pleasure of her mouth. Her full breasts pillowed his chest. Her gentle hands urged him closer, making his blood run heavy and hot.

Shuddering, he deepened the kiss, a powerful surge of hunger battering his resolve, driving any thought of resistance from his head. He needed to feel her, touch her, explore every feminine part of her.

But this was wrong. He had to do the right thing here, no matter how erotic she felt. She deserved better than this. *Better than him.* He had to gather every scrap of decency he'd ever possessed and be the man she needed him to be—not the sorry man he'd become.

Using all his willpower, he ended the kiss. He closed his eyes to block out the sight of her, knowing he was too damned weak to resist. His body throbbed. His erratic pulse bludgeoned his skull. *She was willing. Aroused.* Everything male inside him clamored to do what they both desired.

But somehow he managed to stand. "We both need sleep." Sensual hunger roughened his voice. "You can take the master bedroom. I'll use the room down the hall."

He made himself turn and limp off. *He'd done the right thing.* He'd had to protect her, even from himself.

So why did he feel like hell?

Haley woke up hours later. She lay in the queen-size bed, staring into the pitch darkness, wondering what had dragged her from her fitful dreams. Truthfully, she was shocked she'd managed to sleep. Despite her exhaustion, she'd thrashed in the bed for hours, so fired up after that kiss, so plagued by questions about Sully that she'd finally given up, resigned to a long night staring at the walls. And yet, somehow she'd drifted off.

She rolled onto her back and groaned, her skin still so sensitized that even the brush of the sheet felt like torture, making her burn for Sully's touch. She'd never been more aroused or frustrated in her life. Why had he stopped? She couldn't have made her intentions any clearer. And the way he'd kissed her... He hadn't just worshipped her, he'd devoured her. As if he needed her in order to breathe.

She'd never been kissed like that. She'd never imagined it could be that way. And it had nearly killed her when he'd stopped.

The floorboard in the hallway creaked. Her heart faltered, then galloped hard. But the footsteps continued, and she recognized Sully's limp. He was pacing the hallway. *Unable to sleep.*

She sat up and held her breath, waging an internal debate. She should stay in bed. He'd clearly had his reasons for ending that kiss. Whatever nightmares afflicted him, whatever internal ghosts he battled, she had no business pushing him toward something he didn't want.

But he *had* wanted it. She hadn't mistaken the urgency in his kiss or the obvious bulge in his jeans. He was more than willing and able, which led her to conclude one thing. He was trying to act noble. He thought he was protecting her.

But she could take care of herself.

She threw aside the covers, then paused again. Did she really have the right to interfere, though? She should respect his decision and give him space. It wasn't as if they had a future. They'd been thrown together in extreme circumstances, and when this ordeal was over, they'd go back to their separate lives.

But he'd listened to her. He'd consoled her. He'd held her when she'd cried.

Now it was her turn to comfort him. Sully was suffering; his endless pacing proved that. And it wasn't in her nature to ignore a person in need. Whether it led to sex or not didn't matter. She couldn't turn her back on him now.

Rising, she tugged down the hem of the long T-shirt she'd found in the dresser, then padded barefoot across the room and into the hall. The lights were out, the hallway empty now. Her heart battering against her breastbone, she crept to his open bedroom door.

He stood at the window, wearing jeans, his naked back to the door. He'd opened the drapes, and the full moon illuminated the swamp behind the house and cast a silver glow over the room. She skimmed the line of his powerful shoulders, the slope of his muscled back. His feet were bare, his hair a tousled mess. An acute sense of loneliness seeped from him in waves.

This was a man in pain. Her heart ached, the need to hold him a tangible thing.

She didn't think she'd made a sound. But all of a sudden, he turned his head. Their gazes locked. Hunger pulsed between them, jump-starting her pulse. Her blood roared in her ears.

"Go back to bed." His voice came out rough.

She stepped through the doorway and into the room. "I can't."

"Haley..."

She crossed the room. He turned toward her, his

strong jaw set, his body tensing like a gunslinger's at high noon. She stopped a foot away.

For a long moment, she drank in the sight of him—the slashing lines of his tortured face. The hollows and shadows of his whiskered cheeks. The thick ridges of muscle bunching his shoulders and arms. He was beautiful, virile. Definitely all male.

Her heart doing somersaults, she closed the remaining distance between them, conscious that she was naked beneath her T-shirt, that every cell in her body craved this man's touch.

She reached up and skimmed her fingers down his rough-hewn jaw, intoxicated by the feel of him, the sexy scratch of stubble turning her pulse maniacal. He looked rough, rumpled, gloriously muscled, his harsh angles accentuated in the shadowed room. The moonlight bathed him in silver, exposing a network of tiny lines feathering his skin.

Scars. She touched his chest, tracing her finger over the muscles padding his breastbone, down his impressive washboard abs to a cluster of scars beneath his ribs. Her throat turned thick at the suffering he'd endured, the horrors he must have seen. The burdens he still carried inside.

He caught her wrist, trapping her hand against his hard chest. Her gaze snapped back to his. For several charged seconds, neither moved, the desire ricocheting between them rooting her in place.

"Be damned sure of this," he finally growled.

She crowded close enough to feel the heat radiating from his naked skin. "I'm sure."

His gaze didn't veer from hers. She had no trouble reading the hunger in his eyes, the same wild craving that burned inside of her. Then he released her wrist and cradled her face, his gaze turning so hot, so savage and raw, she was sure that she'd combust.

And then he kissed her again. His mouth slanted over hers. Insistent. Ravenous. The kiss of a starving man. And she gladly surrendered to his need, shivering and melting against him, running her hands over his shoulders knotted with muscles, wanting him so desperately she nearly cried out.

He braced his calloused hand over her jaw, changing the angle of the kiss and penetrating her mouth with his tongue. Thrills skidded inside her, like heat lightning crackling inside her veins. She clung to his corded neck, her thoughts growing muddled, her senses narrowing to this one man, this single moment in time and the frantic need for him clawing inside.

She wanted his hands on her skin and breasts. She wanted to feel his hard muscles flexing around her, stoking the maelstrom swirling inside. And she wanted his mouth everywhere, on every intimate part of her, until she exploded with bliss.

He slid a hand down her back, pulling her closer, holding her against the vee of his thighs. Her knees went weak, the rigid feel of him igniting her flesh. She moaned against his mouth, the desire building inside her nearly impossible to withstand.

Their mouths still fused, their kisses growing more desperate, he walked her backward to the bed. They landed on the mattress, and he trapped her beneath him, his delicious weight pinning her down. And then he kissed her again, sending glorious sensations spiraling through her, laying waste to her self-control. But despite her frantic moans, he took his time, running his hands over her face, her belly, her breasts, as if inventorying every inch of her body, like a sculptor examining his work.

She gasped and arched against him, the feel of his big, rough hand on her breasts too exquisite to bear. Moisture pooled between her thighs. Her body softened and trembled, on fire for his torrid touch. She stroked his back, his shoulders bunched with muscles, frantic to get closer yet.

He tugged her long T-shirt over her head. His eyes burned, his breath turning hoarse, his face taut as he ravished her with his gaze. Her heart swelled, his desire for her touching something inside her, affecting her in a way she couldn't explain. Then he renewed his sensual onslaught, laving his way over her skin in a sensual brand, scattering a trail of sparks in its wake. She grew insane with a feral hunger, lost to the sensations rushing and colliding inside her, all thoughts driven from her mind, except one—the raging need to draw him inside.

Then he paused, lifting himself slightly away from her, his gaze sweeping her in the moonlit bed. "You're beautiful."

She knew it wasn't true. But the reverence in his husky voice convinced her he thought so. Her heart yielded another notch.

He stood and removed his jeans. The air caught in her throat at the sight of him fully aroused. She skimmed his flat, rock-hard belly, his wide shoulders roped with sinews, his chiseled biceps and corded thighs. He was glorious, perfect, the absolute masculinity of him robbing her of breath.

Kneeling over her, he took her mouth again, and she yielded completely, giving herself over to his electric touch. Their kisses turned even more urgent, her heartbeat erratic, her need edging toward delirium now.

But then he stopped. His breath sawed in her ear. "Hell. I don't have protection."

"We don't need it. I can't get pregnant, remember?" The pain of it welled in her chest.

He fingered her hair, his dark gaze softening on hers. "I don't… I'm clean, Haley. You don't have to worry about that."

"I'm not. I trust you." She did. Sully would never harm her. This man would never break his word or lie to her. She might not know the particulars of his life, but she knew one thing. His honor meant the world to him.

He took her mouth again. And then he entered her in one powerful thrust, the feel of him so exquisite that she cried out. Her pulse turned frenetic, the need for him throbbing inside her with a recklessness she couldn't contain. He plunged and withdrew, bringing her closer to insanity with every stroke, to that exquisite moment when hunger exploded into a pleasure too fierce to endure.

And then it broke. Waves of ecstasy pumped through her, the rapture relentless. She let out a strangled cry.

Sully stiffened, his deep groan mingling with hers, and hurtled them both into paradise.

She awoke from a doze some time later, still nestled in Sully's arms. Her eyes closed, she listened to his rough, strong breath as he slept beside her, little flashes of pleasure still bursting inside her, remnants from the most incredible night of her life.

Not that she could claim a lot of experience with men. There had been Jeremy in high school, of course. But she'd only dated sporadically since then. It had been too hard to maintain a relationship on the run. And when she *had* connected with someone, it had inevitably petered out, more her fault than his. She'd always held back, never revealing her past, never allowing anyone beneath the surface of her life. She couldn't. It was too dangerous. She hadn't wanted to take the risk.

Until Sully. He was the first person she'd told the truth. She'd given him her trust, her body, her heart.

Stunned, she snapped open her eyes. She rolled her head toward him, taking in his strong jaw, slack in sleep, the dark lashes resting against his stubble-roughened cheeks, the column of his sinewed throat. He had one arm thrown out to the side, and his muscles glimmered in the moonlight, the play of light and shadows emphasizing his banked strength. She ran her gaze over his chest, lingering on the scars disappearing beneath the sheet. He was insanely male, every inch the warrior.

And she was sinking fast.

But she had to be careful. She still knew little about him. He refused to discuss his family. He refused to reveal any details about the war. He hadn't even talked about the time he'd spent here, in his grandparents' home, other than giving her the basic facts.

And she knew better than most the pain a one-sided relationship could cause. She couldn't put herself through that kind of torture again. This had been sex for him, a temporary release from the nightmares he suffered.

Even if it had felt like more.

Struggling to get a grip on her unruly emotions, she rose on her elbow and studied him again, his rugged appeal scrambling her pulse. She ran her fingers over his scars, her heart aching at the pain that he'd been through.

He shifted, exposing his knee. She glanced down, her breath catching at a horrific web of scars puckering his thigh. No wonder he limped. What kind of injury had caused that much trauma? How much agony had he been through? Is that why he'd received his Purple Heart? And what about the Silver Star? How had he earned that?

He opened his eyes, his sleepy gaze capturing hers. For several seconds, she stayed trapped in his gaze, the thought of the pain he'd borne tearing her to shreds inside. "What happened to your leg?"

His eyes instantly shuttered, the change in him so abrupt that she pulled back. He sat up and swung his legs over the side of the bed.

"Sully…"

"I don't want to talk about it."

"But—"

"Leave it, Haley." His words were sharp, the finality in his voice like a slap, shutting her out. But she'd been around enough runaways to recognize the pain behind his anger—even when he hurled it at her.

He reached down and pulled on his jeans, then tugged his T-shirt over his head. "I'm going out for a while."

"What?" She frowned at the still-dark window. "Where are you going? It's the middle of the night."

"Just out. Get some sleep. I'll be back before it's time to leave."

She gaped at him, stunned, as he scooped up his gun and shoes and left the room. His footsteps receded in the hall. He rummaged in the kitchen, banging cupboards. And then the back door opened and closed.

Dazed, she rose and went to the window. Sully limped across the deck and into the yard, the silver moonlight glinting off the bottle in his hand. He headed across the lawn, then merged with the shadows bordering the swamp. A moment later, he disappeared from view.

Still reeling, she picked up her discarded T-shirt and put it on, then perched on the edge of the bed, trying to stifle the jab of hurt. His reaction shouldn't have surprised her. She never should have asked him about his wound. She'd foolishly butted in where she had no right, provoking him, like prodding an injured bear. Of course he'd lash back.

And so what if he did? So what if he wouldn't reveal what caused that pain? She had no place in his life. Sully was a loner. He had every hallmark of a man at odds with the world. He had ghosts to defeat, issues he needed to resolve—serious issues that didn't involve her. The sooner she recognized that, the better off she'd be.

Because if anyone knew the futility of trying to compete with an addiction, it was her. She could never win that battle. Lauren had taught her that.

No matter how much it hurt, no matter how much she yearned to help him heal, she had to resist the urge to meddle in his private life. She had to think of herself for once, keep her distance and protect her heart.

But she had a feeling it was far too late.

Chapter 10

Sully limped down the narrow trail through the wetlands, a bottle of whiskey in one hand, the full moon
lighting his way. Not that he needed the light to guide
him. He'd grown up on the bay, spending nearly as much
time at his grandparents' house as he had in his own suburban Virginia home. Every twist in the winding path,
every creak and crack in the aging house inundated him
with memories—memories he'd tried like hell to forget.

He reached the weathered dock perched at the edge
of the water, a narrow channel that wended through the
marsh grass to the bay. Taking a seat on the wooden oar
box, he unscrewed the cap on the bottle with trembling
hands. Then he guzzled down several deep swallows
of whiskey, desperate to quell the shakes. He paused to
catch his breath, then took another vital drink. Hissing,
he wiped his mouth on the back of his hand.

He'd screwed up. Badly. He never should have come

to his grandparents' house. But he hadn't expected this tide of emotions, this overpowering yearning for a happier time. And having Haley here compounded the problem, reminding him of all he'd lost—his honor, his idealism, his dreams.

Even worse, he never should have touched her, no matter how incredible she'd felt. She'd needed comfort, a steady shoulder to lean on, not a night of blinding sex. But he'd succumbed to the wild hunger burning inside him, unable to resist her allure. And then he'd acted like a total jerk, bolting from the house like a soldier diving for cover during a firefight, treatment she didn't deserve.

He scowled at the rowboat bobbing beside the dock, the inky water lapping its sides. He'd panicked, pure and simple. He hadn't wanted to answer her questions and admit his shame. He couldn't bear to see the pity in her gorgeous eyes when she'd learned the truth—or her contempt. And he definitely didn't want to confess his addiction, proof of the failed man he'd become.

The cold wind whispered in the sedge. He knocked back another slug of whiskey, the irony hitting him hard. He'd wanted to conquer evil when he'd gone to war. Instead, *it* had defeated *him*. And night after night, the haunting images mocked him—the children with their eerily blank eyes. The drab mud huts of the village, the haze of their cooking fires permeating the air. The women squatting in the dirt, their faces hidden behind their veils, too terrorized to make a sound. The men leaning against the doorways in their pakul hats, their skin broiled into leather by the desert sun, making it impossible to tell their age.

And then the mujahideen in their ratty scarves, their black eyes burning with hatred, their RPGs screaming through the air. The sounds were the worst—the shrieks of the dying children. The cries of the faceless women, slaughtered without a thought. The shouts of Sully's men as they scrambled to mount a defense, their blood forming crimson splashes in the rocky sand.

Sweat dampening his face, Sully gulped down even more whiskey to stop the endless barrage. He focused on the water slapping against the boat, the tall reeds bowing in the wind, the distant call of an unseen bird. But the full moon gazed down from the midnight sky, its ancient eyes filled with horror, never letting him forget.

Bringing Haley here was a mistake, all right. Being around her, seeing how courageous she was, was forcing him to face the ruins of his life—exiled from his family, barely existing in an empty row house, addicted to alcohol.

And the truth was, he didn't like the man he'd become. He wasn't proud of his pointless life. He had no purpose, no ambition, no goal. He spent his days wallowing in self-pity, anesthetizing the pain with booze, devoid of self-respect.

He didn't have a clue how to get it back.

But he did know one thing. He had to apologize to Haley. He'd had no business shutting her out like that after the most incredible night of his life. Somehow, he had to explain.

Dreading the confrontation, he screwed the cap on the half-empty bottle and rose. Then he limped back down the path toward the house. The wind had picked up, rustling the marsh grass and making shadows flicker across the yard. But something about the silence penetrated his senses, rousing him from his troubled thoughts. *It was too quiet*. The hushed night pulsed with that same unnatural stillness that had gripped the village before the attack.

He stopped in his tracks. Goose bumps prickled his neck. His senses sharpening, he set down the bottle of whiskey and tugged out his sidearm, scanning the shadows flanking the house.

The soft crackle of leaves drew his gaze to the bedroom window and everything inside him tensed. A man crouched beneath the glass, his form barely visible against the house. Then he slunk toward the deck, passing through a sliver of moonlight, revealing the rifle slung over his back.

An E-13. Sully couldn't mistake its distinctive shape, even in the weak light. *The gang had caught up.* But how? No one had followed them here; he'd made damned sure of that. So how had they found this house? Had they investigated his background? Were they keeping a watch on his family? What kind of resources did they have?

His mouth thinned, a hot rush of anger threatening his self-restraint. They'd gone too far. They'd made this war personal now. No one attacked his family—let alone a woman he cared for—and survived.

His adrenaline rising, he crept silently through the shadows, keeping to the perimeter of the yard. That gang member wouldn't have come alone. He must have a lookout or two stationed around the house. Sully had to neutralize the intruder, extract Haley and escape without tipping the other men off.

Pausing, he listened intently, trying to hear around the blood pressure thundering through his skull. *Still no sign of the other gang members.* The intruder jiggled the latch on the sliding glass door and slipped inside.

Sully didn't hesitate. He raced across the deck and

ducked inside. The man stopped and started to turn, but Sully's momentum gave him an edge. He slammed the butt of his gun into his skull, aiming for the sensitive artery behind his ear.

The man grunted and staggered off balance, but he was stronger than Sully thought. He grabbed hold of his rifle and whipped around.

But Sully was prepared. He bunched his free hand into a fist and slammed a right cross into his jaw. The gang member stumbled backward and crashed against the wall. Sully followed and grasped his throat. He bore down hard, trying to cut off his air supply, and bashed him against the wall.

Incredibly, the man fought back, landing a blow to Sully's solar plexus. Pain exploded inside him, but he tightened his grip and held on. There wasn't a chance in hell he'd let him win.

The man's fist connected with his jaw. Furious, Sully seized his arm and jerked him forward, then rammed his elbow into his neck. The gang member crumpled, and Sully took advantage, plowing his fist into his nose.

The man screamed and covered his face. Determined to take him down, Sully knifed his knee into his groin, adding a kick to his ribs to finish him off. Their would-be killer slumped unconscious onto the floor.

His lungs sawing, Sully shook the sweat from his eyes. Then he knelt and searched their attacker, unearthing several spare magazines. He pocketed the ammo, slung the rifle over his back, and rose.

"*Sully!* Are you all right?"

Still laboring for air, he wheeled around. Haley rushed toward him from the hallway, her eyes huge in her bloodless face. *She was safe, thank God.*

Exhaling, he gave her a nod. "We need to get out of here. I doubt he came alone." Luckily, she'd already dressed and grabbed their supplies. "Wait by the back door."

Hurrying now, he strode into the kitchen and grabbed the oar box key from its peg, then joined her at the sliding glass door. "Wait until I give you the signal, then run to the dock. There's a path through the swamp." He pointed to the far right corner of the yard, then pressed the key into her palm. "We'll use the rowboat. This opens the box with the oars."

He inched open the door and listened. *Silence.* He scoured the yard, searching the shadows along the reeds. *Still nothing.* He stepped outside, then crept across the deck to the side of the house. A man stood watch near the street.

They'd have to take the chance.

He signaled for Haley to go. She slipped outside and darted across the lawn toward the marsh. He waited until she'd disappeared, then turned on his heel and followed, sprinting across the grass.

But a shout broke out. Swearing, he raced down the narrow path. They'd just run out of time.

His feet pounded the trail. Cursing the moonlight that exposed them to view, he put on a burst of speed, reaching the dock in a few more strides. Haley stood in the boat, inserting the oars into the locks.

"I'll row." He untied the line and leaped inside. Then he sat and grabbed the oars while Haley shoved them away from the dock. He turned the boat into the shallow channel and rowed with all his might, knowing the reeds wouldn't conceal them for long. The channel was too open, the moon too bright. They had to get deeper into the marsh before those gang members reached the dock.

The men crashed through the swamp. Putting even more power behind it, Sully pulled on the oars, propelling them toward the channel's bend. "Get down," he warned.

Haley slid off the thwart and crouched. "Give me your gun."

"Can you shoot?"

"If I have to."

Pausing, he pulled out his sidearm and handed it to her. "Watch for the recoil."

"I will." She turned to face the stern.

Sully hauled on the oars, his gaze locked on the dock. Sweat dripped into his eyes. The voices drew closer yet. The narrow channel twisted and he lifted one oar, angling toward the coming bend.

Two men bounded onto the dock. Spotting the fleeing rowboat, they raised their guns and aimed.

Haley fired. Her shot barked across the marsh, missing the men, but it was enough to drive them back. They dove backward off the dock, scrambling for cover, while Sully finished turning the boat. In one mighty pull, he catapulted them behind a tuft of reeds.

Now he had the advantage. He knew this swamp. He'd fished it with his grandfather. He'd spent hours during his childhood searching for tadpoles along the banks. He'd snuck out here as a teenager to smoke and drink, even losing his virginity in a nearby cove.

He steered unerringly through the twisting channels, the quiet splash of the oars and the cold wind rustling the grass the only sounds. After a moment, he paused to blot the sweat blurring his vision and glanced at Haley again.

"You can get up now." He kept his voice low, knowing sound would carry across the water at night.

Still holding the gun, Haley rose and took her seat, the moonlight shimmering in her dark hair. Then her gaze connected with his, and for an instant, the world seemed to fade away. His heart tumbled, the primal urge to protect this woman rising inside him with a force so strong he lost the capacity to breathe.

"What now?" she whispered.

He blinked, not sure what had just happened. But whatever the hell it was, he'd analyze it later when they were safe. "We can't go into the bay. They'll spot us from the shore. And we can't go back to the house for the car."

He caught the mast of a sailboat out of the corner of his eye. *The local boatyard.* It was closed at night, but if Lenny Myers was still the watchman…

He frowned, pained to realize he didn't know. The Vietnam War veteran had been a major influence in Sully's life. His stories of courage and honor had inspired him to enlist.

And yet, he'd never visited him since he'd been back. He'd been so ashamed of his failures that he'd neglected an aging friend—a friend who never would have turned his back on *him.* Not pleased at that unflattering insight, he steered the boat toward the yard.

Perched at the edge of the peninsula, the boatyard was more a repair shop for local skipjacks than a fancy marina, although it still boasted a couple-dozen empty slips. Sully scanned the travel lift hulking in the moonlight, the marine railway beside the machinery shop. Lenny's old Mustang sat beside a dry-docked crab boat and Sully released his breath.

"I know the night watchman," he told Haley. "I'm sure he'll lend us his car."

She shot him a curious look, which he ignored. He knew she deserved an explanation—and an apology for fleeing the house after they'd made love. But he'd do that later, after they'd escaped. He'd already messed up once, nearly getting her killed. He didn't intend to do it twice.

He glided alongside the pier and eased off on the oars. "I'll get it," she said, handing him back his gun. She took hold of the mooring line and wrapped it around the cleat, expertly securing the boat.

He arched a brow. "You're a sailor?"

She grabbed their bag of supplies and scrambled onto the dock. "One of my sister's boyfriends had a yacht."

Right. He stowed the oars in the bottom of the boat and hopped out. He shot a glance at the gate, making sure they were still alone, then led the way past a Chesapeake deadrise workboat to the machinery shop.

He rapped on the metal door. A man called out, and Sully ushered Haley inside. He spotted the old soldier huddling beside a space heater, wrapped in blankets, and stopped. Lenny's ponytail had turned gray. His cheeks had sunk, emphasizing the angular shape of his skull. Even his shoulders looked smaller, frailer, proof of his seventy-odd years.

But his face wreathed into a smile as he rose. "Well, look what the cat dragged in. Sully Turner." His grin widening, he hobbled toward them, his eyes still bright, the usual cigarette odor permeating his clothes.

An unbidden warmth spread through Sully's chest, and he limped across the room. Damn, but he'd missed this man. He'd grown up listening to his stories, idolizing him as the hero that he was, a man who'd put his life on the line for a cause he'd believed in, in a war few people valued or cared to recall.

Lenny clasped his hand and thumped his back. "I heard you made it home. About time you stopped by."

"Yeah. It's been too long." Sully's throat tightened with a barrage of emotions—pleasure at seeing Lenny, guilt that he'd stayed away, shame at the shape he was in.

And he knew that Lenny could see it, that the vet had sized him up in an instant, noting the fine tremors shaking his hands, the disillusionment in his bloodshot eyes, the dark circles testifying to his sleepless nights. Lenny understood too well the crippling memories soldiers brought home, their problems integrating back into civilian life. And Sully had no doubt he recognized that same lost quality in him.

"So," Lenny said, his voice uneven. "It's like that, is it?"

His throat turning even thicker, Sully managed to nod.

But then Lenny's gaze went past him, and his smile returned, a gleam brightening his faded eyes. "You brought along a beautiful woman. My lucky night."

Still feeling raw, Sully turned and introduced them. Haley's face was pink from the cold, her chestnut hair tumbling over her shoulders in disarray. She'd pulled on a sweatshirt over her jeans, but it did little to hide her curves.

Sully moved his gaze down her breasts and hips, remembering every damned detail about her, her scent, her taste, every sigh and shiver she'd made. And that possessive feeling rolled through him again, the overwhelming need to hold on to this woman and keep her from harm.

She stepped forward and shook Lenny's hand. Shifting his thoughts back to their current problem, Sully tightened his grip on the rifle strap. "We're in danger," he told his friend. "It's a long story, but we need a car to get away."

Lenny's smile vanished. Suddenly all business, he fished in his pocket and tossed him some keys. "Use my truck. It's out back. I just filled the gas tank and changed the oil."

No questions asked. If a buddy was in trouble, a fellow soldier always came through. That lump blocked his throat again. "Thanks, Lenny."

"Just promise you'll come back and tell me about those medals you earned."

"I will." He'd be back, all right. He owed Lenny much more than that.

He turned and followed Haley to the door. But then he stopped and looked back at his friend. "Be careful. We've got gangbangers from the city on our trail."

Lenny patted his waistband, a wide smile revealing the gaps in his teeth and adding crinkles around his eyes. "I can't wait. They can make my day anytime."

Sully grinned back. Clint Eastwood had nothing on Lenny Myers. Those punks didn't stand a chance.

Reassured, he exited the building, the cold bay air buffeting his face. "Back here." Skirting a forklift, he led the way to Lenny's late-model pickup truck. He unlocked the doors and they climbed inside.

The truck reeked of stale tobacco. Trash from fast-food meals littered the dashboard and floor. Grimacing, he stowed the rifle behind the seat and strapped himself in. "Sorry about this. I know it's not much to look at."

Haley buckled her seat belt. "As long as it runs."

"It will." He inserted the key and the old truck purred to life, like Lenny himself. The old vet wasn't much to look at, but he was rock steady where it counted—inside.

Suspecting the gang wouldn't be far behind them, Sully tore out of the marina and crossed the low bridge spanning the inlet to the marsh. Then he veered down a wooded back road, heading west through the eastern-Maryland countryside toward D.C.

Haley glanced back at the deserted road, then met his eyes. "Where should we go?"

Somewhere the gang couldn't find them—wherever the hell that was. "Keep your eye out for a hiding place—a dirt trail or somewhere we can turn off. We're too exposed out here with our headlights on. We need to hole up until dawn." They could blend in with the D.C. commuters then.

But as he sped away from the bay, a heavy feeling settled inside him, a certainty that had nothing to do with the deadly gang. He could no longer ignore the brutal truth.

He'd made a mistake tonight. He'd been so damned self-absorbed, so caught up in his addiction that he'd left Haley alone in the house, exposed. While he'd sulked in the swamp, drinking and licking his wounds, the gang had nearly gunned her down. If that wasn't a dereliction of duty, he didn't know what was.

He'd nearly gotten her killed tonight. Thanks to his weakness, she could have died. *Never again.* From this moment on, no matter what it took, no matter what kind of suffering he had to endure, he was done with alcohol for good.

Chapter 11

Half an hour later, they jolted down a rutted tractor trail through a stand of woods, lurching and bouncing though potholes and over rocks. The old truck rattled and creaked. The headlights danced crazily across the leafless trees. Then they broke through the woods into a clearing. In the center was an old tobacco barn, its roof caved in, brush sprawling against the doors, missing boards making Swiss cheese out of its sides. Beyond the barn lay a dried-up cornfield littered with broken stalks.

"This looks good," Haley said. They hadn't passed a house in miles.

"Yeah. I doubt anyone comes back this way. We can rest for an hour or two." Sully pulled the truck around, backed into the shadows beside the barn and turned the engine off.

Silence filled the cab. Haley stared out the windshield, letting her eyes adjust to the dark. The moon was still out, shimmering over the fields as it inched toward dawn. Then the cold wind blew, whistling through a space in the passenger-side window. She cranked the flimsy handle, but the glass hung at an angle, making it impossible to close the gap.

Giving up, she dropped her head against the seat rest and closed her eyes, surrendering to the exhaustion deadening her limbs. The night had thoroughly drained her—the frenzied flight through the swamp, the horror of those gang members gunning for them, the incredible feel of Sully's arms...

She turned her head and studied his profile, memorizing the aggressive slash of his jaw, the sexy quirk of his eyebrows, the way his morning beard stubble darkened his cheeks and throat. She curled her hands, resisting the urge to run her hands over his sandpapered jaw, to kiss the worry lines bracketing his sensual mouth, to slide her body against his heat. Envisioning his hands on her, she shivered hard.

"Cold?"

Just the opposite. She burned at the thought of touching him again. But she wasn't about to admit that, not after the way he'd bolted from the house. "I'm okay."

"I'll see what's in the back."

He pushed open his door and got out, admitting a blast of frigid air that did nothing to cool her thoughts. Then he pulled up the hatch on the truck bed and rummaged through his friend's supplies. He came back a moment later, a pile of blankets in his arms. "These might help. They smell as bad as the truck, though."

"I don't care." Leaving a couple for him, she wrapped one blanket around her shoulders and draped another over her legs. "Believe me, I've used worse."

A Kiss to Die For

"When you ran away, you mean?"

"Yes." She'd endured plenty of uncomfortable nights—starving, freezing, scared. Nights when she'd huddled against her friends, so cold she feared she'd never warm up again. "We had to stay on the move, so we were always searching for shelter. Eventually we started spending winters down south, but at the beginning we were so damned cold." And she would never take shelter or warmth for granted again.

Sully's gaze captured hers, the sympathy in his eyes drawing her closer, the banked heat jump-starting her pulse. She didn't regret making love to him. It had been the most glorious night of her life. But it changed everything between them. She couldn't look at him now without remembering how he'd kissed her, the erotic way he'd made love—and the tender way he'd held her, making her feel cherished and safe.

But it was the torment in his eyes that really gutted her heart. She wanted so badly to heal this embattled man. Everything about him cried out for comfort—comfort she ached to provide.

But she knew better than to push. For every step he took forward, he'd probably take several back. She'd worked with enough troubled teenagers to know. And with killers anticipating their moves, this wasn't the time to delve into his past.

"Speaking of running away…" He cleared his throat. "I'm sorry about the way I cut out back there."

"You don't need to apologize."

"Yes, I do. There's no excuse for how I acted. I shouldn't have left you alone."

His gaze stayed on hers, the intensity in his eyes causing her pulse to stumble hard. The last thing this man needed was more guilt. "Sully, I'm fine. And I can protect myself. I'm used to it. I've been on my own for years."

He reached out and took her hand, lacing his strong fingers with hers. "You shouldn't have to be alone."

His quiet words rumbled through her, eliciting a host of emotions she'd locked away long ago—regret, hope, a longing for the kind of love she'd never have.

She twisted her mouth into a smile. "Yeah, well, I learned to accept reality a long time ago—who I am, what my parents are like, what I can never be. And I don't waste energy wishing for things that I can't have."

He nodded, his gaze on their entwined hands. He ran his thumb over her wrist, the warm caress soothing, steadying, making her feel that she wasn't alone.

"The war changed me, Haley. What happened there, in Afghanistan, I don't want to talk about that. But it was bad." His voice turned raw. "I don't know why I survived. I should be dead right now. And when I came back home, I couldn't cope."

The agony in his voice made her heart flip, and she longed to pull him close. "I started to drink," he continued. "It was the only way I could make it through the nights. I thought it would beat back the flashbacks and help me forget."

"Did it?"

He hesitated, then shook his head. "No. I still have the flashbacks. But now I'm addicted to alcohol, too."

She clung to his calloused hand, sensing what this admission cost him. She wondered if it was the first time he'd voiced it aloud. "Have you decided what to do about it?"

"Yeah." He grimaced. "Stop drinking for one thing. I nearly got you killed tonight."

"That wasn't your fault. You didn't bring the gang to the house."

"But I wasn't there to protect you when they showed up."

"You were there when it counted."

"But what if I hadn't been?" Raw fear rang in his voice, his eyes so bleak that it wrenched her heart.

And suddenly, she realized he wasn't talking only about her. His fears went beyond the gang, beyond the danger shadowing their heels, to whatever had caused those flashbacks that plagued his nights. He believed that he'd failed someone. This courageous man was tortured by guilt.

But she knew him. Maybe she didn't know much about his childhood or family. Maybe he hadn't shared many details about his past. But she knew the essence of who he was.

And she'd bet her life on one immutable fact. Sully would fight to the death to protect the people he loved. He would never willingly give up. Whatever had happened in Afghanistan wasn't his fault. How could he ever have doubts about that?

Unable to resist, she twisted around to face him and cupped his jaw with her hand, willing him to understand. "Sully...you've saved me so many times. Even when you didn't know me, you risked your life for mine. You've come through for me time after time. And you're the bravest man I've ever met."

"You're wrong. I'm not who you think I am."

"You're *exactly* who I think you are."

His Adam's apple dipped. His stark eyes burned into

hers. Then he slid his hands into her hair, his tremors torching the hunger inside her, the need to feel him a primal ache.

Her gaze dropped to his mouth. The dark night pulsed around them, cloaking them in a private world. And right or wrong, she needed this man with a desperation she couldn't define. "Sully…" Swallowing hard, she lifted her gaze to his. "Make love to me again."

He closed his eyes and groaned. "Haley…"

"Please don't turn me down. I need you."

His breath came out in a rush. His eyes burned into hers, his blatant hunger scorching through her like liquid fire. And then he surrendered with a groan and pulled her to him, slanting his mouth over hers, the hard feel of him making her shudder, his desperation like a lightning bolt triggering hers.

His lips devoured hers. His tongue plundered her mouth, igniting a maelstrom she couldn't contain. She shoved her hands through his tangled hair, felt the muscles rippling along his shoulders and back, aching to move closer yet.

But the gearshift blocked her way.

"Hold on," Sully muttered. "I'm coming over." It wasn't easy, but he scooted awkwardly over the gearshift onto her seat and dragged her across his lap. Then he claimed her mouth again, his kisses potent, lengthening, luring her deeper into a sensual morass she had no intention of trying to escape. Her thoughts grew blurred, her reality narrowing to this one man, the delirium growing inside her, the naked hunger making her crazed.

Desperate to feel him, she broke the kiss. Then she wriggled around on the seat to face him and straddled his muscled thighs. She tugged her T-shirt over her head and tossed aside her bra.

His gaze fell to her breasts. His jaw turned taut, the hunger that wracked his face flooding her with heat. Her body moistened, the erotic hardness between her thighs making her crazed.

His big, calloused hands covered her breasts. Thrills shuddered through her, igniting a conflagration of need. Then his mouth replaced his hands. Her head fell back, her breath coming fast, the ecstasy threatening to drive her insane.

After an eternity, he lifted his head. "Can you get your jeans off?"

Rising, she yanked down the zipper, bumping her head in the cramped space. She managed to shove off the rest of her clothes, then knelt over him again as he undid his fly.

Their eyes locked. For a moment, time seemed suspended, her heart tatting a frenetic beat, her emotions so muddled she couldn't seem to form a thought.

Except one. She needed this man, needed him with an intensity that shocked her, with a need that went far beyond sex, far beyond this single moment in time.

Her pulse rioting, she rose on her knees, then slowly took him inside her, inch by glorious inch, the hard, pulsing feel of him so overwhelming she started to shake.

He made a low, ragged sound deep in his throat. Then he crushed his mouth against hers. Unable to stand it, she gave herself over to the primitive instincts, to the madness clawing inside her, to the sheer pleasure driving her wild.

Her arms tightened around his neck. She rocked and

shivered against him, her desperation coiling so tightly inside her she wanted to scream. Sully pulled down on her hips and thrust against her. Insistent. Relentless. Inexorable. Driving her to the edge of desire.

And then her control dissolved. Torrid pleasure zapped her, a jolt so intense that she cried out. She went rigid in his arms, then shattered into a million sparkles, ecstasy lashing her veins. Sully's hoarse cries echoed her own.

For several minutes afterward, she didn't move. Her heart ran a tattered race. She couldn't seem to catch her breath. Then Sully lifted her chin and kissed her, the kiss tender and gentle and deep, unlike anything she'd ever felt before.

He might not want her, but he needed her. Just as she needed him.

Then he pulled the blanket over her back, drew her head to his neck, and closed his eyes. And for a long time, she nestled against him, relishing his strength and warmth, trying to sort out what had occurred. But her body was too thoroughly sated, her mind too fuzzy to figure it out.

She managed to doze. But reality eventually crept back along with the cold night air, dispelling the magic, tugging her out of the sensual cocoon. Because no matter what had just happened with Sully, no matter how glorious he'd made her feel, they still had killers searching for them.

She disentangled herself with a sigh and began gathering her clothes while Sully did the same. "So how do you think the gang found us?" she asked, tugging on her pants.

"Hell if I know. They didn't use a tracking device this

time. And they couldn't have followed us to the house. We would have noticed that."

She put on her bra and T-shirt, then tried to give Sully space as he scooted over the gearshift again. She knocked her head against the roof and winced. "You think Foley was involved?"

"I don't see how. We saw him leave."

She frowned at that. "He could have phoned someone and told them what we were driving and where we were."

"We still would have noticed a car."

"Once we left the freeway, sure. But they could have followed us until we exited without us noticing. And if they knew who you are, who your family is, that your grandparents lived out here... They could have figured it out."

But that raised even more questions. Exactly who *was* this guy? What kind of power did he have? And who else had they put at risk?

Worried now, she slipped on her shoes. "Should you call your parents? Make sure they're all right?"

Sully exhaled. "I don't know. I don't want to scare them. I guess I could call my sister and have her check things out."

"You have a sister?"

He nodded. "There are six of us kids. I'm the youngest."

She waited, but he didn't elaborate, leaving her to fill in the gaps herself. She assumed they lived nearby. His grandparents had a home here and Sully had spent vacations at their house.

He'd also mentioned that his family wanted to see him—which made sense. Big families tended to be close-knit. It was hard to live like a loner with that many people around.

So what would cause Sully to isolate himself from the people who loved him most?

She gazed into his eyes, dying to ask, but still unwilling to pry. He'd tell her when—if—he was ready, and not before. "I always wanted a big family," she said, instead. She would have given the world for someone who'd cared.

Embarrassed at her maudlin turn of mind, she rummaged in the sports bag and pulled out one of the disposable phones. "Here."

He turned it on and frowned. "There's no signal bar. I'll walk back to the road, see if I can pick up a signal there."

He pushed open the door and climbed out. He took the rifle from behind the seat and slung it over his back. Then he handed her the pistol she'd used in the boat. "Keep this. And lock the doors. I won't be long."

He paused. The moon had shifted, shadowing his face, and she couldn't read the expression in his eyes. But then he ducked his head back inside the cab, dragged her toward him and kissed her, a deep, hungry kiss that obliterated every thought. Then he turned on his heel and limped away.

Stunned, she didn't move. She stared at the woods where he'd disappeared, the night sounds settling around her—the wind whistling through the window's crack, the creak of branches swaying nearby. An owl hooted from the barn, the lonely sound echoing her thoughts.

She'd give the world for someone who cared, all right. *Someone exactly like him.*

She dragged the blanket around her, then leaned back

against the seat and closed her eyes, knowing she was doomed. She was in way over her head here and drowning fast. How on earth could she protect her heart?

"You're sure about this?" Haley asked.

Sully drove into Falls Church, Virginia, a few hours later, maneuvering though the morning traffic heading into D.C. "We need to go on the offensive and take him by surprise. It's the only way we can be sure we're not walking into a trap."

"I guess."

He didn't blame Haley for feeling nervous. They were stuck in a game they didn't understand, at the mercy of an unknown enemy—who somehow managed to anticipate their moves. It was time to seize the initiative and opt out of the deadly game. They couldn't risk another attack.

And Foley owed them answers. Intentionally or not, he must have tipped off the gang. It was the only explanation that made any sense.

Sully turned off the busy highway, drove a quarter mile down a tree-lined side street and entered the condominium complex where Special Agent Foley lived. An online search for his phone number had yielded his address. And given the early hour, they expected to find him at home.

Sully shifted down a gear, slowing to read the numbers on the gray, two-story condominiums. Housed four to a building, each unit had a private, single-car garage in back, a common yard in front.

Haley leaned forward. "There it is. The one at the end. And there's his car."

Foley's faded hatchback sat in the driveway by the

small garage. Sully pulled in behind it and they both climbed out. Traffic on the nearby beltway hummed in the quiet air.

Sully glanced at the E-13 but decided to leave it in the truck for now. No point scaring the neighbors or alerting the cops. He followed Haley around the side of the building to the front door, his feet crunching in the frozen grass.

Haley rang the bell. A dog's frenzied barking erupted in the unit next door. Blowing on his hands for warmth, Sully eyed the adjoining door, the cheerful wreath reminding him of Thanksgiving—and the family he refused to see.

Steering his mind from that painful thought, he leaned over Haley's shoulder and tried the buzzer again.

"He has to be home," Haley said, her breath forming puffs of frost in the air.

His gaze traveled over her chestnut hair, down the curves covered by her bulky coat. His body warmed, the need she'd awakened threatening to sidetrack his thoughts. But if he didn't pull himself together, they'd both be dead.

Stepping back, he craned his neck to see the second-story window. "The bedroom light is on." And two *Washington Post*s were rolled up in plastic sleeves on the door stoop, one for the neighbor, the other for the ATF agent. "He couldn't have left without his car."

A small groove creased Haley's brow. "Maybe he's in the shower."

"Maybe."

The neighbor's door opened just then. An older woman wearing a bathrobe and slippers stuck her head out. "Morning." She stepped onto the door stoop and picked up her newspaper, then scurried back inside.

"Excuse me," Haley called before she shut the door. "Do you know if Mr. Foley's at home?"

The woman paused and peered back out. "He should be. He doesn't usually leave for work until seven." She shot them another smile and closed her door.

Growing impatient, Sully reached out and tried the doorknob. To his surprise, it turned.

Haley blinked. "It wasn't locked?"

"Apparently not." *Which was odd.* People in law enforcement didn't tend to be lax about security. They knew too much about local crime. And Foley didn't seem the laid-back, open-door type.

A sense of uneasiness stirring inside him, Sully scooped up Foley's newspaper and went inside. Haley followed a second later and closed the door.

Foley hadn't been kidding about the divorce cleaning him out. His furniture consisted of the basics—an old sofa, a giant-screen television, and a coffee table crowded with empty beer bottles and the remnants of frozen meals. There was no kitchen table, no artwork on the walls, just stained beige carpet in what was definitely a rental pad.

Haley walked into the tiny kitchen and turned around. "I don't hear any water running upstairs."

She was right. The place was as silent as a morgue. Another jitter prickled his nerves.

Haley frowned. "Maybe he fell asleep with his light on and he hasn't woken up yet."

Or maybe something far more sinister was going on. Sully set the newspaper on the coffee table and drew his sidearm, then gestured for her to fall in. "Stay behind me."

He crossed the small living room to the stairs and started up the carpeted steps. Halfway up, a floorboard creaked, and he stopped. His pulse quickening, he motioned for Haley to wait.

His heart thudded hard. He listened, but a car driving past the building was the only sound. And then a whimper reached his ears, the moan of a man in pain.

Foley. Sully took the remaining steps two at a time to the landing and glanced around. Three bedrooms and a bathroom straight ahead. The sound had come from the right.

"Foley?" he called out. "Are you there? It's me, Sully Turner." If the ATF agent was armed, he didn't want to risk getting shot.

Foley didn't answer. Signaling for Haley to stay back, Sully quickly checked the other bedrooms to avoid a trap. Then he nudged the master bedroom door open with the barrel of his gun and peeked inside. Foley lay on the carpet in a pool of blood.

"Oh, hell." He glanced around, then rushed inside. "Call for an ambulance," he told Haley, but she'd already picked up the bedside phone.

He stuck his gun into his waistband and knelt. "Foley!" He lifted the agent's wrist and checked his pulse. It was faint, but there.

But for how long? He took in Foley's chalky face, the bullet hole in his chest, the carpet saturated with blood. Sully's gut sank. Shot at close quarters, the special agent would never survive.

Just like the men in that desert sand.

Sully closed his eyes, battling the memories, fighting off the crippling despair. The men were gone. He wasn't in Afghanistan anymore. Foley needed his help.

"Foley," he demanded. "Talk to me."

The ATF agent moaned. His eyelids fluttered, then opened a slit, but he didn't seem to focus on him.

"It's me, Sully." Gripping his shoulder, he gave him a shake. "Come on. Wake up. You have to tell me what happened."

The agent opened his eyes again. He moved his bloodless lips, murmuring something Sully couldn't hear. Then he groaned and closed his eyes.

"Damn it." They couldn't lose him now. "Stay with me, buddy. Open your eyes again."

Miraculously, he obeyed. "Need…" he whispered.

"What?"

"Money. Wife…she…" His eyes rolled back in his head. His mouth went slack as he slipped into unconsciousness again.

"Damn." Sully felt his pulse, but it was growing even fainter now.

Haley hurried over, her eyes dark with concern. "An ambulance is on the way. They said they'd arrive in three minutes."

"We'd better go."

"What? We can't leave him!"

"We don't have a choice."

"But—"

"It's too risky. We don't know who the good guys are."

Still looking torn, Haley gave him a nod. "You're right." Reaching over, she stripped the blanket from the bed, then tucked it around Foley to keep him warm.

"Help's on the way," she whispered to the injured

man. Then she rose and fled the room. Sully jogged after her down the stairs and out the door.

But as he climbed inside the truck and started the engine, their predicament finally sank in. They'd spoken to the neighbor. She could identify them to the police. And their prints were in the house—on the newspaper, the phone.

A siren wailed. Sully floored the accelerator and roared out of the parking lot, disgusted at his mistake. Not only did they have the gang to contend with, but now the police had an excuse to bring them in.

They'd just become the prime suspects in Foley's attack.

Chapter 12

"Foley died." Thoroughly shaken, Haley set the cell phone on the small table between them and hugged her arms. "Brynn just found out from Parker. He was dead by the time he got to the hospital."

Fighting back the nausea roiling inside her, she stared out the window at the parking lot and swallowed hard. They'd stopped at a coffee shop off I-95, in desperate need of a washroom and a plan. But no matter how hard she'd scrubbed her hands, no matter how much hot water or soap she'd used, she couldn't wash away the horrific images—Foley's blood, his gaping wound—or the suspicion that this was all her fault, that she'd somehow caused his death.

She dropped her gaze to her uneaten muffin. Her stomach in total rebellion, she pushed it aside. "I can't believe he's dead. Poor Foley."

"We don't know that he was innocent. He might have been mixed up in this."

"Even if he was, he didn't deserve to die—especially like that." In an agony of pain, suffering and alone.

"What else did Brynn say?" Sully asked.

She picked up her foam cup, but her hands trembled so hard that coffee slopped over the rim. She set it back down and wrapped her hands around it, soaking in the warmth. "It's just what we expected. The neighbor told them about us. She even described our truck. She must have been watching from her window. Now the police have put out an alert for our arrest."

It was worse than that. She'd never heard Brynn sound so scared. Foley's death signaled a new level of ruthlessness on the killer's part. Attacking a law-enforcement officer was an act of impunity, inviting much closer scrutiny—meaning he wasn't worried about getting caught. Either he had absolute confidence in his abilities to evade the police, or he was willing to sacrifice everything to murder them.

"I don't understand why, though," she continued. "It's not as if we killed him. Parker knows that."

Sully rubbed his bristled jaw. His T-shirt was a mass of wrinkles. He hadn't shaved in days. And yet, the shaggy hair and heavy beard stubble only made him look darker, sexier and far more dangerous, like that avenging angel who'd swooped in and saved her from the shootout on the street. "He might not have a say in it. And the case against me is pretty strong—strong enough to bring me in for questioning, at least."

"I don't see how."

"I was at Foley's condo. I showed up at your shelter

when the gang appeared. And I was at the gala when the bomb went off."

"Right. Guarding me."

"I've got a psych record, Haley. I went through treatment for PTSD. They could claim I snapped. And we're carrying around a stolen weapon, that E-13."

"But—"

"I'm not saying the case would hold up. But they have enough cause to detain me. And once I'm in custody…"

The person behind this would kill him. And her. Without Sully's protection, she wouldn't survive for long.

Feeling even more overwhelmed now, she rubbed her tired eyes. What a disaster. This case got worse by the day. They had no idea what was going on, no idea who to trust. They were flailing around, pursued by everyone, completely on their own.

Fighting back a swell of panic, she struggled to think. "Why do you think the gang killed Foley?"

"He was the lead investigator tracking those missing E-13s. Maybe he had a good lead."

"That storage receipt, you mean."

"Probably, yeah. It would have been nice if Foley had told us who he suspected, though, or at least mentioned the shooter's name before he died."

She thought back to those moments in Foley's bedroom, trying not to remember the blood. "What exactly *did* he say to you?"

Sully made a face. "He complained that he needed money, and that his ex-wife had cleaned him out."

"That's an odd thing to say on his deathbed."

"He was out of his head with pain."

"You don't think she could be involved in this?"

"The ex-wife? I doubt it. I would have bet on *him* killing *her,* not the other way around. He was bitter enough about the divorce settlement."

Haley couldn't argue that. And the police would surely question her. An ex-spouse was an automatic suspect, especially after a nasty divorce.

She picked up her blueberry muffin and forced herself to take a bite. It tasted like sawdust, and she set it down. "So what now?"

Sully took a swallow of coffee, then leaned back in his chair. "My money's still on your father. He works with gang members. We saw them at his house. He had those weapons in his storage unit, or so we think. But I haven't ruled out the senator yet. He's got the connections, and he used to be in a gang." He paused. "Did Brynn say if they'd identified that label we found?"

"She didn't know anything about it. Foley hadn't mentioned it to Parker."

"What about the storage-unit receipt?"

"Parker didn't know about either one." An awful thought made her pause. "What if Foley didn't tell anyone about it, not even at the ATF? What if that's why he was killed, for the evidence—and now it's gone?"

Feeling even sicker, she pressed her hand to her mouth. They'd broken into her father's safe, endangering their lives to find proof of the gang's activities—and the evidence had disappeared. Now they had no proof, nothing to use for a search warrant against her father, not a single clue to guide their way.

Sully dragged his hand down his face, then sighed. "You're right. It's probably gone. So we need to find something else. There has to be something we've missed."

"Like what?"

He lifted his powerful shoulders in a shrug. Looking as frustrated as she felt, he powered up his laptop and turned his gaze to the screen.

Haley forced down a gulp of coffee, but her mind instantly swerved back to Foley and the gruesome sight of him dying beside the bed. Not wanting to go down that dreadful route, she shifted her attention to Sully again. She studied the worry lines crossing his brow, the grim slant of his sensual mouth, the fatigue shadowing his eyes, testimony to his sleepless nights.

Exactly what had he seen in Afghanistan? What horrors still haunted his sleep? How on earth could he have witnessed the atrocities of war and still get through the days? *He didn't.* He'd told her that before. He'd ended up not just addicted to alcohol, but suffering from debilitating post-traumatic stress.

Her gaze dropped to his lean hands as he typed on the keyboard. They looked steadier than hers right now. She felt chilled to the marrow and numb from the constant trauma—and her experiences didn't come close to matching his.

But she needed to pull herself together and focus. "What are you looking for?" she asked.

"I pulled up some images of the senator. I thought you might know who these people are."

She scooted her chair closer, and he turned the screen her way. "There's my father." She pointed to one of the photos. "And Gwendolyn Shaffer, of course." Going across the screen, she named several people, mostly politicians and socialites who moved in her parents' crowd. "There's my mother."

"Where did they take that shot?"

She tilted her head. Her mother and the senator stood beside a Christmas tree. She studied the woodworking on the walls, the ornate gold rug, the elaborate window treatments and chandelier. "It looks like the White House. They must have gone to a reception there."

Leaning forward, she peered at two men standing behind them, just on the edge of the shot. "I think that's the ambassador of Jaziirastan in the background. The one with my father. We saw him at the charity ball."

She sat back in her chair and sighed. "I don't see how this helps us, though. What are the chances that a clue is going to jump out at us?"

"So what do *you* suggest?"

"I don't know." Feeling overwhelmed, she spread out her hands. "Whoever the killer is, he's smart. He's evaded capture for at least fifteen years. I doubt he's going to make a mistake so obvious that we'll notice it right away."

Sully tilted his head, conceding her point. "All right. Then maybe we need to look at this from another direction."

"Like what?"

"Let's look at the victim, the guy who died in the warehouse."

"Allen Chambers?"

Sully leaned forward, resting his forearms on the table. "What do we know about him?"

She thought about that. "Not much. He was a junkie, a heroin addict. And he was from Virginia. Dumfries, I think." Less than an hour from where they were.

"But why was he killed? Was he part of the gang?"

"No, I don't think so." Haley tried to recall what Parker had told her about the case. "I don't think they

ever figured it out, exactly. They assumed it was a ven-
detta, that maybe he owed the gang money for drugs,
or something like that. It might even have been random,
part of a gang initiation rite. Why?"

"I thought it might give us a clue."

"Sure. But if the police couldn't figure it out…" And
they'd spent years investigating the murder, with far
more resources than Sully and she had.

He tapped on his keyboard again. "How old was
Chambers when he died?"

"Middle-aged. In his mid-to-late forties, I think."

"Did he have a criminal record?"

"Not that I know of."

"He probably did, to pay for his drugs. Most junkies
end up resorting to crime."

"I'll call Brynn again and ask…if you think we can
risk the call."

"Go ahead. I doubt it'll make a difference at this
point. And they can't trace the burner phone." He
frowned at the screen again.

Haley forced down a sip of coffee, then placed the
call. "She doesn't know," she told Sully when she'd hung
up. "She'll ask Parker and call us back."

"I found Allen Chambers' obituary. The newspaper
had it archived."

She leaned toward Sully to see. The obituary didn't
have a photo, just a brief write-up about his life. He was
from Dumfries, Virginia, as she'd thought. He'd been
valedictorian of his high school and attended college at
William and Mary. "Prestigious school." Chambers
was survived by his parents and a couple of siblings. The
family had requested donations to Georgetown Univer-
sity Law Center in lieu of flowers.

Her heart sped up. "Wait a minute. Why George-town Law?"

Sully's gaze cut to hers. "What do you mean?"

"The part about the donations. It doesn't say he went to Georgetown Law. Why not send donations to William and Mary, instead?"

"Maybe a relative went there. Or maybe he went there for a year or two and dropped out."

"Maybe." She checked his birth date again, and her heart took another swerve. "He was a year younger than my father."

Sully's gaze sharpened. "You think there's a connection? That they knew each other in law school?"

"I don't know. But I think it's worth our time to find out."

They arrived in Georgetown close to noon. Clouds had gathered as the morning wore on, turning the sky a murky gray. Haley glanced at the students scurrying past, the Capitol Police car cruising down New Jersey Avenue, moving too slowly for her peace of mind. Inhaling deeply, she struggled to steady her nerves. She hated this paranoia. She'd lived with it for so many years—always looking over her shoulder, always worrying that a killer lurked around the next corner, forever wondering if people were looking at her for a reason or if her imagination was working overtime.

"Are you all right?" Sully asked, walking beside her.

"I'll feel better when this is over."

Except she wouldn't be with him.

Trying not to think about that part, she entered Mc-Donough Hall, a four-story stone building with lots of glass. She knew she'd have to deal with the ending at some point. They had no future together, despite her burgeoning feelings for him. But that could wait. They had a professor to visit first.

"Which floor?" Sully asked.

"The second. Let's take the stairs." She veered into the stairwell and started up.

"You think this guy will know anything?" Sully asked.

"I hope so." She'd made several phone calls on their way up Route 66. The records department had refused to answer her questions, citing privacy concerns. They wouldn't even confirm that Allen Chambers had attended the school.

But several phone calls later, she'd lucked out. She'd managed to get an appointment with a professor emeritus who'd taught here for decades before he'd retired. He still maintained an office in McDonough Hall, coming in to do research twice a week. Haley knew it was a long shot. Even if Chambers had been a student, the professor probably wouldn't remember him. But it was the only chance they had.

They exited the stairwell and headed down the hall, past bulletin boards crowded with notices and clusters of students queued up beside office doors. Some leaned against the walls, while others sat, studying, on the floor. They all had sallow, sleep-deprived faces and carted backpacks bulging with books.

Professor Diehl's office was at the end of the corridor. Haley checked the number on the half-open door and knocked.

"Come in."

She led the way inside, stopping to avoid knocking over a stack of books on the floor. Professor Diehl sat behind one of the two desks crammed into the tiny room. Overstuffed shelves lined every wall.

The professor was older than she'd expected, probably in his nineties, with narrow, hunched shoulders and age spots on his face. His hair was sparse and white, sticking in wispy tufts to his shiny scalp. But the faded blue eyes behind his wire-rimmed glasses were sharp.

"Professor Diehl? I'm Haley Barnes. This is Sully Turner. We'd like to talk to you if you have a minute."

The professor waved his gnarled hand toward a couple of chairs. "Have a seat."

They moved the books to the floor and sat. The professor cocked his head, studying them. "So how can I help you?"

"We're looking for information about a man who attended school here some years ago. At least, we think he was here. We thought you might remember him if he was."

The professor leaned back in his chair, making it creak. "I can try. I've got a pretty good memory for names and faces. Not as good as it once was, of course."

She doubted that. His shrewd eyes didn't miss a beat. "It would have been nearly forty years ago. His name was Allen Chambers."

Surprise lit the professor's eyes. "Chambers? Yes, of course I remember him."

"Really?" She exchanged glances with Sully, sudden hope blazing inside. "That's amazing."

"Not really. The brilliant ones always stick out."

"What can you tell us about him?"

His bushy brows gathered. "Why do you want to know?"

"It's complicated," she admitted. "But basically, we're

investigating the circumstances surrounding his death. We'd just like to know more about him, what he was like, that sort of thing."

The professor steepled his hands, tapping his index fingers against his lips, obviously trying to decide what to divulge. But then he shrugged. "I suppose there's no reason you shouldn't know about him. He was a wonderful student, intuitive, curious. He was editor in chief of the Law Journal, if I remember right."

He rose from his chair with effort, stepped awkwardly over a pile of papers, then hobbled to the bookcase and searched the shelves. "Ah, here it is." He tugged at a stack of magazines halfway up.

Sully leaped to his feet, reached around the professor and grabbed the pile before it fell. "Here, let me get those."

"Thanks. I'm not as steady on my feet as I used to be." His shoulders stooped, the professor returned to the desk and sat down. Sully placed the magazines on the desk and retook his seat.

"Do you remember if Allen Chambers graduated?" Haley asked.

"Yes, indeed. He was valedictorian. Brilliant, as I said." He shuffled through the magazines, the blue veins in his hands standing out like roots on an ancient tree. "Of course, he had a lot of competition. That was a particularly strong class."

Haley nodded, not surprised. Most law students were competitive. And they couldn't make it into a prestigious school like Georgetown without both intelligence and drive.

"What did he do after graduation? Do you know?"

The professor continued thumbing through the pile.

"That was a real tragedy. He never practiced law. Didn't even take the bar exam that I know. I heard later that he'd gotten addicted to drugs. But I guess you know how he died." He shook his head, regret in his eyes. "A terrible waste of a gifted mind."

Haley snuck a glance at Sully. His arms were crossed, his expression unreadable, his gaze on the magazines. She wondered if the professor's words had hit home. The causes were different; unlike Allen Chambers, Sully had a valid reason to drink—but he was addicted, too.

The professor picked up a magazine. He straightened his glasses, then peered at the cover and flipped a page. "This is it." Smiling, he turned it so they could see. "Our alumni magazine. One of our other students that year made the cover. Alfred Riggs. He's a senator now."

Her pulse suddenly erratic, Haley stared at the photo of a much younger Alfred Riggs. "Were they in the same class—Allen Chambers and Alfred Riggs?"

"Yes. As I said, it was quite a class."

Her heart began to thud. "Then you might remember my father. Oliver Burroughs. He was the senator's classmate, too."

The professor's bushy white eyebrows rose. "Of course I do." He tapped his finger on the magazine. "They were a trio, you know, always together."

"They were friends?" Her voice came out as a squeak.

"Yes, and they were quite a group. Each one so different."

Hardly able to believe her ears, Haley reminded herself to breathe. "In what way?"

The professor folded his hands again. "Allen Chambers loved the law. He loved the theory, the moral and ethical questions, the historical and cultural context...."

He lived it, breathed it. It was a real passion for him."
His smile turned wry. "A student like that is hard to forget. It's why I taught, to connect with a mind like his.

"Alfred Riggs was different. He was a few years older
than the others. He'd done a tour in the military, I think.
He was smart, but the law wasn't a passion for him. He
saw it as a stepping-stone, a means to a better career,
nothing more. Not that there's anything wrong with that.
But I wasn't surprised to see him run for office. He
makes a much better politician than an attorney."

"And my father?"

The professor hesitated, as if choosing his words.
"He wasn't quite the caliber of the other two. Not that
he wasn't capable, of course, but…"

Sensing the reason behind his reserve, she gave him
a smile. "Don't worry about hurting my feelings. My
father and I are estranged. We had a falling out some
years ago."

The professor nodded. "Oliver was shrewd. And very
determined. He had the willpower and drive to succeed.

"But he saw the law as something flexible, mallea-
ble. Something he could manipulate to his own ends.
We teach that to an extent. Defense attorneys have to
defend their clients, regardless of their guilt. It's how
our system works. But that type of lawyer isn't as interested in justice as he is in power."

"That's him, all right." He'd just described her father
perfectly. Her respect for the professor rose.

Turning his attention back to the magazine, he
flipped through several more pages, then stopped. "Ah,
here we go."

Haley got up and went to the desk. Sully joined her
a second later, looking over her shoulder at the photo

on the page. A dozen students had assembled around a statue outside. She picked out her father right away. He stood to the side, his arms crossed, looking belligerent even then. Alfred Riggs was beside him, laughing with another friend.

"I suppose Senator Riggs was popular," she said.

"Yes, quite. A natural politician, as I said. And not an easy man to forget."

"So which one is Allen Chambers?"

He ran his crooked finger over the group. "There he is, in the back row. Fifth from the left." He handed her the magazine.

She counted off the students, then froze. Her heart made a funny thump. The air felt sucked from her lungs, her head turning strangely light.

"What's wrong?" Sully asked, grabbing her arm. "Are you all right?"

Oh, God. She had to leave. *Right now.* Panic surging inside her, she dropped the magazine. "No, I...I'm kind of dizzy. I...I need air."

"Sit down," the professor said. "Wait until you're stronger."

She shook her head, too desperate to get away. "No, really. I'll be fine. I just need some air. Thanks so much for your help."

"My pleasure. Not many people come to see me these days."

"We appreciate it," Sully said, his hand still gripping her arm.

"If there's anything else you need, let me know."

Frantic, Haley broke loose from Sully and bolted out the door. She lunged into the nearest stairwell, then sank onto the top step, resting her forehead against her knees as she tried to breathe.

Sully lowered himself beside her and gripped her neck. "Inhale," he ordered, forcing her head down. "You're white as a ghost."

Fitting, considering that she'd just seen one.

"What the hell happened back there?"

Still feeling dazed, she wheezed in air. Then she lifted her head and met his eyes. "That man…Allen Chambers. I know him. I've seen him before."

"Where? When?"

"Right before I ran away. At my father's house."

Chapter 13

Haley huddled on a log beside the campfire, inhaling the fragrance of the wood smoke as it dispersed in the crisp night air. The wind kicked up, making the flames flicker and sway, and she shifted closer to feel their warmth. She'd never enjoyed camping, not after the years she'd spent on the streets. She had too many bad memories of sleeping in the open, feeling defenseless and exposed. But after hightailing it out of Georgetown, worried that the police might spot them, camping at the C&O canal seemed the safest choice.

She finished off the last of her hotdog and stuffed her napkin into a plastic bag. Then she glanced at Sully sitting beside her, the reddish gleam from the firelight gilding his face. Thankfully, he'd had enough cash left to buy a tent and food, along with other supplies. And this time of year, the campground was empty, especially with rain clouds gathering in the sky. They'd be lucky if it didn't snow.

Shivering again, she held her hands near the flames to savor their warmth. The woods around them rustled and creaked. The Potomac River—invisible in the stygian darkness—roared and tumbled along its nearby bank. The campground was nestled below the towpath, tucked in a hollow behind the trees.

No one had followed them here. No one could have predicted where they'd go. And no one could find them if they tried. The canal stretched for two hundred miles on the Maryland side of the river, its access points obscure. They were safe—for now.

"So tell me about Allen Chambers," Sully finally said.

Her gaze on the fire, Haley drew her legs to her chest and rested her chin on her knees. "It was the night I told Jeremy I was pregnant. I told you I'd snuck out to see him. After we talked—after he dumped me—I was a wreck. Angry, scared. I didn't know what to do. I wandered around for a while, but eventually I went back home. I went in through the garden, the same way I'd gone out.

"My parents were having a party. It was chilly, so the guests were all inside. But as I came up the path, I heard voices. My father was outside, arguing with Allen Chambers. Not on the patio. Near the fountain, a little ways from the house."

"You saw them?"

She nodded. "The garden lights were on. It was dim, and Chambers had his back to the house, but I caught sight of his face. I didn't recognize him. In fact, he struck me as kind of odd."

"In what way?"

"He didn't look like a guest. He was scruffy. He had sloppy clothes, like a homeless person, and his hair was all a mess.

"But I didn't pay much attention to him. I was too absorbed in my own problems." Her childhood had just ended, her world abruptly fallen apart. "I assumed he was a client."

"Maybe he was. If he had legal problems, he'd probably go to your father for help. They'd been friends at school, and your father was practicing law."

"I guess." They still didn't know if Allen Chambers had a criminal record. Parker hadn't returned their call. And without reception at the canal, they'd have to wait until morning to find out.

"Could you hear what they said?" Sully asked.

"Not really. I could hear their voices, and they were arguing. I know that much. At least my father was. He sounded angry. But I wasn't really listening. I was too scared that he'd see me and I'd get in trouble for sneaking out. And I kept thinking about Jeremy and how he'd acted, how he was nothing like I'd believed. I just ducked behind the shrubs and hid."

Sully reached out and added another branch to the campfire. The flames flared, bathing her with welcome heat. "It's funny how the worst memories are the most vivid," she added. She could envision that scene even now—the terror clutching her gut, the certainty that no matter what Jeremy did or thought, she was going to keep their child.

She turned her head. Pain flickered through Sully's eyes. *His memories were worse than hers.*

The burning branch shifted again. "So what happened next?" he asked.

"I waited until Chambers left. He went out through the back—more proof that he wasn't a guest. My dad watched him go, then stood on the patio, smoking a cigarette. I thought for sure he'd seen me, that he was trying to decide how to punish me, or that he was waiting for me to come out. But he finally went back into the house.

"I stayed there a while longer until I figured it was safe. Then I snuck inside. I was halfway down the hall, almost to my father's library when I heard him in there, talking to my mother. I turned around, but she came out before I could get away."

"What did she do?"

Haley exhaled. "She marched me into another room and demanded to know where I'd been. There was no point lying. She could see that I'd been crying. And the way I was dressed…it was obvious I'd been outside. I even had leaves stuck to my back from hiding in the hedge.

"She was livid. I've never seen her so mad." She'd clenched her lips so tightly they'd gone chalk white. "Not only had I disobeyed her rules, but I was pregnant. And the father was totally unacceptable, not even close to coming from our class. I thought she would have a stroke. Luckily, Gwendolyn Shaffer showed up."

Sully's head rose. "Where did she come from?"

"She was at the party, I guess."

"What did she do?"

"What she always did. She smoothed things out. She sent me to my room, told me to take a shower and go to bed. She stayed to talk to my mother. I assume she calmed her down so she could go back to her guests."

Sully frowned. "Was the senator there?"

"I don't know. I didn't see him, but I didn't go into the party. I just ran upstairs. I can check my mother's records later and find out."

The wind came up, sending frigid air down her neck. Shivering, she raised her collar on her coat. "So what do you think?"

His gaze met hers. "This doesn't exactly clear your father. It still looks like he's the one behind all this."

"But why would he head a gang?"

"Money, probably. Gangs usually deal drugs, and there's a lot of money in that. And it could explain why Chambers was there. Maybe he'd come to pick up drugs."

"My father didn't need money. I told you, my mother's family was loaded."

"They were in shipping, right?"

"Right. Tobacco, sugar, military supplies during both world wars. They'd sold the business before I came along, so I don't remember any of that. But my mother was an only child. She inherited everything—the money, the house in Guilford. The one in St. Michaels, too."

"But did your *father* have money?"

"No, not like her family. But my mother wouldn't have married him if he was broke. She's too worried about her social standing. Status is everything to her."

Sully dragged his hand down his face. "All right. So he didn't need money."

"He didn't have a motive, either. Why would he kill Allen Chambers if they were friends?"

"I guess we need to know why they argued."

She shrugged. "It could have been something simple.

Maybe he'd invited Chambers to the party. My mother would have been shocked if he'd shown up dressed like that. She could have had my father turn him away. Or maybe he'd come for a handout if he was broke."

His expression thoughtful, Sully turned his gaze to the fire. "How long after that was he killed?"

She thought back. "A couple of months. I ran away a few weeks after the party, and it wasn't too long after that."

"And Gwendolyn Shaffer? When did she go overseas?"

"About the same time. Just before I ran away, I think. So she was out of the country when the murder took place."

"All the more reason to suspect your father. And if he knew you'd been in the garden and thought you'd seen him with Allen Chambers, who he later murdered…"

Raindrops splattered her cheeks. Chills chased over her skin. "He'd have the perfect reason to want me dead."

But *why* had her father killed Allen Chambers?

She was no closer to answering that question two hours later as she sat cross-legged inside the tent, studying her mother's files. Rain drummed against the roof. The wind thrashed the sides, making the light from the lantern sway. She'd hooked the external disk drive to the laptop, but the battery was draining fast. And she still didn't have a clue.

She ejected the disk she'd finished studying and added it to the pile. She still couldn't believe her father was the one who'd had Allen Chambers killed. But the evidence seemed to suggest it, and she knew better than to ignore the facts. Wishful thinking couldn't erase reality, as she well knew.

Sully opened the tent flap and limped inside, bringing with him a burst of cold air. His eyes connected with hers, making her heart do a little dance. Raindrops glistened in his hair and dripped down his whiskered face. "Here." She tossed him a T-shirt. "I'm using it as a towel."

"Thanks." He ran it over his hair and face. Then he peeled off his jacket and sat down beside her on the sleeping bag. "Have you found anything interesting?" He took off his boots and set them aside.

"Not really. The senator was there that night. So was Gwendolyn Shaffer." But they'd already known about her. "No other names popped out at me.

"But talk about obsessive compulsive. My mother documented everything—the silverware, the color of the candles, which songs the musicians played. It's ridiculous. She also threw a lot of parties." Haley motioned toward the disks she'd gone through. "After I left home, she got even worse. She had parties constantly, even when my father was out of town."

Sully turned his head. "How do you know he wasn't there?"

"I told you, she wrote everything down. She even included the seating charts, showing the senator in my father's place."

"You think that's significant?"

"No. He'd be the logical one to act as her escort if my father wasn't around. It's the number of parties that strikes me as odd. It wasn't that long after Lauren died."

"Maybe that was her way of coping. People react to grief in different ways."

"I guess." Giving up on the disks, she turned off the laptop, stuffed everything into the sports bag and zipped it up. Then she rolled up her jacket to use as a pillow and lay on the sleeping bag, listening to the rain hammer the tent. Sully lowered himself beside her, his wide shoulder aligned with hers.

"The thing is," she continued. "I was suffering, too. I loved Lauren. I know it's different for a parent to lose a child, but she was my sister, and we were close. I was grieving as much as they were."

And instead of consoling her, they'd shunned her, making her feel even more bereft.

Sully turned on his side to face her. He reached out and stroked her hair, his voice dropping to a husky rasp. "And then you lost your baby, too."

Her throat turned tight, a swift stab of pain hollowing her heart. He was right. She'd lost everything. Even her future, the children she'd never have.

"The worst part is the guilt," she confessed. "Not just about Lauren. But I keep wondering, if I hadn't run away, maybe my baby would have survived. Maybe not. The STD might have made me miscarry regardless of where I was. But if I'd had treatment in time..." Her mouth wobbled. "It's hard not to wonder, not to blame myself."

"I know." He ran his knuckle along her jaw. Then he played with her hair again, sliding the strands between his fingers, bunching the ends in his trembling fist. He swallowed, his Adam's apple dipping in his whiskered throat, his eyes turning distant and dark. "I lost my best friends in Afghanistan. And it was all my fault."

Her breath caught. She didn't answer, but her heart galloped through her chest. She wanted so badly to learn what happened, for him to reveal his past. But she didn't want to push and scare him off.

Letting go of her hair, he rolled onto his back and rested his forearm across his face. "It was my third tour there." His voice was so low she had to strain to hear above the rain. "The fighting was bad, but you learn to deal with that. You tough it out and go on. As long as you believe in the cause, if you think you can make a difference and help the world, then you can justify the cost."

She lifted herself onto one elbow and studied his profile, how the low light glowed on his swarthy skin. Her gaze traced the cords standing taut in his neck, the dip at the base of his throat, his strong cheekbones and chiseled mouth. She could see him as an idealistic young soldier, determined to defend the helpless and protect the world. He was still that way. He just didn't think so anymore.

"After a while, though, it started to seem pointless. We'd clear a village, liberate them from the insurgents, and as soon as we left, they'd come right back. Even worse, they'd kill whoever had helped us, so in the end we made things worse. And so many soldiers died, so many decent men. You start to doubt what you're doing, wondering if it's worth it. These people…they'd been living there for centuries with the same culture, the same beliefs. Who were we to try to change them?

"The women and kids were the hardest to take. The women…they were like ghosts. Silent, hidden behind their veils. Too scared to look at you, let alone talk."

"I know what you mean," Haley murmured. "My friend Nadine, the other runaway. Her family is Middle Eastern. She told me stories of what it's like."

"Yeah." The rain picked up, the wind gusting against the tent. "I told you, I have a big family—brothers and sisters, lots of nieces and nephews. The kids I saw in Afghanistan were about their age, but their eyes…they were blank, *dead*.

"And what kind of life did they have? Living in mud huts with no education, no hope. Especially the girls. Illiterate, forced into marriage—sometimes even before puberty, then later dying in childbirth. They're lucky to survive to forty.

"And those kids…they'd seen everyone around them die. They were numb to it. A dead body didn't even faze them. And we were just another invader to them, another group of oppressors, just one more in an endless line. No wonder they didn't trust us to help."

He lapsed into silence again. The storm bore down harder, tugging at the stakes securing the tent. Not knowing what to say, Haley took Sully's hand, trying to lend him silent support.

"I got the idea to help them," he finally said. "I still thought we could win them over, that if we just showed them some kindness… So I got permission to repair a school the Taliban had bombed. We had a local translator, an interpreter. He knew the tribal elders and agreed to organize it.

"We knew there were risks. There were insurgents in the area. But he assured us they weren't close by, that our last engagement had sent them packing and they'd retreated into the mountains to regroup. Our intelligence backed him up. The chain of command okayed the mission. We still took precautions and had air support on standby in case anything went wrong."

She tightened her grip on his hand, dreading the story she knew would come. She wanted to tell him to stop.

His body had tensed, pain emanating from his strong frame. And she couldn't bear to see him suffer.

But he went on. "The village was in a valley, more like a narrow canyon with ridges along the sides. We couldn't get the MRAPs in. Those are the armored vehicles we used. The road had washed out during the rainy season, and we were afraid they'd get hung up. So we left a couple of men to guard them. The rest of us dismounted and went in on foot. Our interpreter led the way in an old truck filled with supplies."

He closed his eyes. His breath came shallow and fast. He clung to her hand, lost in the memories of that fateful day.

"The villagers watched us come in. The men waited in their doorways. The women were squatting outside their huts, tending their fires. The kids were like statues, standing there looking at us with those eerie eyes. That's when I felt it, that something was wrong. I yelled for the men to halt just as the shooting broke out."

He stopped, the anguish in his voice eviscerating her heart. "It was an ambush. We didn't have a chance. They killed everyone—the women, the kids. Hell, they'd put them there as decoys, slaughtering them without a thought. And my men…"

He worked his jaw. Sweat glistened on his brow. He pinched the bridge of his nose, obviously fighting to regain control.

"What did you do?" she whispered.

He let out his breath. "I was bringing up the rear. I saw them get mowed down. It was goddamned hellfire. It happened so fast…. The interpreter had tipped them off.

"I called in a TIC—Troops in Contact. The command

mobilized the Quick Reaction Force. But it was already too late. They'd died on the spot." His voice broke. "I couldn't leave them there. I couldn't let the insurgents mutilate what was left of them. So I ran back for help. The guys we'd left with the MRAPs were heading in."

"You went back to the village?"

"There were three of us. One died on our first trip in. It was just Jason and me after that. He drove and manned the guns. I ran out and retrieved the bodies while he provided cover. That's when I got shot."

First trip? "How many times did you go back?"

"Five."

She gaped at him in horror, unable to imagine the courage that took—his leg badly injured, his world exploding around him, his comrades dying or dead.

"Jason got killed on the last run. We'd picked up our last buddy and turned around. The rotary wing had just arrived and we thought we were in the clear. The insurgents were on the run. He turned his head to make a wisecrack—his way of coping with that hell—and a second later, he was dead. We'd enlisted together. He was my best friend."

Her heart aching, she pulled him close. She stroked his hair, his back, rocking against him as if to absorb his pain. It wasn't enough. Sully needed and deserved so much more. His courage humbled her. Amazed her.

No wonder he'd earned the Silver Star!

And to witness all those deaths… Her eyes burned, her throat turning so thick it was all she could do to speak. "Their deaths weren't your fault."

"It was my idea to rebuild that school. I set it up. I convinced them to go."

"But you didn't *make* them go." Her voice turned

fierce. "They were willing. They knew the risks. You said you took precautions. And *you* didn't cause the ambush. You didn't pull the trigger. You weren't the one who killed those kids."

"But if I hadn't decided to go there, to try to help the villagers, they'd be alive."

She locked her eyes on his. "You don't know that. There's a lot you can't control, especially in a place like that. And even if it were true, it doesn't mean what you did was wrong. You tried to make a difference, to make the world a better place. It was still a worthy cause. And your friends…" Her voice cracked. The tears she'd struggled to hold at bay burned behind her eyelids and dampened her cheeks. "They wouldn't blame you, Sully. They would never blame you for that. And they'd be grateful you brought them home."

Sully closed his eyes. He rested his forehead against hers. His trembling hands gripped her head, as if he'd shatter if he let her go.

The rain pummeled the tent. The wind keened in the pines outside. The lantern flickered, then dimmed, draping them in a shadowed haze.

And then he shifted his head and kissed her cheek, her eyes, her jaw, trailing shivers over her skin; the sexy roughness of his jaw, the heat of his mouth scorched her cells, sparking an instant blaze of desire.

Her hands tightened around his neck. He worked his way down her jaw to her throat, lingering over the pulse point beneath her ear until she moaned. And then his lips captured hers, the kiss tender and wild, gentle and deep. A kiss filled with wonder and reverence and need.

His big hands cradled her skull. He shifted again, changing the tempo of the kiss, spurring her pulse into a faster beat. But there was something different in the way he kissed her. This wasn't just lust. This wasn't just a release from the danger dogging their steps. This wasn't even comfort or possession or need. She couldn't name it, couldn't even think with his tongue teasing hers, his hands inching toward her breasts, her senses on fire for his touch.

But she sensed it, reveled in it, craved it.

He made her feel complete.

And then he turned and swept her beneath him, and his mouth turned carnal and hot. Her thoughts blurred, her body erupting with pleasure and the world around them ceased to exist.

What had she done?

Haley opened her eyes a long time later, still entwined in Sully's arms. Her leg was sprawled over his. Her hair spilled over his chest. She'd snuggled against him during the night, one arm hooked around his waist, her cheek resting against him, relishing the strong, steady beat of his heart.

But lying there in the predawn darkness with the rain lulling them to sleep, she couldn't deny the truth. She'd fallen in love with Sullivan Turner—head over heels, body and heart.

And their time together was nearly done.

She inhaled sharply, a flurry of panic threatening to overwhelm her at the thought. But she had to face facts. In a few hours, morning would break and their bubble of intimacy would come to an end. They had to make plans. They had to figure out how to confront her father. They had to find a way to arrest him and end the terror for good.

But after that—assuming they survived—could they have a future together? Did their time together really have to end? A relationship wouldn't be easy. They still had obstacles to overcome, even without the dangers they now faced. Sully had an addiction to fight. He'd already acknowledged he had a problem. He'd crossed another threshold last night by confessing his feelings of guilt. But the road to sobriety wouldn't be simple, even if he'd already begun to heal.

And she had baggage of her own, namely a gang contract on her head. It would take time to get the word out that the killer wasn't calling the shots and the bounty no longer applied. And she had a bigger, far more important obstacle she couldn't change—she could never have kids.

But foolish or not, impossible or not, she loved this wounded man. And for the first time she could remember, she allowed herself to hope.

Chapter 14

"You're sure about this?" Haley asked.

Sully sat in the driver's seat of the pickup truck, his eyes narrowed on the restaurant. "We can't keep running. We have to take the lead and throw him off guard. It's the only way to win."

And they didn't have much time. The odds of their survival diminished with every passing day. Foley's death had driven that home. They couldn't keep fleeing and camping out, no matter how amazing the nights.

Sully glanced at Haley sitting in the passenger seat beside him. He studied her thick, glossy hair, the lovely curve of her cheek. Her lips were smooth and full, her throat a graceful arch. And the way she'd felt when he'd come inside her...

He closed his eyes and stifled a groan. He'd been fighting the memories all morning, trying not to dwell on the time they'd spent in the tent. How she'd listened to him, held him, even cried for him.

She'd given him a precious gift. She'd helped him see that what had happened in Afghanistan wasn't entirely his fault. Not that his guilt was gone. It would probably never completely disappear. But she'd lifted the mill-stone weighting his heart and brought him back from the walking dead.

And maybe, just maybe, if he stayed sober, if he got a job and cleaned up his act, he could be worthy of having her in his life.

But this wasn't the time to dwell on that. They had a mission to complete first. And no matter what it took, he had to keep her safe.

Opening his eyes, he studied the restaurant. It was just off interstate 70 in Frederick, Maryland, an hour from both Baltimore and D.C. Parker McCall had suggested the place when they'd called him, confident no one would find them here. And it wasn't far from the canal where they'd camped out.

"Parker's already here," Haley said.

Sully glanced at the car they'd driven to the gala and gave her a nod. The cop had arrived on time.

But a heavy feeling of reluctance chained him in place. Not that he doubted his plan. His gut told him their only chance for success was to be decisive and act. The problem was that once they went inside, they couldn't turn back. They were coming out of hiding, giving up their fugitive status and turning themselves over to the police. They had to trust Parker, the system, the other cops on the force, despite their pursuer's power.

It was like walking into that canyon again with the

insurgents lurking behind the ridge. But this time, Haley's life was at risk.

But damned if he could figure another way out.

Haley reached for her door. "We'd better go in. We're already ten minutes late."

"Yeah, let's go." His steps dragging, he climbed out of the truck. The rain had slowed to a dismal drizzle, but the air hadn't warmed, and the punishing chill seeped through his clothes. He glanced at Haley as they walked to the entrance, marveling that she never complained. She'd been hungry, cold and scared during this entire ordeal, but she'd worried about comforting *him*.

Shifting his focus to their surroundings, he led the way inside. He spotted Parker at a table by the window, facing the door. The cop's eyes connected with his, hovered briefly on Haley, then continued sweeping the room. *A typical cop—suspicious, alert, aware.*

Slightly reassured, Sully limped across the room to the table. Sergeant Delgado, the gang expert, sat to Parker's side. Across from them was Gwendolyn Shaffer, the senator's chief of staff.

Sully stiffened, unable to mask his surprise. Why was she here? He knew Haley trusted her. And Gwendolyn Shaffer knew all the key players involved. Maybe Parker had invited her along, hoping she could help them gain insight into their characters and clarify this murky affair. But in Sully's mind she was a wild card, an unknown, even a possible suspect. He intended to stay on guard.

Gwendolyn Shaffer rose and greeted Haley, her eyes lighting up with a smile. She sounded sincere, murmuring words of concern, but he'd seen her in action before. In the circles these people moved in, they all acted like long-lost friends while they plotted each other's demise. Haley had said as much.

He took the seat next to Haley's. Without warning, he flashed back to another breakfast, in another restaurant, only a couple of days ago. A lot had happened since then. Foley was dead. The gang had attacked them twice. And he'd made love to Haley multiple times.

The waitress arrived and poured their coffee. Sully took his black, managing to gulp down several swallows without spilling too much. He'd gone thirty-odd hours without a drink now, and the tremors were getting worse. His head ached, his stomach was on the verge of revolt and he felt jumpy enough to bolt.

Another reason to end this ordeal, so he could concentrate on cleaning up his life.

Parker began. "I've been filling Ms. Shaffer in on the case, telling her what we've learned so far and what we suspect." He directed his gaze at Haley. "First off, I looked up Allen Chambers's background. As far as I could tell, he didn't have a criminal record or any prior arrests. In fact, I couldn't find evidence of legal problems of any sort. I searched for liens, debts, taxes owed, but he wasn't on the grid. Except for his drug addiction, he was clean."

Haley put down her coffee cup. "Then he probably wasn't my father's client. So we don't know why he was meeting with him in the garden that night, or why they were arguing."

Gwendolyn Shaffer stirred. "I'm not sure I'm following this right."

"It happened when I still lived at home," Haley explained. "You were at our house for a party. I'd snuck out to see my boyfriend. My mother caught me coming back in."

Gwen nodded. "I remember that. It wasn't long after Lauren died."

"That's right. I'd seen my father talking to a man in the garden just before I came inside. His name was Allen Chambers."

The cop pulled a photo from his pocket and slid it to the older woman. "Did you see him at the party?"

Gwendolyn shook her head. "I don't think so. It was a long time ago, but he doesn't look familiar."

Sully took another drink, pondering that. Unless she was the killer, there was no reason why she would know Allen Chambers. She was younger than the senator and Haley's father. She hadn't attended law school with them.

"You never saw him come to the office when you worked for my father?" Haley asked.

"No. But again, that was a long time ago."

"Were you around when he died?" Sully asked.

Her eyes sharpened. "No. I was in the Caribbean. Trinidad and Tobago. I had a Fulbright scholarship and spent the spring semester there."

"We had another development," Parker cut in. He pocketed the photo, then met Sully's gaze. "I tried to call you last night, but couldn't get through."

"We couldn't get reception."

This time Sergeant Delgado spoke up. "We finally arrested Markus Jenkins."

Sully recognized the name. "The leader of the Ridgewood gang." The one a corrupt prison official had released from jail. "Is he the one who put the bounty on Haley?"

Delgado nodded. "Yeah. He admitted it. He lawyered up right away, but he was willing to make a plea bargain. We interviewed him yesterday afternoon."

"What did he say?" Haley asked.

"He ratted out Foley, for one thing."

"The ATF agent?" She sounded stunned.

"It seems Foley helped steal the missing weapons."

"What? But why? Don't tell me he was a gang member?"

"No. Apparently he needed money. His wife took him to the cleaners during the divorce, and he was scheduled to retire in a couple of years. Seems he didn't like the idea of living the rest of his life on whatever he had left.

"He'd been monitoring the weapons as part of his job," Delgado continued. "So when the gang approached him about a deal, he agreed."

Sully considered that. "Smart move on their part. Find a weak link, someone ripe for corruption, and get him to take the risk—and the blame—if anything goes wrong."

Parker gave him a nod. "We'd suspected an inside job. The security surrounding those guns was tight. But we didn't have a clue until now, especially since Foley was investigating the case." He shook his head. "No one suspected him. He'd had a good career, no blemishes on his record."

Until he'd found a temptation he couldn't resist.

Parker turned to the chief of staff. "Didn't Senator Riggs have something to do with the gun manufacturer, Walker Avionics? I saw a picture of him with Walker hanging on your office wall."

"That's right. The senator facilitated an arms deal with them about a year ago."

"What kind of deal?" Sully asked.

"Jaziirastan wanted to buy weapons for their military. We helped them jump through the legal hoops to make the deal go through. Jaziirastan got its weapons. Walker Avionics got more business, which brought in hundreds of jobs. And when these new weapons go into full production, they'll help the area even more."

Sully could imagine. Every military and criminal organization in the world would want those high-powered guns.

"And of course, we're interested in other sorts of trade with Jaziirastan, too," the chief of staff added. "They're a vital interest to us."

Sully raised his brows. He'd been to Jaziirastan. It was a small country perched on Afghanistan's border. Their main export was opium, which kept their economy afloat.

He rubbed his jaw, doubts about the senator flitting through his mind. "It's interesting that the senator, a former gang member, brokered a deal with the company that manufactured those guns—the same weapons the gang now has."

Gwen aimed her razor-sharp gaze at him. "The senator's gang involvement ended in high school. I can assure you he's completely aboveboard."

Haley shot him a warning glance. "We know that, Gwen. Senator Riggs is a wonderful man. But I have another question about those weapons. Is there a reason the gang wanted those guns specifically?"

Delgado, the gang expert, spoke up again. "For one thing, the black market value is through the roof. But I don't think they wanted these for resale. Markus Jenkins claimed they sent the weapons to a drug cartel south of the border. He didn't know why they wanted them, but he had the impression the weapons were payment for something, that there was some sort of deal going on. But that wasn't his business. He was a middleman. He just had to get the weapons from Foley and pass them to the cartel. But it seems Jenkins has a weakness for guns. He gave in to temptation and kept a few E-13s for himself."

Sully grunted. "And then he used them to shoot at Haley and that pregnant teen."

Haley sighed. "And like idiots, we told Foley everything we knew. We even gave him the evidence we'd found—the label and that receipt. He must have loved that. Talk about a gift!"

"So who killed Foley?" Sully asked.

Delgado shrugged. "That's the question. We're assuming that whoever is behind all this ordered the hit, thinking he knew too much. Maybe once Foley stopped being useful, he was killed. Markus Jenkins denies carrying out the hit. He's not revealing anything about that."

"Who's his lawyer?" Haley asked.

Parker grimaced. "Your father's firm is representing him."

Silence gripped the group. The waitress stopped by and asked for their orders, but no one wanted to eat.

"That's really strange," Haley said when the waitress had refilled their coffee cups and left.

"What's strange about it?" Parker asked. "We already knew he had gang members for clients."

"Not that. The plea bargain. If my father's the one masterminding all this, he wouldn't want Jenkins to talk. He isn't that sloppy. He'd want to protect himself."

Sully looked at her. "That's a damned good point."

He still thought her father was guilty. But advising Jenkins to accept a plea bargain didn't make sense if he was involved.

But how could Burroughs *not* be involved? He had the gang connections. He'd rented that storage unit with the Walker Avionics label inside. Gang members had shown up at his house to kill them.

His gaze traveled to Gwendolyn Shaffer. She frowned into the distance, looking lost in thought.

"You're sure the senator isn't involved in this?" he asked her.

"I told you—"

"We can't afford to make a mistake," Parker said. "Whoever's behind this is trying to kill Haley."

The chief of staff seemed to deflate, her bluster gone. "I know." She let out a sigh. "I can't imagine the senator harming Haley, though. He speaks about her fondly all the time.

"And in our old neighborhood, where the senator and I come from, everyone was in a gang. It didn't really mean anything. And he wasn't violent. I definitely can't see him ordering an execution. That's too cold-blooded for him."

"He's smart enough to run a gang," Sully pointed out.

"He's also busy running the government."

"But he does have the contacts," Parker said. "He's good friends with Haley's father and could have maintained his gang connections that way."

Gwen folded her arms. "I'm positive the senator's not involved. I do all his scheduling. I know who he's meeting with all the time. I even make his medical appointments. If he was meeting with gang members, I think I'd know."

Sully still didn't buy it. The senator could hide his involvement plenty of ways. But arguing with Gwendolyn Shaffer was getting them nowhere. Her loyalty to the senator ran too deep.

"How about Haley's father?" Parker asked her. "You worked for him for years. You think he could be directing all this?"

She hesitated, looking torn. "Oliver Burroughs has always treated me well. I have a lot of respect for him professionally, and I'm also his friend, so it's hard for me to imagine him that way."

She shot Haley an apologetic look. "But if I had to choose…I can see him in that role more than I can the senator. He knows Walker. He met him through the senator. And he knows everyone in the justice system, so he probably knows Foley, too."

For that matter, so did Gwendolyn Shaffer. She not only had access to the senator's connections, but she was friends with the Burroughs family. She'd socialized with them for years. She probably knew as many people in high places as Burroughs and the senator combined.

"All right." Parker straightened in his seat. "So we're going to focus on Burroughs. We need to act quickly and bring him in for questioning before anyone else gets killed. But we have a problem. We don't have any proof. And he's a lawyer, a powerful one. I can't arrest him on a trumped-up charge. It'll never stick. He'll go screaming to the commissioner and I'll end up fired."

"So what do you suggest?" Haley asked.

"We need proof."

"What kind?"

"Ideally, I'd like to get a confession on tape, an admission of guilt." Parker hesitated, his eyes on her. "You think you could confront him? We could send you in with a wire."

"What?" Sully straightened. "No way in hell. She'll be too vulnerable. She's not taking that kind of chance."

"Exactly what were you thinking?" she asked Parker.

Sully stared at her. "Haley, forget it. You're not going to confront a criminal."

"Parker won't let him hurt me."

"You're right," Parker said. "Brynn would kill me if her friend got hurt." He flashed her a quick smile. "The safest place to meet would be at his house. We can keep traffic out of the area."

"It's too isolated," Sully argued. "Once she's inside that mansion, how will we know what's going on?"

"I'll be wearing a wire," she said. "And my father's hardly going to shoot me in his house."

"Why wouldn't he? He put a bounty on your head, remember?"

"I still can't see him doing it himself."

"Does he have guns?" Parker asked her.

She shrugged. "A couple of old revolvers from my mother's family, heirlooms from one of the wars, I think. But they're mounted on the wall."

"Can he shoot?"

"I don't know."

"He can, actually." Everyone's eyes shifted to Gwendolyn Shaffer. "The senator belongs to a hunt club. He takes Burroughs there to shoot from time to time."

Sully worked his jaw. "All the more reason not to do this. Getting hold of a gun is easy. Hell, his clients could give him one."

"We didn't see a gun in his study," Haley said.

"You said yourself that the house is huge. He could keep it anywhere."

She let out a sigh. "Look. We can worry about that part later. Our biggest problem is getting him to talk to me. I asked him for help at the gala and he refused. He wouldn't even hear me out."

"Right," Sully said. "And he isn't a fool. He isn't going to just blurt out his role in all this."

"I think that's where I come in," Gwendolyn said.

Everyone turned to her.

"He'll agree to meet with me. We're on good terms. He won't suspect a trap that way."

"But do you feel comfortable doing it?" Haley asked. "He's your former boss, your friend."

Sully closed his eyes. Leave it to Haley to worry about Gwendolyn Shaffer when her life was on the line.

"I'll have to go with you. Otherwise, he's not going to let you in. In fact, maybe I should go in alone."

Sully nodded at that. Not that he wished Gwendolyn Shaffer any harm, but he didn't want Haley involved.

But Haley still shook her head. "No. I'm the one with the bounty on my head. If anyone's going to confront him, it's me."

"Then I'm going with you," Sully said.

"You can't. He'll never talk to you. Gwen and I have to go in alone."

"We'll work out a script," Parker said, pulling out his notepad. "Ways to get him to say what we need. But I have to get permission first. We'll need to get teams in place, a surveillance van. And we'll put you both in bulletproof gear." He started making notes.

Sully scowled, a bad feeling crawling through his

gut. Two women confronting a killer alone was suicidal. Didn't anyone see the lunacy in this besides him?

Gwendolyn pulled out her cell phone and started tapping on the screen. "Today's too crazy for me. Tomorrow's good. We need to find out if Burroughs is in court and what his schedule is."

"I'll check on that." Parker jotted something else down.

"What about my mother?" Haley asked.

"Good point. We'll need to get her out of the house. I'll have someone work on that." He looked up. "All right. We've got lots to do and not much time. I suggest we get to work. I'll be contacting everyone and coordinating the operation once we get the go-ahead, so expect my call."

They all began scraping back chairs. "I'd like you both to stick with me," Parker told Haley. "I'll need you to talk to some people. You can stay at my house tonight. I'll get a security detail to stand guard." Not waiting for an answer, he gathered up his notepad and went over to pay the bill.

Still hoping he could dissuade her, Sully helped Haley to her feet, then trailed her to the parking lot. He hung back while she said goodbye to Gwendolyn Shaffer, nodding at Delgado as he drove away.

A minute later, Haley returned to his side. Sully tried to stay calm, but every instinct he possessed urged him to whisk her to safety fast. "Listen, Haley. You don't have to do this. We can figure out some other way to get the evidence we need."

"I'll be all right."

"They can't make you do this. There has to be another way."

"I want to do it. It's the fastest way to end this mess."

"I don't like it. Too much can go wrong. And I don't like the idea of Shaffer going in there with you. We don't know her well enough."

"I've known her most of my life. And she's perfect for this role. She used to work for my father. She's still his friend. She can convince him to meet with us."

"But—"

"You said we need to take the lead, right?"

"Right." And no plan was ever perfect. But putting Haley at risk...

"Then we need her help. My father trusts her."

Gwendolyn Shaffer drove past in her Mercedes and tooted her horn. His dread mounting, Sully watched as she exited the parking lot, then merged with traffic and drove off.

Halcy's father trusted her, all right.

But the real question was, *could they?*

By the time they assembled in the alley behind the Burroughs mansion in Guilford the following afternoon, Sully was a wreck. Ironically, flashbacks hadn't kept him up all night for once. Neither had the nausea and headache from the alcohol withdrawal. Instead, he'd spent the entire night anguishing over Haley's safety, envisioning everything that could go wrong—while Haley slept beside him like a rock.

But Sully had to give Parker credit. The man was not a slouch. He'd worked late into the night putting the operation together. He'd secured the proper permissions. He'd had a legal team triple-check their plans.

And he'd posted commandos disguised as gardeners all over the grounds. A cop with a leaf blower was cleaning the driveway. Another was trimming the shrubs near the door. A SWAT team worked just outside the front gate, pretending to resurface the street. They'd not only blocked off road and hauled in paving equipment, but sprayed something that stank like asphalt over the surface, doing a credible job of fooling *him*. Parker even had a man keeping watch on Haley's mother, who was currently at her plastic surgeon's doing who knew what.

He'd also taken steps to protect Haley. She wore a bulletproof vest under her top. He'd outfitted her with a wire another team in a van could hear. He'd worked with her for hours, going over the questions she should ask her father and instructing her on what to avoid. He even had a helicopter on standby to assist in the take-down, in case anything went wrong.

In short, Parker had planned for every contingency.

Except one. Gwendolyn Shaffer had failed to show up.

"Any sign of her?" Parker asked, trotting over, still wearing his sling.

Haley shook her head. "No. I haven't seen her."

"Damn. She's half an hour late. And if we don't get moving…"

A dark sedan turned into the alley. "Oh, good. That must be her." Parker started toward it as it pulled up behind Sully's pickup truck and parked. A second later, Senator Riggs climbed out of the passenger door and headed their way, his burly bodyguard close behind.

Sully frowned. What the hell was he doing here? The senator wasn't part of their plans.

"Where's your chief of staff?" Parker asked him.

The senator stopped. "She's not here?"

"No. You haven't heard from her?"

The senator shook his head. "She didn't come in this morning. I haven't seen her all day. She told me about the plans yesterday, so I thought I'd see if I could help in any way. She would have called if she got tied up."

"It's not like her to be late," Haley said, sounding worried. "She's always on time."

Parker swore. "We can't wait. If we don't do this now, Burroughs is going to leave. And who knows when we'll have another chance?"

Haley stepped toward him. "I'm ready. I can go in alone."

"The hell you will." Sully couldn't keep the outrage from his voice. "If she's not here, we call it off."

"No, we don't." She turned around and met his eyes. "Look, Sully, I know you're worried, but nothing is going to go wrong. I'll be back in no time with the proof we need."

He didn't like it. Foreboding roiled in his gut, the same premonition of danger he'd had in Afghanistan before the insurgents attacked. "Then I'm going with you."

"You can't. He'll never open up with you around."

"Damn it, Haley—"

"Sully, you can't. We've gone over this a million times. I'll be lucky enough if he talks to me."

"I'll do it," the senator said. "I can get Oliver to talk."

"Sir?" The senator's bodyguard shook his head. "I don't advise that. I need to keep you in sight."

"I'll be fine."

"But—"

"Oliver's an old friend of mine. I've known him for years. He's not going to do anything rash."

"We don't know that. If he's desperate—"

"Look. We need answers. I can take Haley in there

to get them. I'll carry a sidearm if you think it's necessary, but I don't need protection from him." He turned to Parker again. "What do you say?"

"I don't know." Doubt pulled at his voice.

"I promise you I'll be fine. We both will. I won't let Haley get harmed."

"All right." Still looking reluctant, Parker turned to the cops milling behind him. "Five minutes, everyone." He turned back to the senator. "This way. I'll fill you in while we get you armed."

Sully stood motionless, feeling as though his world had spun out of control. This was wrong. For all they knew, the *senator* was the one they were after. Why didn't they see the danger? How could they let Haley take the risk?

But then she walked up and embraced him. For a moment, he indulged himself, holding her soft body close, never wanting to let her go. "Haley…"

"Don't worry. I'm going to be all right." She released him and stepped away. But the flash of fear in her eyes belied her words.

And suddenly, he understood what she was doing. She was protecting him. If anything went wrong, if Burroughs turned violent and attacked, she didn't want Sully to have to take him down and live with the burden of having caused her father's death. "Haley, listen—"

"I've got to go." She hurried to join the senator, then walked with him down the alley toward the house. Sully watched her go, her head erect, her hair swaying against her back, that innate gracefulness in her stride. Emotions tumbled inside him—helplessness, pride in her courage, terror that she wouldn't survive.

And love.
He loved her.
And now he might lose her—forever.

Chapter 15

She was scared. Terrified, if she wanted to admit the truth. Despite what she'd told Sully, she did *not* want to confront her father. And she desperately wanted Sully by her side. She felt way too alone and exposed.

But she wasn't alone. Senator Riggs was with her, and he was armed. Besides, Parker couldn't have planned this operation more carefully. Cops swarmed the grounds. He had a SWAT team poised to pounce. One word from her, at the slightest sign of danger, and they'd storm into the mansion, their weapons drawn. Nothing could possibly go wrong.

Trying to keep up with the senator's long strides, she hurried past the police officers posing as the paving crew and up the drive to her parents' front door.

Where was Gwendolyn Shaffer? That question nagged at her the most. "I can't believe Gwen's not here," she said. "This just isn't like her."

The senator nodded at a cop trimming a tree. "I know. I'm worried about her. I hope she didn't have an accident. As soon as we're done here, I'll start making calls."

Haley gave him a grateful nod. The senator was right. They'd work on finding Gwen when they were done. Right now she had to focus on getting her father to confess to his gang involvement—without jeopardizing the case.

But as she climbed the steps to the porch, more doubts flooded her mind. What if they had this wrong? What if her father wasn't the killer? But who else could he be? Senator Riggs?

They stopped at the front door, and she angled him a glance. He pushed on the doorbell, making the chimes in the foyer peal. Then he shot her a friendly smile, probably meant to bolster her confidence. But suddenly, he seemed like a stranger with his expertly cut gray hair, his professionally whitened teeth, his meticulously tailored slacks.

Why hadn't she ever noticed how fake he looked?

She mentally rolled her eyes. She was acting ridiculous. She'd known the senator since childhood. He wasn't the criminal who wanted her dead. She was letting her imagination run away from her—which proved how spooked she was. She had to pull herself together fast.

Her father cracked open the door. "Well, hello, Alfred." Surprise mingled with delight in his voice. "What are you doing here? I thought Gwen was stopping by."

Smiling, he pulled the door open wider to let him in. But then he caught sight of her and stopped. "What do you want?" Every trace of pleasure disappeared from his voice.

"We'd like to talk to you," the senator said before Haley could answer. "It's important."

Her father didn't move. He stood blocking the doorway, his lips drawn tight, his gaze burning at her with contempt. And for one unguarded moment, Haley was a child again, awkward, gawky, overweight. Wanting desperately to please her parents, to be the child they desired. Wondering why she couldn't make them love her, unable to understand what she'd done to deserve their disdain.

It took all her willpower not to buckle and flee. But she steeled her jaw and held his gaze, refusing to look away. She wasn't that child anymore. And no matter what he thought of her, she refused to cower or run away.

After what felt like an eternity, he turned back to Senator Riggs. "Of course. Come in. It's cold out there today." He moved back from the door, his false joviality grating on her nerves. Her knees trembled as she stepped over the threshold and went inside.

Ignoring her, he closed the door, then accompanied the senator down the hall, chatting about an upcoming party he planned to attend. Haley lagged behind them, her palms clammy, her steps echoing on the marble tiles. *Could the policemen in the surveillance van hear them?* Of course they could; Parker had tested the equipment multiple times. But even more doubts assailed her the farther they moved from the door.

Desperately missing Sully, but knowing she'd done the right thing to dissuade him, she followed the men into the study. Her father gestured to the armchairs, then took his seat behind the desk.

He held up a box of cigars. "Care for a smoke?" he asked the senator.

"Thanks, but I'd just as soon get to the point."

Her father set the box back down with a shrug. "So what's this about?"

The senator leaned forward in his chair. "Did Gwen stop by today?"

"No. She was supposed to. I was expecting her when you rang the bell. Why do you ask?"

"She was supposed to meet us here."

Her father spread his hands. "Well, as you can see, she didn't come."

Senator Riggs turned to her and her pulse began to race. It was time to make her father talk.

She forced herself to meet his eyes. "I wanted to talk to you. I tried to ask for your help at the ball, but you wouldn't listen. That's why Gwen was supposed to come, and why Senator Riggs is here now. I need information, and they're trying to help."

Her father's mouth hardened, a sure sign he wasn't pleased. He had no qualms about manipulating others, but didn't appreciate that she'd done the same to him. He leaned back in his chair and crossed his arms. "Go ahead."

"I told you I was in danger. You realize that car bomb at the gala was meant for me."

He snorted. "That's a bit far-fetched."

"Not at all. There's a gang contract on my head, a bounty. The Ridgewood gang has offered a reward to bring me in, preferably dead."

Her father's expression remained blank. She didn't know what she'd expected—surprise, dismay, maybe a glimmer of sympathy or even guilt. But her father's disinterest hit her like a brutal slap. "I don't see what this has to do with me," he said.

"Don't you?"

A flush crept up his face. His eyes remained locked on hers. "Would you like to explain that remark?"

She knew that tone of voice. He used that deadly softness in the courtroom right before he mounted an attack. It always destroyed his opponents. It used to terrify her.

No more. She inched up her chin. "You've represented members of that gang. In fact, Markus Jenkins is your client right now."

"And?"

"And I needed some questions answered. I was hoping you'd help."

He shifted his gaze to the senator, then back to her. "I told you, I can't discuss my clients."

The senator crossed his leg. "We aren't asking you to betray their confidence, Oliver. We just need answers to some questions, particularly since we're such old friends."

Her father leaned back in his chair. His eyes narrowed another fraction, as if he was considering the pros and cons. Then he slanted his head. "You can ask whatever you like. I'll answer what I can."

The senator ceded to her again. Haley swallowed hard, determined not to blow this. It could be their only chance. "I'm sure you remember the night you found out I was pregnant. You were here, in the study, when I came in from outside. There was a party going on. It was just after Lauren died."

Her father's expression filled with pain. His gaze darted to the picture on the corner of his desk. Haley knew what it was—a photo of her parents and Lauren—and it summed up Haley's life. Left out. Never part of the trio. Never valued for who she was.

And it hurt, more than she wanted it to. Even now her father grieved for Lauren. This study was practically a shrine to her memory, with pictures of her everywhere—on the walls, the desk, the bookshelves. Always Lauren. Always adored. Never forgotten.

Why couldn't her father have loved her, too?

She forced herself to breathe around the raw ache gripping her chest. It didn't matter anymore. She didn't need this despicable man's affection. That time was done.

She unclenched her jaw. "That night. When I was coming home through the garden, I saw you talking to one of your former classmates. Allen Chambers."

Her father's head reared back. "You were there?"

"I was hiding in the bushes. I didn't want you to see me sneaking in."

He heaved himself from the chair and walked to the window, then stood there for a moment, looking out. A cop was cutting the hedges nearby, but the thick exterior walls muted the noise.

Her father turned around. "Go on."

"You were arguing." She paused, giving him a chance to explain, but her father didn't take the bait. He'd spent his life coaching witnesses. He knew better than to talk. She suddenly realized that getting him to say something incriminating was going to be harder than she'd thought.

"You know he died a short time after that. A gang executed him."

"I remember. But what does this have to do with me?"

Faltering, she rose and went to the unlit fireplace. Sully was right. This wasn't going to work. Her father would never admit his guilt.

But maybe if she went off script…

Parker would be mad. The other cops would have a heart attack if she deviated from their plan. But she had to end this ordeal right now.

"When Lauren and I were little we used to watch you work. We'd hide in your storage room and peek out."

Confusion clouded his eyes. "I know that. I could hear you giggling in there."

"Sometimes we hid under the couch, instead."

He glanced at his watch. "Is there a point to this?"

"We learned about your secret drawer, the one under your desk. The one where you keep the combination to your safe."

He turned still. She'd caught his attention now. "And?"

"And I came to visit the other day when you weren't around. I decided to check your safe. I found a receipt inside, a receipt to a storage unit. You Save Self-Storage."

He stared at her.

"The same storage unit where you put those stolen weapons. The E-13s. The ones the Ridgewood gang used to try to kill me. The ones Roger Foley helped steal."

His eyes bulged. "What are you talking about?"

The senator joined her at the fireplace. For the first time, he spoke up. "We're talking about a gang leader, Oliver. The same man with influence inside the police force. A man who had Allen Chambers executed in that warehouse. A man who arranged to steal those assault rifles and put a contract on his daughter's head."

Her father's jaw went slack. He stared at the senator, then at her, his head swinging back and forth between them like a cornered animal trying to pinpoint the greatest threat.

"Where's Gwen?" the senator demanded, stepping closer. "Why isn't she here?"

"I told you—"

"Where the hell did she go?"

"You think I hurt her?" Her father gaped at him. Then he let out a strangled laugh. "How can you think that? I haven't seen her in days."

But Senator Riggs didn't relent. "Why did you kill Allen Chambers?"

"I didn't. You're crazy. My God. What's wrong with you today?"

For a split second Haley almost believed him. He sounded genuinely stunned. But she knew he could act. He routinely feigned outrage in court, summoning anger and indignation to sway the judge.

"I heard you arguing with him," she said. "You had a motive to kill him." She was guessing, but he didn't need to know that.

His expression instantly changed, his eyes menacing now. "Arguing about what? What did you hear us say?"

Realizing her bluff had backfired, she clamped her lips.

"Tell me." He strode toward her with furious steps. "What did you hear that day?"

Understanding the danger, she took a quick step back. But the fireplace mantel blocked her escape.

"Stay away from her," the senator warned, but her father didn't back off. He loomed over her, his big body trapping her against the fireplace, his eyes burning with anger and something more. Guilt? Fear?

What was he trying to hide?

She lunged sideways to scoot away. But he reached out and gripped the neck of her shirt, winding it around his fist until she couldn't breathe. "Stop," she gasped. "You're hurting me."

The senator tried again. "Get your hands off her, Oliver."

"Or what? Mind your own business, Al. You might be a senator, but this is my house. And she's my daughter. I'll do whatever the hell I want."

He jerked up his arm, lifting her onto her toes. Haley clawed at his hands, trying desperately to loosen his hold. Her vision began to fade. She lashed out with her foot, but his shin was like cement. His hot breath swept her face, making her dizzier yet.

Suddenly the senator slammed into him from the side. Knocked off balance, her father released her, and she stumbled back against the mantel, smacking her head.

Stars burst behind her eyes. She hauled in a much-needed breath. Her father whirled and charged at the senator, crashing into him with a grunt. Both men fell to the floor. Then they battled and rolled, twisting and grappling for supremacy, the sickening sound of fists striking flesh making her flinch.

An armchair crashed into the desk. A Tiffany floor lamp fell, then shattered, flinging shards of colored glass over the floor. The senator caught hold of her father, struggling to get him into a headlock, but he lost his grip and fell back. Still fighting to clear her vision, Haley scanned the room for a weapon, desperate to end the fight somehow. "Help," she gasped into the wire. "He's—"

Her father leaped to his feet. He had the senator's wire in one hand, his gun in the other. The veins in his flushed face bulged. Haley had never seen him look so incensed.

"What the hell is this?" he demanded. "You came here armed?"

Wheezing, the senator crawled to his knees. "Put the gun down, Oliver."

But her father whipped around and looked out the window. "Christ. Those guys are cops, aren't they? This is a trap. You came here to set me up."

"Listen—"

"No, *you* listen." He waved the gun between them, and Haley went stone still. He looked wild, out of control. The slightest move could make him snap.

He aimed the gun at her and she blanched. "Get over there next to him. Now!"

Where were the cops? Surely they'd heard her plea for help. She shot a frantic glance at the door.

"I said *move!*"

Not seeing any choice, she started across the room. But her foot hit the glass from the broken lamp. She slid, lost her balance and flailed her arms.

The gun barked out. Fire scorched her arm and she shrieked.

The door crashed open. Her father wheeled around as several armed officers stormed in. "Drop the gun!" someone shouted.

Her father's gun went off again.

The officers fired back.

Her father froze. For a moment he seemed suspended, his eyes filled with disbelief. Then he turned, and she saw the blood pumping from his wounds. Horrified, she clamped her hand to her mouth.

"I didn't kill anyone," he said. His face sheet white, he collapsed on the floor.

And then Sully burst in, lunged across the room like a madman and crushed her against his chest.

She never wanted to let him go.

He was never letting her out of his sight again. Sully paced around Haley's room in Baltimore's Shock Trauma hospital, still unable to get the previous day's horror out of his head. Hearing that shot, seeing the SWAT team charge into the house and being unable to rush in and save her... He'd aged decades before he'd reached her side.

What would he have done if he'd lost her? He loved her. He needed her in his life.

This woman had saved him. She'd taught him to forgive himself. She'd convinced him that he'd done the best he could with the intelligence he'd had that horrific day in the desert sand. More important, she'd shown him that it was better to make mistakes than cower inside a bottle, reliving his failures and wallowing in the past. He would never regain the idealism he'd once had—he'd grown too jaded for that—but Haley had taught him that there were still battles worth fighting in this world.

And then he'd nearly lost her.

Never again.

He passed a shaky hand down his face and glanced at the bathroom door. She was inside, getting cleaned up, ready for the hospital to discharge her. They'd kept her overnight, more for protection than anything else. Her wound was superficial, barely a nick in her right arm. Even so, Sully had stayed with her overnight, sleeping in the chair beside the bed.

One good thing had come from the ordeal. He'd been so frantic with worry over her safety that he hadn't dwelled on his own physical discomfort. And the withdrawal symptoms were finally beginning to ease.

Haley emerged from the bathroom just then. Her face was pale but freshly scrubbed. She'd brushed her shiny hair. She wore the clean clothes her friend had dropped off, and the green sweater brought out her gorgeous eyes.

His throat suddenly thick, his emotions skidding around like a car on ice, Sully limped to her side. He didn't say a word, just gathered her in his arms and held her, so damned grateful she'd survived. She slid her arms around his neck and squeezed him back, while an eternity passed by.

"It'll get better," he promised. "The memories will start to fade."

"I know. It's just…it seems so pointless. He didn't have to die."

He eased back and searched her face. "I'm sorry." He knew it had to be tough. Even though Burroughs had directed that gang and tried to kill her, he was still her father. She shouldn't have had to watch him die.

Sully had listened to the takedown live in the surveillance van. He'd heard Haley's statement later to the police. And everyone had concluded the same thing. Her father had panicked when he realized she knew about Allen Chambers. Whatever they'd argued about that night long ago, Burroughs hadn't wanted anyone to know. So he'd attacked her, needing to shut her up.

Why Burroughs and Chambers had argued in the garden was still a mystery, one they'd probably never solve. But it seemed likely that Burroughs had ordered Allen Chambers's death.

"Any word on Gwen's whereabouts?" she asked.

"No." He hated breaking the bad news. She obviously

cared about the missing woman and wanted to see her safe. "Parker called while you were in the bathroom. They're searching for her, but they don't have any leads."

Her eyes troubled, she gave him a nod. "Did he say anything else?"

"The ATF is trying to track down the weapons, but they think they're already south of the border."

"I guess that's not a surprise."

"No. But they need to figure out what the cartel has planned." He paused again. "They told your mother about your father's death."

"How is she taking it?"

"Not great. About how you'd expect. Parker said a doctor was helping her cope. Are you going to call her?"

She sighed. "I don't know. I'll have to think about that. Maybe eventually, once I figure out what to say." She glanced toward the door. "Can we leave now?"

"We have to wait for the wheelchair to arrive."

"That's a bit much for a scratched arm, don't you think?"

"Hospital rules. Parker's bringing the bodyguards, too." Even though her father was dead, Haley still had that bounty on her head. Until that threat ended, until they could convince the gang the reward was canceled, they'd have professional bodyguards watching their backs. And not rent-a-cops, either. Haley's friend Brynn had sprung for the real deal—highly trained, former black-ops guys.

Haley edged her hip onto the bed. Sully sat beside her and held her hand. "How's your arm?"

"Wonderful. They pumped me full of painkillers and antibiotics. I can't feel a thing."

"Think you can lift a fork?"

She tilted her head to meet his eyes. A small smile played around her lips. "I hope you're not suggesting hospital food on Thanksgiving."

He slashed her a smile. "I can manage better, if you're up to it."

"I think," she whispered, "that as long as you're with me, I can do anything."

So could he. Anything except let her go.

Chapter 16

Haley had no idea where they were heading. Sully refused to give her a clue. But he'd shaved for the occasion. He'd donned clean jeans and trimmed his hair. And he was definitely sober. His hands were steadier on the wheel, the whites of his eyes nearly clear. *He looked good.* And when he glanced at her, the intensity in his burnished-gold eyes made her senses reel.

Frankly, she didn't care where they went. All she wanted to do today was forget. She didn't want to think about her father's death. She didn't want to think about Gwendolyn Shaffer and where she might have gone. And she definitely didn't want to think about the bounty on her head, or the gang members who still might want her dead. She'd deal with all that stress tomorrow. Right now, she wanted one selfish day for herself. She wanted to forget the horror, forget the pain and simply spend time with the man she loved.

They exited I-95 in Fairfax and entered an aging, tree-lined suburb filled with swing sets in the big backyards. Multiple cars filled the driveways. Kids played touch football in the streets in spite of the frosty air. Sully drove unerringly through the neighborhood, not even glancing at the street signs, then pulled up to a two-story brick colonial at the end of a cul-de-sac and parked.

Mature trees towered over the house. Neatly trimmed azalea bushes bordered the drive. She climbed out and surveyed the aging house, taking note of the shiny red door, the decorations taped to the windows—paper turkeys shaped like children's hands.

Her heart missed a beat. She stopped on the cracked sidewalk and turned around.

"What's wrong?" Sully asked.

"Who lives here?"

He looked down to meet her gaze. "My parents. Is that a problem?"

Problem? "No, of course it isn't a problem." But it was an enormous step for Sully. He'd avoided his family for months, ashamed of the man he'd become. That he now was willing to face them—at a holiday dinner, no less—spoke volumes about how he'd changed.

"Are you sure you want to do this, though?"

"Yeah." His voice turned gruff. "If you'll go in with me."

She reached out and squeezed his hand. Her chest felt suddenly full. "There's nothing I'd rather do more."

Their hands still linked, she accompanied him to the door. Sully paused on the small cement stoop, a sliver of trepidation flitting through his potent eyes. But then he squared his broad shoulders, swung open the door, and accompanied her inside.

They walked into total pandemonium. Haley had never seen anything like it. Children raced around. A yipping Jack Russell terrier chased them, making the children squeal. Adults laughed and chatted in clusters around the crowded room, while one harried mother darted over to capture a fugitive toddler who threatened to fall. A young boy curled up in a corner armchair, lost in a book, oblivious to the chaos rocking his world. The mouthwatering smell of roasting turkey filled the air.

For a minute, they just stood there, no one paying attention to them. But then a few heads turned. A hush fell over the crowd, bit by bit, like dominoes toppling in a row. Finally silence gripped the crowd, a stunned expression on every face. And then they erupted in joyous cries, rushing forward to hug Sully. He was mobbed.

"Uncle Sully!" a little girl shrieked. She pushed through the crowd and flung herself into his arms. Grinning, he swung her up and held her upside down, and she let out a piercing squeal. More kids raced over, leaping on him like metal filings on a magnet, clinging to his arms and legs. He tipped his head back and laughed.

Haley's eyes burned. A huge lump wedged in her throat, making it impossible to breathe.

And then an older woman hurried into the room. She was short and plump, with gray hair and a pretty face. She wore an apron over her slacks. She came to a halt. Her hand flew to her mouth. Her eyes widened and brimmed with tears.

Sully set the children down. The crowd parted, and he slowly limped to her side. "Mom."

The small woman rushed into his arms. She clung to him and sobbed. "Sully, Sully, Sully."

Haley sniffed and blinked like mad, but hot tears brimmed in her eyes. Sully stood with his head bent, his eyes closed, while his mother wept in his arms. Overcome with emotion, Haley stood riveted—witnessing the kind of love her parents had never shown her, not once in her entire life.

A middle-aged man strode through the back door and into the room. *Sully's father.* Haley didn't have any doubts. He was an older version of Sully—tall and broad shouldered, still handsome despite his years, with the same heart-stopping, whiskey-gold eyes.

Sully lifted his head. Their eyes connected from across the room. The man's mouth tightened and a bright sheen filled his eyes. Sully's mother released him and wiped her tears.

The men met halfway across the room. Sully's father hugged him, then thumped him on his back. "Welcome home, son," he said, his voice gruff.

Haley bit her wobbling lip, trying desperately not to lose it completely and weep. A woman her age came over and handed her a tissue. She was crying, too. "I'm Meghan," she said. "One of Sully's sisters."

"Haley Barnes."

Sully turned and cleared his throat. His eyes met hers, and her heart swelled so much she feared it would splinter apart. "Hey, everyone. I have someone I'd like you to meet."

Three hours later, it was Haley's head she thought would burst. She'd met Sully's two brothers, both with his trademark eyes. One owned a construction company.

The other was a nuclear engineer. His three sisters were all gorgeous and had equally varied careers—one was a research biologist, another an elementary school teacher and the last one a smoke jumper who put out forest fires. Haley had already forgotten their names, let alone those of their respective mates.

And she had no clue which child went with which adult. But it didn't seem to matter. They all joined in, wiping hands and noses, tying shoelaces, tickling and telling jokes. There seemed to be a constant mass of kids moving amoeba-like through the house, back and forth, up and down the stairs. And the Jack Russell terrier kept making everyone laugh, especially when he leaped up and stole the pumpkin pie off a toddler's plate. At least Haley could remember the dog's name—J.R.

But now the commotion had begun to subside. The women sat at the table, talking about their kids. The youngest children had crashed, while the older ones played outside in the fenced backyard. The men, including Sully, were in the den, cheering a football game on the big-screen television. The dishes were done, the mountains of food eaten or stored in the fridge. Sully's mother had even delivered meals to the bodyguards waiting outside.

Haley marveled at it all, wondering if Sully realized what a treasure this was. He had the family she'd always dreamed of—lively and down to earth, engrossed with squabbles and laughter and tears. And love. These people truly cared about each other.

Sully's parents had given their children an incredible gift—the capacity to love. Haley's parents had lacked it. They were shallow, manipulative and self-absorbed. All the wealth in the world hadn't given them this generosity and kindness of spirit, a selflessness that Sully's family had in spades. She doubted they even realized how unusual that was.

Needing a moment alone, she wandered into the living room and studied the photographs hanging on the walls. They hadn't been taken by well-known photographers like the ones at her parents' house. Some were clearly amateur work. There were school photos, team photos, pictures of newborn babes. She lingered over a shot of a teenaged Sully looking awkward in a tux, standing beside a girl. In another, a much younger Sully proudly held up a fish he'd caught, his grin revealing missing teeth.

Then she spotted another photo. It sat in a place of honor by itself on a special shelf. It was Sully in his formal army uniform. He looked impossibly young, far too young to march off to war. And so somber. Next to the photo was a display case containing his Silver Star and Purple Heart.

"That picture was taken when he graduated from boot camp."

Haley turned. Sully's mother, Diane, stood beside her, smiling wistfully at the photo. "It was a hard day for us. We were so proud of him, and yet so scared about what he might go through."

Haley pressed her hand to her abdomen. If her child had survived, she couldn't have stood the thought of him marching off to war. And yet, how could a parent not be proud of a child that brave?

She studied the medals. "He told me what he did in Afghanistan. I can't even imagine the courage that took."

Diane's smile turned tender. "He was always the warrior, the one who fought the bullies and stuck up for the weaker kids. I asked him once why he did it. He was nine years old, and he'd come home from school with a bloody nose. He said that somebody had to do it, and it might as well be him."

Her eyes misted. "He never changed. He always stepped up to act. And whatever he did—going to war, rescuing his fallen comrades, even exiling himself from us—he did what he thought was right. He stayed true to his moral code."

Haley swallowed hard, a thick ache unfolding in her chest. "He rescued me, too. He didn't even know me, and he risked his life to save mine. I owe him."

"And I owe you."

Haley turned her head. "Me? Whatever for?"

His mother reached out and touched her hand. "We saw him after he got back, after the hospital discharged him. He was a broken man. Not just his leg, but his spirit. His soul was gone. And his eyes… It killed me to see him in that kind of pain. And then he disappeared. You have no idea how helpless we felt, wanting so badly to help him, but he shut us out. But now he's changed. You brought him back."

"You're wrong. It wasn't me. He healed himself."

"But you were the spark." She wrapped her arms around Haley and gave her a hug. "Thank you so much for giving me my son back. I owe you a debt I can never repay."

Haley's vision blurred. She shut her eyes, fearing she just might weep again. "He's a special man."

Diane gave her another squeeze, then stepped back and studied her face. Her eyes softened even more. "You love him."

She couldn't deny it. "It's not...we don't..."

His mother smiled again. "You'll sort it out. And I want you to know that whatever happens, you're always welcome here. This is your home now, too."

Her throat closed up. An awful pressure gripped her chest, making it impossible to breathe. "Thank you." She wondered if Diane had any idea of the impact of those simple words. That she was welcome here. That this was her home. Her own mother had never said them once.

"Grandma!" a child called out from the other room. Sully's mother shook her head. "It never ends." She patted Haley's cheek and hurried away.

Her thoughts whirling, her emotions ragged, Haley wandered to the den. But instead of going in, she hovered in the doorway and watched Sully lounging in an armchair across the room. One young nephew sat on the floor at his feet, making motor noises and running a small truck over his shoes. A toddler had claimed Sully's lap. She chattered at a page in a book.

Sully looked relaxed—his legs stretched out, his head resting against the back of the chair, his eyes on the television screen. And her heart took another fall. He didn't just have the kind of family she'd always dreamed of. He was the *man* she had always yearned for, the one she loved.

"Unka Sully," the little girl demanded, poking his chest.

"Oh, sorry." He tore his gaze from the screen and turned the page, adjusting the book so she could see.

Haley inhaled swiftly as the essence of this man came into focus, like a blurred picture suddenly becoming clear. He would make the perfect father. Sully was kind, patient and strong. A man who wrestled and played with his nephews. A man who spent his afternoon turning the pages for his young niece.

A man who'd sacrifice everything for the ones he loved.

And the irony hit her hard. She had finally found the perfect man. A man who accepted her, who thought she was beautiful, who valued her for herself. And while he hadn't said the words yet, she could feel his love in his kiss.

But he needed more than she could offer. She couldn't have children. She could never give him the family he deserved.

His mother had said it all. Sully did the right thing, no matter how difficult, no matter the cost to himself.

Now she had to follow his example. No matter how much it destroyed her, no matter how much it devastated her heart, she had to do the right thing and let him go— and sacrifice the happiness she'd always dreamed of so he could go after his.

Something was bothering Haley. Sully sent her a side-long glance as he limped toward the pickup truck, lugging the care package his mother had pressed into his hands. "This thing weighs a ton. She must have packed us enough food to last a month."

Her lips curved up, but the smile didn't reach her eyes. She'd been like that for the past hour, troubled, distracted, distant. Like a lightbulb that had suddenly dimmed. She was still gracious and polite. His family had been nuts about her. Hell, *he* was nuts about her. He was so crazy in love it was all he could do to keep from blurting it out.

So what the hell had gone wrong?

They reached the truck and he unlocked the door. He set the food on the floor, then waited for her to get in.

"Listen, Sully…"

He cocked his head.

"We need to talk."

His belly tensed. Suddenly wary, he leaned back against the truck and crossed his arms. "That sounds ominous."

He knew her well by now. He recognized her nervous tells—the furrowed brow, the way she twisted a loose strand of her hair around her finger, how her gaze flitted past, not quite settling on his.

A cheer erupted from the neighbor's house. Someone had scored. A motorcycle sped past on a nearby road, the whine of its engine slowly fading away.

Her gaze finally returned to his. "I'm going to have one of the bodyguards take me back to Brynn's. I think…it's time we parted ways. You're not in danger now. I'll be all right, too, or at least I will be before too long. There's no reason you need to hang around with me."

He didn't move. The muscles in his jaw turned tight. "No reason?"

She hugged her arms. She shifted her weight from foot to foot. "All right, fine. It's just that, there's no point. We don't have a future together."

"And why is that?"

Still hugging her arms, she shook her head.

"I love you, Haley."

Her gaze flew to his. She pressed her hand to her mouth, pain darkening her hazel eyes. "Don't do this, Sully."

"Don't do what? Don't care about you? Don't love you?"

"Yes."

"It's too late. I've fallen in love with you."

Her face paled. "Sully..."

He pushed away from the truck and stalked toward her. Then he clasped her jaw and tugged, forcing her to meet his gaze. "Tell me you don't feel the same way."

"I can't," she whispered, tears springing to her eyes.

"Then what the hell's the problem?"

"I'm wrong for you, Sully. I can't offer you anything long-term. Look at your parents."

"My parents?" He frowned. "What do they have to do with this?"

"Everything. They're the perfect example of what parents should be. Of what *you're* going to be. And what you need. A family, marriage, kids.

"I can't give you that, Sully. You know I can't have kids. I told you that before. The scarring was too extensive. And I saw you with those children today. You'd make the perfect father. You deserve more than a barren wife."

His temper stirred. "Don't you think I should decide what I need?"

"You can't. Right now you think it doesn't matter. Maybe you even think you don't want kids. But what if you change your mind? I've seen a bad marriage, Sully. I grew up watching my parents, so I know how a bad one looks. I've seen how the coldness makes you shrivel inside. I know the way it kills your soul, the way it destroys your life.

"And I couldn't bear to do that to you. I know you, Sully. You'd be loyal to me to the end, no matter what the cost. You'd never divorce me. You'd never admit that you'd changed your mind. But it would get worse and worse until you ended up miserable. And it would kill me to see you like that. To know I did that to you."

"Bull." He planted his hands on his hips. "My knee is a mess. I'll always walk with a limp. Does that mean you'll change your mind about me?"

"It's not the same. A limp doesn't alter your life."

"You want life altering? Then how about this? I've got post-traumatic stress. I'm an alcoholic. I'll have to battle my addiction every day for the rest of my life. Is that going to change your view of me?"

"Of course not."

"We all carry scars, Haley. But yours don't define you, any more than mine define me."

"You're wrong. They *do* define us. They make us who we are."

"And I love who you are." Desperate to convince her, he cupped her face with his hands and gazed into her gorgeous eyes. "Haley, you're everything I've ever wanted. You're beautiful, sexy, brave. I don't care about having kids. If we want them someday, we can adopt. I want you to marry me."

Her eyes glistened with tears. "I can't do it. I love you too much to destroy you."

His temper flared. And suddenly, he felt pissed off. He released her face and scowled. "This isn't about what's best for me, Haley. Don't think for a minute it is. It's about *you. Your* insecurities, *your* doubts in yourself, *your* fears."

"It's not—"

"Go ahead and run away. Go ahead and pretend

you're being a martyr, that you're doing this for my own good. But it's a lie. This is all about you.

"I've laid it on the line for you, Haley. You've seen who I am. I told you I love you. I told you I accept you the way you are, that I don't care whether or not you can have kids. But you won't believe it. Well, that's your weakness, not mine. And I've got to tell you, Haley. Running away like this? It's the first cowardly thing I've seen you do."

Tears brimmed in her eyes. Her face contorted with pain. "I'm so sorry, Sully."

She walked over to the closest bodyguard and climbed into his car. The guard shot him a questioning glance and Sully motioned for him to go. A moment later they drove away.

Sully stood on the sidewalk for what felt like eons, his eyes on the corner where the car had disappeared. His entire body trembled. He wanted to snarl and rage. He loved her, damn it. And she loved him. How the hell could she throw that away?

Cursing, he turned on his heel and strode back toward the house. But instead of going inside, he detoured to the detached garage that sat behind the house. He stormed inside and slammed the door, then stomped through his father's hangout to the dorm-size refrigerator tucked under the workbench.

He jerked open the door and looked inside. Bottles of beer crowded the shelves. His stomach seethed, a wrenching pain hollowing his chest where his heart used to be.

He yanked out a bottle and popped the cap. Then he raised the bottle to his lips, the scent of the beer offering comfort, tempting him to forget Haley, forget the world and let the alcohol numb the ache.

His hands shook. He stood motionless, the bottle just inches from his mouth, a war raging inside his head.

And then he hurled the bottle against the floor. The glass shattered, spraying beer all over the room. He collapsed into his father's beat-up armchair, his eyes on the frothing beer as it raced along the cracks in the cement.

No amount of alcohol was going to heal this pain.

Chapter 17

"Why don't you talk to him? It's been three weeks."

Haley slumped on the bar stool at Brynn's kitchen counter, cradling a cup of tea. "Why? What good would it do?"

Brynn leaned across the granite counter, her auburn hair shimmering beneath the pendant lights. "What *harm* could it do? You're miserable. It wouldn't make you feel any worse."

Haley frowned at her tea, sorely tempted. She missed Sully desperately. She spent every waking hour reliving the memories, dredging up every last detail about him—his amazing kiss, the deep timbre of his husky voice. The way his cheeks went taut, his voice turning even rougher when he was aroused. The excruciating pleasure she'd experienced in his arms.

And the nights… She kept hallucinating that he was

lying beside her, hearing him breathe, inhaling his scent, her body so on fire for him that she wanted to weep.

"You look like hell," Brynn added.

Haley sighed. "Thanks."

"Well, you do. You've got huge bags under your eyes. You keep staring into space. You walk around like a zombie and you look all strung out."

"I know. I've looked in the mirror. But I repeat, what good will it do?"

Brynn's eyes gentled. "He told you he loved you, sweetie."

Propping her elbows on the counter, Haley pressed her fingers to her aching head. "You should have seen him with those kids, Brynn." A spasm knifed through her, the pain unbearable, even now. "He was so great. I had to let him go. What else could I do?"

"Did he say he cared about having kids?"

"No. And he probably doesn't right now. But what if he does later? What if he changes his mind—and then he's stuck with me?"

"And what if he doesn't?" Sighing, Brynn came around the counter to her side. She sat on the stool beside her and slid her arm around her waist. Then she rested her head on Haley's shoulder, the way she used to when they were teens.

"Listen, Haley. Neither of us won the lottery with our parents."

"You can say that again." Brynn's childhood had been horrific, even worse than hers.

"Yours did a real number on you," Brynn continued. "Your mother's a witch, and your father...well, he obviously wasn't worth much." She lifted her head. "But

Haley, you *are* worth something. Sully is lucky to have a woman like you."

Haley smiled. "You're my best friend, Brynn. Of course you're going to say that."

"That's not why I'm saying it. Sully's right. This is about you not believing in yourself. You spend all your time helping others—the kids in the shelter, me. And you don't do anything for yourself."

"Oh, please. I'm not exactly a martyr."

"Prove it. Take Sully at his word. He loves you. And if it's true love, it doesn't come with conditions or strings. You know he's not perfect. You've accepted his flaws and he's done the same with you. And why wouldn't he? You deserve him, Haley. And you deserve to be happy. You just have to believe it now."

Haley considered that. Intellectually, she knew Brynn was right. But feeling it, making herself believe it… "How do you suggest I do that?"

"Confront the past. That's what I had to do. That's what Sully did. He went home and faced his family.

"You've been avoiding everyone. You haven't talked to the senator. You haven't spoken to your mother. You've never discussed your father's death. You need to get closure before it eats you alive."

"How can I do that? We don't even know what happened to Gwen."

"I know." Brynn reached out and squeezed her hand. "Life isn't tidy. If you wanted a perfect life, you'd be like your mother with her crazy lists. Just tackle what you can."

"I don't know."

"It's up to you." Brynn rose. "You can choose not to

act. But if you don't confront the past, you're going to lose Sully forever. And you'll have to live with that."

The problem with good advice was that it was hard to ignore.

It was even harder to follow.

Haley dragged herself out of bed the next day at the crack of dawn. She showered and choked down some breakfast, then had her bodyguard, Victor, drive her to her mother's Guilford estate. Not that she feared the gang as much anymore. No one had tried to kill her since her father died. Sergeant Delgado had used his gang unit contacts to spread the word, making sure the gang knew the bounty no longer applied. Parker figured in another couple of months they could dispense with the bodyguards for good.

Victor pulled in at the mansion's front gate. A decorating crew had arrived at the estate, leaving it ajar. Victor parked on the turnout beneath the porch and they both got out. At this early hour, she was confident her mother would be at home.

Even so, it took a moment for her to gather her courage. She lingered beside the car, looking at the house her ancestors built. The weak morning sunlight glinted on the lead-paned windows. A cardinal flitted past and landed on a dogwood tree, its red wings bright against the bare branch. The sound of hammering came from the garden behind the house, the workers' voices carrying in the crisp air.

A host of emotions bubbled inside her, but Haley didn't ignore them for once. She acknowledged them one by one—the disappointment, the sorrow, the rage. Her feelings about this house, this family were complicated, a morass of confusing, disturbing thoughts.

Her childhood hadn't been fair. No amount of wealth could ever make up for the utter lack of love. But Brynn was right. She needed to face the past and let it go, including her resentment toward her parents.

With the bodyguard in tow, she walked up the flagstone path to the portico. She caught a glimpse of the crew stringing lights on the patio behind the house. More workers tackled the garden, using a cherry-picker truck to reach the highest branches of the old blue spruce. Her parents had always hired a company to decorate for the holidays. They wouldn't dream of doing it themselves.

She climbed up the wide stone steps. Small potted trees had been placed between the pillars, their white fairy lights twinkling even now.

Haley paused, the scene striking her as bizarre. Her father had just passed away. The scandal of his criminal activities hadn't died down. And yet, her mother was carrying on as if nothing had happened. She was planning her usual holiday party.

Talk about ignoring reality.

The front door wasn't locked. Haley inhaled and stepped inside, trying not to remember the last time she'd walked through this door. She stopped beneath the chandelier to calm her nerves and tried for once to be objective, to see the house from a stranger's eyes.

It was elegant, no doubt about that. Every single item reflected her mother's expensive taste. She'd selected every detail with exquisite care, down to the color of the roses in their heirloom pots. Everything matched. Nothing had been to chance. And nothing was out of place.

But while it was beautiful in a sterile way, there was

none of the warmth and love she'd felt in Sully's house. There was no mess, no joy, no shoes in the hallway or jackets slung over chairs. She couldn't even conceive of her mother taping paper turkeys to the windows or tacking crayon drawings on the fridge. She'd have a stroke if anyone tried.

A maid bustled past. "Excuse me," Haley called. "I'm looking for my mother. Is she in the solarium?"

"Yes, ma'am." The maid disappeared down the hall.

Still not certain what she'd say, Haley left the bodyguard to patrol the hallway and headed toward the sunroom. She decided to play it by ear. If her mother kicked her out, so be it. At least she would have tried.

She approached the study door and paused. She made herself look inside, then blinked, stunned at the changes. The rug had been replaced. The broken lamp had disappeared. Instead of cigars, the room reeked of some lemony cleanser, as if her father's death had never occurred.

She shuddered at the memory of the gunshots. And suddenly, that nagging suspicion came winging back, the uneasy feeling that she'd overlooked something important, that something had been off.

What bugged her was that her father had seemed sincere. He'd sworn until the end that he hadn't killed anyone. But that couldn't have been true. When she'd mentioned the argument with Allen Chambers, he'd gone berserk. He'd obviously had something to hide.

But what?

Frowning, she continued down the hall to the solarium. She glanced around the room, taking in the sunshine streaming through the wall of windows, the workers on the patio outside, packing up their supplies. Her mother sat at her Chippendale desk, writing in her journal. Haley could envision her elegant cursive strokes, precise and controlled, like everything else she did. She never strayed out of the lines.

"Mom."

She didn't look up. She was intent on her task, the only sound in the room the steady scratch of her pen. She wore a long satin robe with a mandarin collar, the deep sapphire blue setting off her cornflower eyes and blond hair. It struck Haley again how beautiful her mother was. *How cold.*

Would Lauren have ended up the same way? She'd had her mother's features and drive for perfection. But perfection had a heavy price.

"Mother." She spoke louder this time.

Her mother looked up from her journal. Her eyes went blank for a moment, as if she didn't know who Haley was. *Tranquilizers.* The doctor must have sedated her to the hilt to get her through the grief.

But then she blinked, and her eyes cleared enough to register surprise. "What are you doing here?"

So much for mending fences.

Haley walked over and sat on the dainty chintz chair across from the desk. She'd always hated that chair. The designer fabric was stunning, but it had a hard seat and rigid back, which epitomized her mother's style.

"I came here to talk," she said.

Her mother's voice cooled. "There's no point. Your father and I changed our wills long ago. You won't inherit anything from his death."

Haley's belly clenched. "I don't want to." It was true. There was nothing she wanted in this house. She still had a few fond memories of Lauren, but too much pain haunted these halls. After she left here today, she didn't intend to return.

"I wanted to tell you I was sorry about Dad."

Her mother's blue eyes flickered. She capped her pen and set it down. Then she picked up the ribbon bookmark, lay it precisely along the gutter of the page and snapped the journal closed. She folded her perfectly manicured hands on her neat desk.

"I'm sorry I didn't come sooner," Haley continued. "I should have paid my respects. It was just…" Her father had tried to kill her. How was she supposed to cope with that?

Her mother didn't respond. But her mouth looked pinched, the skin around her eyes tight. Haley didn't want to feel sorry for this woman, but pity still swelled inside. "I'm sure the holidays will be hard without him."

"Not especially."

Haley's head reared back. "Excuse me?"

"I'm better off without him. He was such a disappointment to me."

"But…how can you say that?" Talk about speaking ill of the deceased. He'd been dead three weeks and her mother had already started in on the complaints.

Her mother sighed. "I misjudged him. Oliver had ambitions when he was young. That's why I married him. I thought he was going places, that he'd become the district attorney, then a senator, even the president someday…. But he never followed through."

Haley didn't know what to say. She knew her parents hadn't married for love, but to hear her mother state her ambitions that baldly, and so soon after her father's death…

But maybe her mother was distraught. Not only had

her husband just died, but his criminal activities had come to light. And for someone as status conscious as her mother, that would come as quite a blow.

Still, Haley had come here for answers, and she intended to get them before she left.

"The night Dad died…he was upset about something I'd overheard. An argument, from a long time ago. I'd heard him arguing with Allen Chambers in the garden. That was a man—"

"I know who he was." Her mother's voice turned sharp. "He was a drug addict, a worthless man who deserved to die."

Haley inhaled sharply, her mother's cruel indifference shocking her even more. An addiction didn't negate a man's worth. Sully was an addict, and he was the most admirable man she knew.

But she didn't want to argue with her mother, no matter how reprehensible her views. "Dad was upset when he found out I'd overheard them. I wondered if you knew what they were arguing about?"

"Of course. That man had been blackmailing your father for years."

Haley stared. "Blackmailing him? For what?"

Her mother glanced at the window. The workers had begun to leave, their voices fading as they walked away. "I suppose it doesn't matter now. The truth will come out soon enough. Your father hired Allen Chambers to take the bar exam for him after law school. Your fool of a father couldn't pass it on his own."

Haley gave her head a swift shake, not certain that she'd heard right. "He cheated on the bar exam?" Hysteria bubbled inside her. "Oh, God. Oliver Burroughs, the mighty defense attorney, was a fraud." He'd practiced law under false pretenses for all those years. It would have destroyed them if it had come out. No wonder he'd paid blackmail to keep it hushed.

And it made perfect sense. It fit her father's personality to a tee. He bullied people to win his cases. He'd married her mother to enhance his image and power. If he couldn't pass the exam on his own, then of course he'd cheat. And Allen Chambers was the perfect choice— brilliant, probably in need of money to fuel his drug habit.

"How long did you know about it?" she asked, still trying to grasp it all.

"Not until that night. I was livid when I found out."

"That's right. You were arguing with Dad in the study when I came in. That's what you were fighting about."

"He'd jeopardized everything I'd worked for."

"Everything *you'd* worked for?"

"I couldn't take the chance that it would come out after that. Allen Chambers had to go."

She couldn't take the chance? Haley's heart skipped a beat. That unsettled feeling swirled inside her, her father's words echoing in her mind. *I never killed anyone.*

She took in her mother's flawless face, her spotless, organized desk, the absolute coldness in her eyes. Horror dawned. "It was you." She stared at her mother, aghast. "You had Allen Chambers killed."

But that meant... "*You* were the gang leader? You put a price on my head?" *Her mother?*

"Don't look so surprised. I'm not as useless as people think."

Haley's head spun. "But why would you ever get involved with a gang?" Her mother was an even worse snob than her father was. Haley couldn't imagine her consorting with criminal men.

"Money, why else?"

"But your family was rich."

"Rich!" Her eyes flashed with real emotion now. "Your grandfather bankrupted the company. He lost every cent we had. An entire fortune went down the drain! We only had one ship left, and it was mortgaged to the hilt. The creditors were going to turn us out of the house. Thank God he drank himself to death in time. I took over the business and saved it. I changed our cargo and routes."

Haley felt numb. "You brought in drugs."

"The demand for cocaine and heroin was picking up. People were willing to pay top dollar for high-quality goods. Of course, no one knew I was involved. I made sure no one could trace the drugs to me. But the money finally poured in. I paid off the loans. I made us secure. Then later, when the New York gangs moved in to the area, I sold the ship and retired. It was getting too risky by then. I kept up my contacts, though, in case I needed anything done."

"Like having Allen Chambers killed." Revulsion made her recoil. "And then you came after me."

"I didn't know it was you, not until your friend surfaced a few weeks ago. And by then…I didn't have a choice. I couldn't take the chance that any of you could pin that death on me."

"There's always a choice. You chose to kill Allen Chambers. You chose to import drugs."

"You don't understand. I was going to lose everything, my house, my position in society."

Haley gaped. "Your position mattered to you that much?"

Her mother's eyes burned dark. A flush mottled her face and neck. "It's easy for you to criticize me. But you've never lost anything. You don't even know what it means."

"You're wrong." Haley's voice shook. She curled her hands into fists, struggling not to lash out. She'd lost her baby, her beloved sister. She'd even lost her hopes and dreams. "I loved Lauren. I tried to save her. I was devastated when she died. She was my best friend."

Her mother's face turned pale. For a moment she seemed to shrink and age, looking vulnerable in the remembered pain. But then she shook her head. "Lauren was the final piece of my plan. She was so beautiful, so perfect. I was going to marry her to someone worthy, a royal, like Grace Kelly did. She'd have a title, status, wealth."

Haley stared at her, aghast. How could her mother be so shallow? Lauren had been beautiful inside as well as out. But this woman's impossible demands for perfection had driven her sister to her death.

"When she died, I had to make other plans."

Her matter-of-fact tone took Haley aback. "Plans? What other plans? What are you talking about?"

"Senator Riggs. He'll be president someday, you know. And since he's a widower…"

Haley's mind churned. She struggled to follow the logic, to make sense of her mother's words. Then the photo she'd seen of her mother and the senator at the White House popped into her mind. "You're having an affair with him."

"He was lonely after his wife died, and we've always been friends. He wasn't hard to persuade."

"You're saying you love him?"

"Love?" She laughed. "Don't be absurd. But he's useful. He has contacts I need." She gestured toward her journal. "I collect secrets, little details that could come in handy. Blackmail's quite effective, as your father knew."

Still reeling over the revelations, Haley shook her head. Her mother—not her father or the senator—was the link to the gang. And Gwen...

Her heart plummeted. She gripped the arm of the chair, afraid to ask. But she had to know. "Where's Gwen?"

"Gone now." Her mother opened a drawer. "She was too smart. She came to me that night, asking questions. But she'd already figured it out."

Nausea chugged through Haley's gut. She covered her mouth with her hand, trying to keep from getting sick. "You killed her."

"She had to go. She was going to turn me in."

Oh, God. Poor Gwen. Haley's eyes burned. She blinked furiously, unwilling to shed a tear in this monster's presence. "What did you do with her body?"

"That's not anything you need to know." Her mother rose. A gun appeared in her hand—aimed straight at Haley's heart. Haley froze. Her blood thundered through her skull.

"It's all wrong now," her mother continued, sounding calm again. "Everyone messed up. Your father. That stupid Markus Jenkins keeping those weapons for himself. I can't abide mistakes like that. Now I have to clean this up." She motioned with the gun. "Get up."

Panic surged inside her. She had to bring down her mother, but how? She could probably best her in a fight, but her mother would shoot her if she attacked.

Her gaze darted to the telephone on the desk, the empty patio behind the house. No help there. But her bodyguard, Victor, was in the hall. If she could somehow alert him....

"Now," her mother ordered, and Haley rose. "Walk to the door."

Her eyes on the gun, she complied.

"Now open it. We'll head to the basement. You try anything sneaky and I'll shoot."

Haley gripped the doorknob, her mind spinning through options. Maybe she could lunge through the door and slam it shut.

But her mother stepped close, pressing the gun against her side.

Her heart pounding, she opened the door. The hallway was empty, and her hopes for a rescue tanked.

Her mother jabbed the gun beneath her ribs. "Let's go."

Haley turned and headed down the hallway, but there was no way she was going meekly to her death. She wasn't the obedient child she used to be, and she refused to let this woman win. If her mother shot her in the process, so be it, but she'd be damned if she'd die without a fight. There'd be noise, shouts, bruises and blood. No matter what it took, she wasn't going down those basement stairs.

They stopped at the basement door. Her mother jerked it open, but Victor stood on the landing, blocking their way.

Haley seized her chance. "Watch out!" she screamed and dove.

The gun went off. Haley twisted around and lunged for her mother's legs. But Victor reached her first. He slammed her down and knocked the pistol away, sending it skidding down the hall. Then he cuffed her arms behind her back.

"The police are on the way," he told Haley as she scrambled up. "I was listening in the hall. Are you all right?"

"I'm fine," she assured him, trying to catch her breath.

Her mother awkwardly rose to her feet. She straightened her spine and faced Haley, managing to look imperious even now.

"You've always disappointed me," she said. "That crippled soldier…is the best you can do."

Haley gaped at her in outrage. And at that moment, once and for all, she let go of her need for this woman's love. Haley wasn't lacking. Her parents were the deficient ones, not her. Her father had been a lying bully. Her mother was a despicable woman, as lacking in warmth as this mausoleum of a house.

And wounded or not, Sully was better than all of them put together. Her family didn't hold a candle to that heroic man.

She'd been an idiot. Sully loved her. He wanted her the way she was. Why had she let her old insecurities dictate her life? Why had she cared what her parents thought? She'd based her need for acceptance on people who weren't even worthy. Sully's opinion was the only one that mattered to her.

From this moment on, she refused to let anyone rob

her of the happiness she deserved. She'd lost her sister, her unborn child, years of her life.

But she was not going to lose Sully Turner, the man she loved.

Chapter 18

Sully applied the last stroke of polyurethane to the bottom stair tread. He got down on his knees, checked from different angles to make sure he hadn't left bubbles or brush marks, then rose. He gazed at the finished stairs, satisfaction flooding through him at how well they'd come out.

He'd transformed the row house in the past three weeks. The windows gleamed. He'd sanded and refinished the wood floors in every room. He'd painted the ceilings and walls, top to bottom, and stripped and painted the wood trim. He'd labored night after night, day after day, hour after hour. Every time the craving for alcohol hit him, he'd started sanding or painting again.

Every time he'd thought of Haley, too.

Which hadn't left much time to sleep.

Bending down, he put the lid on the can and tamped

it into place. Then he set the brush on the drop cloth, grabbed a rag and wiped his hands.

A meow caught his attention in the nick of time. He whipped around and nabbed the kitten before he bolted up the stairs. "Oh, no, you don't. You're not getting your paw marks in that finish. You'll just have to wait until morning to go upstairs."

Still holding the cat, he nudged several tall refrigerator boxes into place, blocking off the railings and stairs. Even this little monkey couldn't leap that high.

"Let's find something to distract you, bud." Still carting the little cat, he picked up the drop cloth and supplies, then limped across the room. He hadn't brought in any furniture aside from a kitchen table and a couple of chairs. He couldn't see the point, since he was selling the place come spring.

He dropped his supplies on the kitchen table and released the cat, who instantly began twining around his legs. Then he grabbed a can from the cupboard, dumped the contents into a bowl and refilled his water dish. "There you go."

His own throat parched, he opened the fridge, twisted the top on a bottle of water and chugged some down. Still drinking, he walked back through the room to the front window and looked out. His gaze shot straight to Haley's shelter, as it always did.

God, but he missed her. His alcohol cravings had nothing on his need for her. The desire to drink came at odd moments, fleeting urges he could control. Keeping his hands busy helped combat those.

But Haley… The yearning for her went deeper. It was constant, as much a part of him as his limp. Wake up and miss Haley. Eat breakfast and miss Haley. Work, shower, sleep and still miss her like hell.

And the nights... He dreamed of her, fantasized about her, relived every single detail about her—the quirk of her brow, the perfect curve of her lush breasts, the throaty cries she made when she climaxed in his arms. The need for her consumed him, and it was a miracle he slept at all. When he did manage to catch a wink, he woke up hungering for her even more.

No, the need for her hadn't subsided. And he knew now that it never would. He loved her too damned much.

She was part of him, all right. Now he just had to wait for her to realize that—however long it took.

He'd put up a wreath.

Haley walked up the path to Sully's porch, her gaze on the evergreen wreath hanging on his front door. She knew where he'd bought it. A disabled veterans' group had been selling them by the metro stop. She'd bought one exactly like it an hour ago.

That Sully had bought it didn't surprise her. That he'd hung it on his door gave her hope. It was a sign of a man who'd rejoined the world, a man who planned to hang around for a while and put down roots.

Hopefully with her.

The sound of hammering came from inside the house. Her heart made a little lurch, a flurry of excitement tripping through her as she climbed the steps. The past few days had been sheer torture—her mother's arrest, the media circus surrounding Gwen Shaffer's disappearance, the fallout from her father's misdeeds.

But she'd weathered it all, and now she was finally

done. She'd wrapped up her past life and could move forward. There was nothing holding her back.

Except for one last thing. *She had to claim the man she loved.*

She raised her hand to the door and knocked.

The pounding stopped. Her heart took up the slack, galloping full tilt through her chest. Fastening her gaze on the wreath, she pressed her suddenly moist palms to her thighs.

A second later, the door swung open. Sully stepped into the doorway and stopped. He went dead still. His golden eyes locked on hers, that familiar sizzle of attraction zapping her nerves. On its heels came a wave of longing, a need for him so intense that she started to shake.

Her thoughts deserted her head. She tried to speak, but failed. She just stood frozen in place, absorbing every detail about him, the desire to rush into his arms nearly doing her in.

And he stared back, his face expressionless, his eyes giving nothing away. He'd trimmed and combed his hair. He'd shaved recently, and the slightest shadow darkened his jaw. His shoulders looked impossibly broad, his skin even tawnier than she'd recalled. He'd hooked a tool belt around his lean hips. He had on paint-splattered work boots and jeans.

More important, his eyes were clear, his hands steady. He'd stayed sober. Warmth suffused her heart.

"Haley," he whispered, the raw emotion in his voice telling her what she needed to know. He still loved her. She wasn't too late.

Relief flooded through her. Her heart gave a joyous

leap. Surging forward, she flung her arms around his neck and he pulled her into his arms.

Then his mouth covered hers, and he was kissing her, devouring her, just as she'd dreamed and hoped for weeks. And she clung to him, relishing the hard, real feel of the man she loved. But this time she refused to let him go.

A lifetime later, they came up for air. But he still held her tightly against him, his strong hands gripping her back. "Haley." The low pitch of his voice rumbled straight to her heart. "I was afraid you'd never come."

She locked her hands behind his muscled neck and struggled to find her voice. "I'm sorry it took me so long to come to my senses."

"Just promise me you plan to stay."

"I'm not going anywhere ever again." Her gaze held his. The love she felt for this man ballooned inside her, threatening to burst. He started to haul her inside.

But something brushed against her leg. Startled, she glanced down. A kitten wound around her ankles, then meowed.

A cat and a wreath.

Smiling, she broke away from Sully and picked him up. "Who's this?" He was a pitiful-looking creature with a scruffy gray coat, a shock of white over his missing eye and a crooked tail. She could feel his bony ribs through his fur.

"His name's Gunny. Gunnery Sergeant Jason McKenzie. He showed up one day and decided to stay."

Her voice softened. "You named him after your friend."

"Yeah. This was his house, so it seemed to fit."

Her heart lost its rhythm again.

"Come on in before you get cold," he said.

She hadn't noticed the cold. She'd been too wrapped up in him to care. Still cuddling the cat, she stepped over the threshold and followed him inside.

The scent of fresh paint caught her attention, and she glanced around. Sunshine poured through the sparkling windows. The beautifully finished wood floors gleamed. There wasn't any furniture, but the walls were a soft pewter gray, made even lovelier by the bright white trim.

"You've done a wonderful job on it, Sully."

His eyes met hers. "The work helps control the cravings."

He made it sound easy. She knew it was anything but.

"Come on, I've got chairs in the kitchen. I can give you the tour later if you want."

She put the kitten down, then trailed him into the kitchen, admiring the gorgeous cabinets, more proof of his handiwork. "How come you don't have furniture?"

"I'm going to sell the place this spring. I'll be done fixing it up by then."

"Sell." Her nerves drummed. "You're not leaving the area?"

"No, I'm just ready to sell." He pulled out a chair for her and took the other seat, moving it close so their knees touched. Then he clasped her hand in his, the warmth a balm to her soul.

"This place got me through a lot. Not just the addiction. It helped me work through my grief over Jason and the other buddies I lost. Now it's time to move on and let them go."

She squeezed his hand. "I understand. I've come to

grips with my own troubles these past few weeks." She dragged in a breath, wanting him to know. "You were right, Sully. My insecurities were holding me back. All my life my parents told me I didn't measure up. I knew it wasn't true, but knowing and feeling are different."

Swallowing hard, she held his gaze. "I went to see my mother. I found out she was the one trying to kill us."

"Yeah. The senator told me they arrested her."

"You've talked to him?"

"A few times. I'm sorry about Gwen."

She nodded. She'd miss Gwen and would always be grateful for her kindness growing up. "They still haven't found her body. I feel terrible that she had the misfortune to get involved with my sick family."

Sully let out a sigh. "Sometimes that's the way life is. There are evil people in the world. Some are a world away in a war zone, others closer to home. Good people suffer. We just have to keep fighting back."

"I know. And what my mother did… The police tried to keep as much of it out of the news as they could. They're still investigating the case, so they don't want all the details revealed."

"Did they ever track down the missing weapons?" he asked.

"No. They think there's something big in the works, though, something involving the drug cartel. They think those E-13s were payment for some sort of operation, but they don't know what.

"My mother isn't talking, and Markus Jenkins is claiming ignorance. He might not really know the plan. My mother was good at parceling information. It was safer for her that way. She used Foley for the transaction, then eliminated him so he couldn't talk.

"One good thing is that she kept journals. She wrote down everything about the gang she led—names of her contacts, the dates of the shipments, you name it. You wouldn't believe how many journals she had, stretching back years. They were in a locked trunk in the attic. Indexed and arranged by date."

Sully laced his strong fingers through hers. "You sure you want to talk about this?"

"I'm sure. And you deserve to know." Still gripping his hands, she summarized what she'd learned. How her mother had started importing cocaine and heroin.

"It was really impressive. No one suspected a woman of masterminding a scheme like that, especially one that young. She was barely out of high school when she began. And she was clever. Only one or two people knew her identity at any given time. She kept rotating them, purging the old contacts after she broke the new ones in."

"Purge, as in kill?" Sully sounded appalled.

She grimaced. "Yes." Even now her brutal coldness stunned her. "She was shrewd enough to know that it couldn't go on forever, so she disbanded the City of the Dead. The remaining members joined the Ridgewood gang. She maintained contact with Markus Jenkins, though, and occasionally used him for some odd job.

"And she kept cultivating people. She had extensive lists of contacts and information about them—people she'd met through my father, the police. People the senator introduced her to—politicians, bigwigs in business like Walker. Even diplomats and foreign dignitaries. She used Gwendolyn Shaffer, too."

She paused. "It turns out she wanted to marry the senator."

Sully raised a brow. "Does he know that?"

"Yes, I told him. She thought he might become president someday, and she wanted to be the first lady."

"What about your father?"

"He'd outlived his usefulness, I guess. I don't know if she would have killed him outright. She'd accumulated a lot of incriminating evidence about him over the years. The police are still trying to unravel it all, but mostly he was bribing judges, tampering with witnesses to win his cases. He got drug money from the gang members he was defending and helped launder it through some real-estate deals.

"So she might have intended to let those things come to light and divorce him, play the poor, unsuspecting wife. Or maybe she intended to kill him. No one knows."

Sully seemed to process that. "Did your father know she was the gang leader?"

"We don't know that, either. The senator doesn't think so. He thinks she planted the storage-unit receipt in his safe to make him look guilty in case anything went wrong. She was good at hiding her tracks and making contingency plans."

The kitten wove around her feet again and meowed. Sully released her hands and lumbered to his feet. "It's time to feed him. He gets to be a real pest if I don't stick to the schedule."

Haley rose and went to the counter. She watched with amusement as he pulled a can from the cupboard and opened it up. The kitten darted over to Sully, meowing until he emptied the contents of the can in his bowl.

Haley smiled. The little cat had him wrapped around his finger, just like his nieces and nephews had.

Suddenly the cat's food registered. "You're giving him crab meat? Isn't that a bit much?"

Sully tossed the can into the recycling bin and shot her a sheepish grin. "I didn't know what the hell to give him. I made the mistake of giving him some crab one day, and now he's spoiled."

Typical Sully. He had a soft spot for the underdogs—human or animal. Her heart expanded. She hadn't known it was possible to love this man any more than she already did. But she had a feeling she'd spend the rest of her life learning just how deep it went.

He came back around the counter to her side. "So now that your mother's in jail, is the danger over?"

"It is for Brynn and me. The gang contract is gone. The police worked hard to get the word out on the streets, and we're pretty sure it worked."

She hesitated. "But there is one problem. The media found out about Brynn and me, how we were runaways and met on the streets. They ran an article about it. Brynn went public a couple months ago, so that wasn't news. But there was a leak in the police department that made it worse."

"I'm not sure I follow."

"Somehow, someone figured out that Nadine was the other runaway girl, the third one in our group. I don't know how they discovered it. Maybe my mother let it out. But Nadine's family has been hunting for her all this time. I told you they're Middle Eastern, really traditional people. They threatened to kill her in a so-called honor killing because she refused a marriage they arranged. That's why she ran away from home."

"They live here in the United States?"

"Yes. Her father is a banker. Her brother is a real-estate mogul. I think my father had dealings with him. Anyhow, the senator is trying to get word to Nadine that her identity has been exposed and that she's in danger, but she's in South America working with a charity group, a Doctors Without Borders type thing. And there's no way to get hold of her until they reach a city in a couple of weeks. The area she's in is too remote."

She paused to collect her thoughts. "Sully...I'm sorry I didn't come sooner. I wanted to finish the mess with my parents first. I had a lot to deal with—my mother's arrest, my father's will. It turns out I had a bequest from my grandmother on that side. She put it in a trust fund I didn't know about. It's a nice chunk of money."

"Yeah? What are you going to do with it?"

"I haven't figured out the details yet, but I want to help girls who have bulimia. Maybe fund programs or open a counseling center.

"At first the money bothered me. I didn't want to accept anything from my family, not even my grandmother. But then I decided that it was fitting. I could help people like my sister, maybe have something good come from her death."

Sully smiled. "I think that's a great idea."

"My mother cut me out of her will, by the way. She's selling the house in Guilford to the historical society. They're delighted to get it, especially now that we're so notorious. They can capitalize on that to get some media attention and raise funds."

"Does that bother you, being notorious?"

"Not as much as I expected. If it gets too bad, I can change my name. I've done that before."

"Turner."

"What?"

His gaze captured hers. He shifted even closer, his expression suddenly so serious that her heart began to pound. "Change your name to Turner. Marry me, Haley."

Her heart took flight.

"I know I've got a ways to go, that it won't always be easy, but I'm sober now. And I have a job. It's only one day a week right now. At Walter Reed, I help with post-traumatic stress counseling, addiction counseling, that sort of thing. I'm just an assistant, but I'm going to take classes and get my degree. Make it official. It will take a while, but it's something I'd like to do."

"You'll be wonderful at it."

"There's more. I told you the senator has been calling me. He wants to create a position, an advocacy for wounded warriors, something on the national level. It's still in the planning stages, but he thinks I'd make a good spokesman."

"You'd make a great spokesman." She didn't have any doubts. "I'm proud of you, Sully. You've turned your life around."

"Almost." His gaze captured hers, sending her pulse on a frantic race. "There's just one more thing I need to make everything right. You."

Her heart tumbled hard. She wrapped her arms around his strong neck and gazed at the man she loved. "You've got me."

His hands tightened on her waist. "Then you'll marry me?"

"As soon as I can."

"Right now?"

"I don't think I can wait that long."

He cradled her face in his hands, his mouth just inches from hers. "You've got me forever. That's a promise."

A promise she knew he'd keep.

* * * * *

Don't miss Nadine's story,
SEDUCED BY HIS TARGET,
the exciting conclusion to Gail Barrett's
BURIED SECRETS miniseries!
On sale December 2013, wherever
Harlequin books are sold.

COMING NEXT MONTH FROM

HARLEQUIN®

ROMANTIC suspense

Available September 3, 2013

#1767 MISSION: CAVANAUGH BABY
Cavanaugh Justice • by Marie Ferrarella

Detective Shane Cavanaugh exudes charm and
confidence, but can he break down the defenses of
his new partner Ashley while racing against the clock
to find a missing baby?

#1768 THE MISSING COLTON
The Coltons of Wyoming • by Loreth Anne White

Dead River Ranch is the end of the road for war
correspondent Jagger McKnight. But a thirty-year-old
mystery about a missing baby boy and a warmhearted
nurse show Jagger it's just the beginning....

#1769 THE SNIPER
by Kimberly Van Meter

To protect her, he broke her heart, but when Nathan
intercepts a kill order for his former flame, he'll do
anything to save her—even if she hates him.

#1770 SHIELDING THE SUSPECT
by C.J. Miller

Accused of murder, Susan is forced to rely on her
ex-lover Brady. But they can't let their fierce attraction
distract them, not when the real killer is targeting Susan.

REQUEST YOUR FREE BOOKS!
2 FREE NOVELS PLUS 2 FREE GIFTS!

H HARLEQUIN®

ROMANTIC suspense

Sparked by danger, fueled by passion

YES! Please send me 2 FREE Harlequin® Romantic Suspense novels and my 2 FREE gifts (gifts are worth about $10). After receiving them, if I don't wish to receive any more books, I can return the shipping statement marked "cancel." If I don't cancel, I will receive 4 brand-new novels every month and be billed just $4.74 per book in the U.S. or $5.24 per book in Canada. That's a savings of at least 14% off the cover price! It's quite a bargain! Shipping and handling is just 50¢ per book in the U.S. and 75¢ per book in Canada.* I understand that accepting the 2 free books and gifts places me under no obligation to buy anything. I can always return a shipment and cancel at any time. Even if I never buy another book, the two free books and gifts are mine to keep forever.

240/340 HDN F45N

Name _____ (PLEASE PRINT) _____

Address _____ Apt. # _____

City _____ State/Prov. _____ Zip/Postal Code _____

Signature (if under 18, a parent or guardian must sign) _____

Mail to the **Harlequin® Reader Service:**
IN U.S.A.: P.O. Box 1867, Buffalo, NY 14240-1867
IN CANADA: P.O. Box 609, Fort Erie, Ontario L2A 5X3

Want to try two free books from another line?
Call 1-800-873-8635 or visit www.ReaderService.com.

* Terms and prices subject to change without notice. Prices do not include applicable taxes. Sales tax applicable in N.Y. Canadian residents will be charged applicable taxes. Offer not valid in Quebec. This offer is limited to one order per household. Not valid for current subscribers to Harlequin Romantic Suspense books. All orders subject to credit approval. Credit or debit balances in a customer's account(s) may be offset by any other outstanding balance owed by or to the customer. Please allow 4 to 6 weeks for delivery. Offer available while quantities last.

Your Privacy—The Harlequin® Reader Service is committed to protecting your privacy. Our Privacy Policy is available online at www.ReaderService.com or upon request from the Harlequin Reader Service.

We make a portion of our mailing list available to reputable third parties that offer products we believe may interest you. If you prefer that we not exchange your name with third parties, or if you wish to clarify or modify your communication preferences, please visit us at www.ReaderService.com/consumerschoice or write to us at Harlequin Reader Service Preference Service, P.O. Box 9062, Buffalo, NY 14269. Include your complete name and address.

HRS13R

Ashley St. James has seen a lot of terrible things on the job,
but nothing has prepared the policewoman for the shock she
gets when responding to what should have been a routine call.

But her new partner, Detective Shane Cavanaugh, is
determined to break down the woman's defenses and help her
heal while they race against the clock to find a missing baby.

Read on for a sneak peek of

MISSION: CAVANAUGH BABY

by Marie Ferrarella, coming September 2013
from Harlequin® Romantic Suspense.

"Hang in there," Ashley repeated to the woman, raising her voice
so that the victim could hear her. The terrier was still barking
frantically. "They're coming. The ambulance is coming. They'll
be here any second. Just don't let go."

God, but she wished the paramedics were here already.
They were trained and they'd know what to do to stabilize
this woman's vital signs and get her to stop bleeding like this.

She refused to believe that the situation was hopeless. Despite
everything that she had been through in her short twenty-five
years, there was still a tiny part of Ashley that harbored optimism.

Ashley's heart jumped. The woman's eyelids fluttered, as
if she was fighting to stay conscious, but her eyes remained
closed. And then Ashley saw the woman's lips moving.

What was she trying to tell her?

"What? I'm sorry," she apologized, "but I can't hear what you're saying." Leaning in as close as she was able, Ashley had her ear all but against the woman's lips. "Say it again. Please, your dog's barking too loud for me to hear you."

She thought she heard the woman say something that sounded like "…stole…my…baby."

Ashley couldn't make out the first word and part of her thought that maybe she'd just imagined the rest of the sentence, but she was positive that she'd felt the woman's warm breath along her face as the woman tried to tell her something.

And then it hit her. What had happened to this woman wasn't just some random, brutal attack by a deranged psychopath who had broken into her apartment. This was done deliberately.

Someone had kidnapped this woman's baby before it was even born.

**Don't miss
MISSION: CAVANAUGH BABY
by Marie Ferrarella,
available September 2013 from
Harlequin® Romantic Suspense.**

ROMANTIC suspense

He'd never intended to see her again....

To protect her, he broke her heart,
but when Nathan intercepts a kill order for his
former flame, he'll do anything to save her—even
if she hates him.

Look for Kimberly Van Meter's exciting new book
THE SNIPER next month from
Harlequin® Romantic Suspense!

Available wherever books and ebooks are sold.

Heart-racing romance, high-stakes suspense!

HRS27839

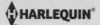

HARLEQUIN®

ROMANTIC suspense

THE DEADLIEST SECRETS CAN'T BE FORGOTTEN

Dead River Ranch is the end of the road for war correspondent Jagger McKnight. But a thirty-year-old mystery about a missing baby boy and a warmhearted nurse show Jagger it's just the beginning....

Look for
THE MISSING COLTON
by Loreth Anne White, the next title in
THE COLTONS OF WYOMING MINISERIES
coming next month from
Harlequin Romantic Suspense!

Available wherever books and ebooks are sold.

Dedication

To Karen Anders, a wonderful friend.

Acknowledgments

I'd like to thank Gail Reinhart and Monique Sherman Hannigan for answering my questions about the Georgetown Law Center. I also owe enormous thanks to my sister, Mary Jo Archer, for her emergency proofreading sessions and unending support.
You're the best!

Books by Gail Barrett

Harlequin Romantic Suspense

Cowboy Under Siege #1672
**High-Risk Reunion* #1682
***High-Stakes Affair* #1697
†*Fatal Exposure* #1757
†*A Kiss to Die For* #1766

Silhouette Romantic Suspense

Facing the Fire #1414
**Heart of a Thief* #1514
**To Protect a Princess* #1538
His 7-Day Fiancée #1560
**The Royal Affair* #1601
Meltdown #1610

Silhouette Special Edition

Where He Belongs #1722

*The Crusaders
**Stealth Knights
†Buried Secrets

Other titles by this author available
in ebook format.

GAIL BARRETT

always knew she'd be a writer. Who else would spend her childhood grinding sparkling rocks into fairy dust and convincing her friends it was real? Or daydream her way through elementary school, spend high school reading philosophy and playing the bagpipes, then head off to Spain during college to live the writer's life? After four years she straggled back home—broke, but fluent in Spanish. She became a teacher, earned a master's degree in linguistics, married a Coast Guard officer and had two sons.

But she never lost the desire to write. Then one day she discovered a Silhouette Intimate Moments novel in a bookstore—and knew she was destined to write romance. Her books have won numerous awards, including a National Readers' Choice Award and Romance Writers of America's prestigious Golden Heart.

Gail currently lives in Western Maryland. Readers can contact her through her website, www.gailbarrett.com.